Lips tasting of wine connected with his, insistent and passionate. Six months ago, he embarked on his solo quest, but it hadn't been so long that he couldn't remember previous intimacies, and those encounters didn't compare to her lavish kisses. *Whew, hot,* he'd go with the flow for a little longer.

She jerked, and then shoved him away. Sadly, the kiss had been a mistake, and from the flash of surprise crossing her face, she'd realized it as well. The pale blue, almost white, towel came loose from her head. She snapped the cloth off. Sexy dark ringlets fell in twisted disarray to her shoulders.

Joe had been lucky enough to catch a joyful kiss and snuggle. He'd delighted in the touch of her lips, the scent of her womanhood, and her wonderful nipples piercing into his thin, sodden shirt. Enjoying the mistake and resulting benefits, he grinned.

The gleam in her eyes went from surprise to anger. With a shaking hand, she wiped her luscious pink mouth.

He stood in a quandary and debated how to explain. Under the circumstances, she wouldn't accuse him of a forced entry.

"Sorry. No lights. I didn't hear a security system buzz. I would've shouted." He took a step. "Instead of coming inside."

She retreated.

Damn. He'd be sleeping in the rain after all.

Mystic Love

by

JJ Keller

This is a work of fiction. Names, characters, places, and incidents are either the product of the author's imagination or are used fictitiously, and any resemblance to actual persons living or dead, business establishments, events, or locales, is entirely coincidental.

Mystic Love

Cover Art by *Angela Anderson*

The Wild Rose Press, Inc.
PO Box 708
Adams Basin, NY 14410-0708
Visit us at www.thewildrosepress.com

Publishing History
First Fantasy Rose Edition, 2016
Print ISBN 978-1-5092-1060-2
Digital ISBN 978-1-5092-1061-9

Published in the United States of America

Dedication

For those who believe in love and defy the odds.

Special thanks: Ericka Scott, Teresa Reasor, Elizabeth Clester, and to you for spending time in my world.

Chapter One

The sports car rounded the corner at breakneck speed.

With a determined stride, a boy chased the foul ball from the field and onto 15th Avenue.

The driver's attention and thumbs were on his cellphone.

Joe twisted and turned and sank into the mattress. He tried to force himself to wake.

The vision continued until he experienced a heart-stopping blow as the car's bumper hit Sam. Joe catapulted upright and used the sheet to clean the sweat from his brow.

Twelve hours later, he stood near the baseball diamond and looked at the sun. The timing seemed correct. He walked the perimeter of the field and glanced along the curving street. Damn, multiple stop signs, the trees matched, and even the sidewalk had identical cracked lifts, from earth eruptions, in two locations. He couldn't see both sides of the avenue at the same time.

Children yelled. Parents cheered and clapped. The distracting backdrop noise altered his recall of the details surrounding the incident. He ran to the nearest intersection and evaluated the scene. The boys covered the field, and the tow-headed batter put on his helmet.

Joe's heartbeat resonated in his ears. There wasn't

any time left. Sam had to be positioned behind the advertisement wall.

The bat cracked against the ball.

"I got it," a pre-teen male said, in a squeaky cracking tone.

"Garth, it's headed toward you," another boy shouted.

He relaxed. Maybe Sam wasn't at the game. A slim lad sporting jersey number nine chased the fly ball. Joe's nerve endings tingled and a rush of adrenaline empowered him. He sped forward.

In the vicinity of the road curve, he spotted Sam running backward.

"No. Stop," Joe shouted.

Sam continued his retreat.

Music blared from a car barreling around the curve. The teen had a cellphone pressed against the steering wheel.

Joe lunged, grabbed the kid, twisted, and then tossed the boy. Sam landed grass side, and Joe hit a sidewalk rise. A burning sharp pain pierced his leg.

Squealing tires and metal connecting with metal vibrated the ground. He ignored the ache in his knee and rolled to the side and stood. The teen's car merged with a fire hydrant and the front fender caved into the driver's door. A geyser shot out the door as the teen crawled from inside.

He glanced at Sam, sitting upright and rubbing his arm.

Joe's heart continued to pound. He took a deep ragged breath. The hurtle and subsequent pavement-hugging fall knocked the shit out of him. Beneath his jeans blood trickled down his leg, but the bumps and bruises were small consequences.

He breathed a little easier. He'd done it. He'd saved the boy from the point of impact and death. As a former police detective, he understood the process of taking statements and confirming information, so he anticipated a cop and reporters asking him a lot of personal questions. He glanced at his motorcycle, parked on the opposite side of the street. The crowd grew larger, sightseers looking for a rush from viewing blood and gore.

He wove through the crowd, mounted his bike, and drove until he crossed the county line. On the side of the road was a sign publicizing an Indian reservation. Why not try to find a primitive solution to his problem?

****

Three weeks later, Cyan, Indiana

As if endorsing Ericka's goal, the flames in the fireplace surged to life. She'd put everything on hold, and focused on the spell. Jacey's phone dinged. She exhaled, releasing the tension in her stomach. She appreciated her best friend's help, but she wanted her to be invested. "Don't answer it," she whispered.

The northwest wind swirled hard. Old metal power lines hit against the brick and stone exterior, adding clamor to the creaky house moans. The clanking increased as a gust of violent wind blew into the room.

Her heart pounded. "This might be my last chance to connect."

"What?" Jacey asked in an annoyed tone of voice. She tapped the face of her phone.

"Could you close the window, please?"

She flipped a long auburn braid over her shoulder, shoved her phone into her jeans pocket, and hurried across the room. Her ebony turtleneck blended into the night, as she lowered the window. "Sticky. Ready to get started?"

"Okay." Ericka hit the light switch, shadowing the room in semi-darkness. The smoky wood scent radiated from the fireplace and helped to set the scene for her desperate attempt to tap into the supernatural and search for a mystic love.

"Do we need all the lights turned down?" Jacey waved her hand. Her wedding ring glimmered in the candlelight. A reminder she'd found unending love as Mrs. Griff Carpenter.

Ericka needed to try to conjure her own slice of happiness. "At any moment the storm could shut down the electricity. Should I turn them off?"

"Yeah. You can always come to our house and spend the night." She leaned over the round table and rummaged through the toolbox of spell charms.

Ericka shook her head. "Thanks, but I'm not staying with you. Newlyweds need privacy."

"All right." Jacey dislodged various Wiccan objects. She picked up a small bag of spices and sniffed. "Found the frankincense."

"It's kind of funny. Our goal was to get rid of the Ames ghost haunting this house. Instead, with any luck, those same tools will call forth a supernatural lover for me."

"Uh, huh. Let's get this circus over with. What's the next step?" Jacey dropped the frankincense and lifted a stick of chalk from the table.

"Let me check." She clutched the paper. "Step One: Have an image in mind of the perfect lover. Got it." She waved to the portrait of the original owner of the house, Kit Ames. "Step Two: Choose time and place. Done. Step Three: Prepare your elements. We need wine, I'll get it."

"First tell me what else Cray Cray said to do, other than draw a circle." Jacey twirled a piece of silken rope.

"Jacey."

"Sorry. All-knowing Priestess."

Ericka cleared her throat. "Step Four: Craft your spell using rhythm or rhyme. Step Five: Bathe in perfumed water and dress in seductive clothing. Nope, not tonight, it's too cold. Step Six: Play music to set the mood, pan music or Barry White, your personal choice."

"Do you need the music?" A floorboard squeaked as she drew a chalk circle.

Ericka waited for her to stand upright. "No. Step Seven and Eight, done. You used a broom to brush away negative energy and to cleanse the area, didn't you?"

"Yep." She wove the red cord through her fingers and winked. "I'm keeping the rope. I like the way it slides through my fingers. I might take it home tonight. Besides, if Kit pops in I want to have the ability to strangle him for having the nerve to return."

"Kit isn't reappearing. I'm going to get a new lover." She wished she'd never told Jacey she'd had a connection with the ghost. "Step Nine: Light candles. White for purity. Red for love. Pink for sex. Stand in the center of the circle and smudge frankincense to scent the air."

She'd tied the rope around her narrow waist. "Okay. I'll smudge."

Ericka bit her lip. "If this doesn't work, will you

help me a second time?"

Jacey winced. "I'm going to support you." Her words were reassuring, but she frowned. She wasn't onboard.

"We sway and chant the spell, six times, until we feel the flow of magic. After the chant, we sip wine from a metal cup and toss the rest into a fire to seal the deal." She smiled, a small help-me-through-this grin.

"I like the drink part."

"I'll go get it then."

"And I'll get things rolling," Jacey mumbled.

She stopped at the threshold of the parlor. "What?"

"I'll smudge the frankincense."

"Okay." She rushed to the kitchen, grabbed the metal chalices, an open bottle of Pinot Noir, and hurried into the parlor. The sacrament table was covered with the items they needed.

"Thanks for getting everything set." Ericka poured wine into the goblets.

Jacey crunched her shoulders forward and back. "Why did the wiccan saleswoman believe you, a person who has never done a spell, could conjure a true love?"

She'd paid a small fortune to take five lessons. "Because I saw and talked to Kit's ghost, I've some magical power."

"How much did she charge you?"

"Enough. She gave me a sense of confidence. Maybe, false confidence." She trembled. Shivers skittered along her spine. She wasn't sure what to do and, even more frightening, what if she achieved her goal? "With zero casting experience, I'm willing to try anything to get that feeling, a zing, a rush of desire and excitement again."

"You'll find love someday." She waved her hand. "You don't need all of this."

"I want to try." Ericka took a sip from the chalice and fingered her triangular-shaped diamond pendant hanging between her breasts. The stone was to be used to deepen a trance. Being imperfect with fractures, would the stone be enough to create mysticism and influence the spell cast?

"Okay. Give me your hand, and we'll chant." She glanced around. "Where's the spell?"

Ericka grabbed the paper from under the toolbox. "Here it is." She put the instructions down. "The final bit is to close the circle. Blow out the candles and wait. Ready?"

"Yep."

"In unison."

"Black flame, light the way. Host of the undead, I beseech thee. Bring my love to me."

Ericka struck a fireplace match. "So mote it be on the count of three." The trio of wicks flared to life on the diamond-shaped red candle engraved with symbols of love.

Thump. Thump. The window opened again. Dense raindrops plopped against the glass and a cool breeze entered the room. The earthy whoosh of air extinguished the candle, leaving the flickering flames behind the fireplace screen to illuminate the room. "OMG. I didn't expect an ethereal response. It came so fast."

"It seems as if the storm is getting closer. Maybe we should call it a night?" Jacey whispered.

Lonesomeness overwhelmed her. *No reason to belabor the point…but what if…* Her heart pattered an unsteady beat. "Can't we finish the chant? Then you can go home to your husband and nice comfortable life." As soon as she said the words, she wanted to withdraw the snarky comment.

Her best friend lurched, as if struck in the stomach.

"I'm sorry. I'm…I just want this so bad. I want—"

She sighed. "It's okay. Ready?"

"Together." Ericka grabbed her hand and said the words she'd been practicing. "The guardian of the Angel of Light and of Air, I call ye forth."

A rush of air brushed over her arm. Her sleeve folded back. An electrifying chill ran along her skin. Could conjuring a lover, rather love, be so simple?

"Lord of the Watchtower of the West, I'm here to call the light to bring forth a love of my own." Her voice shook. Hope existed for her. "And in doing so, I deliver myself from false belief and self-deceit. I am here to open the path."

She lifted the pendant high into the air. "I stand before the deities, Hecate and Persephone, and give you this diamond and partake of this blessing." She removed the necklace and placed the jewel on the table. "Raise your chalice."

Jacey tapped the metal cup against hers. "Drink up."

Ericka drank her wine. "Now we toss the containers into the fireplace." She hurled her cup, and it flew over the screen and landed in the fire. "Here's to hoping."

Flames and sparks shot out as the inferno consumed the remnants of alcohol.

"I understand bringing a supernatural lover to you is important, but—"

"Thanks. I'm…" *Lonely and I want what you've found.*

Jacey's cellphone buzzed. She took it from her pocket and walked closer to the fireplace. She smiled at the screen and whatever the message.

Her tight bond with her husband made Ericka feel the cloak of sadness wrap tighter. "I just want what you and Griff have."

Done with the call, she shoved the phone into her pocket. "Then you need to stop this nonsense and look for a real man."

"I can't. I'm afraid I'll turn out like the rest of the women in my family." She stared at the flames, wishing to get lost in the magic of the chant, to dispel any lingering doubts.

"Just because your mother took off, leaving your dad to raise you and your brother doesn't mean you'll repeat the pattern."

My grandmother, great-grandmother, and great-great grandmother also left their husbands and children. "History repeats itself."

"We've discussed this every time you've dumped a guy."

She snatched the aged paper. "Which is the reason I need to have a non-human lover." She lowered her voice. "I want someone to send me a text that will make me smile and go all dreamy-eyed."

"Oh." Jacey rushed forward and hugged her. "You'll find true love, but not in the supernatural world."

Ericka sniffed.

She took a step back. Her "I mean business frown" appeared, then disappeared. "All the spell books in the universe won't help you. You need to get out more. Date. Caleb Knight, the sheriff, was asking about you. Let's get together this Friday?"

Okay, so she'd try to act normal and ditch the lover-conjuring project. Her throat hurt from holding her agony inside. She swallowed. The lump went into her stomach.

"I think you'll have a lot in common with Caleb. We'll make it a double date."

"Fine," she whispered, already regretting the decision.

"Great. We'll go to dinner, maybe a movie. We'll have a good time." Once again, her voice was its usual happy uplifted tone.

Her friend's unrelenting good cheer made Ericka heavyhearted. The snap of the door hitting the Bombay cabinet in the foyer and slamming shut again drew her attention. "Hey, when you get home will you ask Griff if he'll fix my latch? It only works half the time."

"He will. In the meantime put a chair under the doorknob for security."

Small town life and its trusting people never ceased to amaze her. She walked to the door and grabbed the knob. "Thanks for coming tonight."

"I'll call you with details about the date."

She nodded, but the damn miserable lump in her gut grew. Jacey ran to her car. Ericka waited for her to drive away, and then shut the door and returned to the parlor. She scanned the mocha-tinted walls and crevices. Nothing unusual. No facial imprint came from the boards, no webbed image of a gorgeous man floated into the space. Not even the wide six-inch wall trim had spirit vapor rising from under it.

Strange snakelike mist filtered through the window gap, slithered across the age-darkened parquet, and wrapped cat-like over her ankles. She shook her legs. The cold condensation annoyed her more than scared her.

"Blessed be," she whispered, wanting and needing good karma.

She flipped on the overhead light. After slamming the window shut, she locked it. The mysterious misty ambiance dissipated. The grandfather clock in the corner struck eleven bells. Why couldn't she enjoy human company, date, have sex, all without commitment?

She leaned against the windowsill and gazed at the oil painting above the fireplace. Kit Ames. The artist had emphasized his gleaming black hair and strong jaw. Against the white shirt and red vest, his sun-darkened skin looked lifelike. When she was in the room, her perfect lover's dark gaze followed her. He seemed to ridicule her for trying to do the impossible.

She understood the absurdity of creating a flawless man to have and to hold, but she'd grown tired of a dating pool full of egotists and whiners. What better way to get what she needed than by summoning a man?

"I want to find everlasting love," she whispered into the gloom. No answering murmur came at her plea. No soft gentle caress. She straightened her shoulders and shook off the morose sorrow and longing.

What was wrong with her? She kicked away from the windowsill. Enough time had been wasted spouting silly phrases into an empty room. She'd get her mind off this and focus on work.

She needed to fire her career and clear the name of

the mayor's son. Mayor Ward claimed his son made one stupid mistake and getting into a fight over a married woman shouldn't send him to jail. God willing, the incident wouldn't cost him his future. If she could impress the court and the townspeople with her defense strategy, she'd get more clients, which meant a regular paycheck.

She wiggled the fireplace screen closer to the flames, and shut off the light switch. Grabbing the remainder of wine, she ambled into the library and half-heartedly dove into researching relevant law cases for comparison.

An hour later, her eyes burned from the glare of the computer screen. She stretched, getting the kinks out of her arms, turned off the lights and left the library. She gripped the banister, ascended the stairs, and avoided the fourth stair step. In her bedroom, she stood in the center, closed her eyes, and wished for a tiny bit of love magic to come her way.

She opened an eye and searched the room. Nothing. "Just as well."

She shed her clothes and headed to the shower. As she washed her hair, she categorized the facts of her case. The charge of assault stated any person who attempted or offered with unlawful force or violence to do bodily harm to another person, whether or not the attempt or offer was consummated, was guilty of assault and would be punished. She'd find a way to defray her client's alleged implication.

She recalled previous, relevant trials and climbed from the shower. Rain continued to slash against the bathroom window. Violent rolls of thunder shook the panes. The house's electricity had been updated, but transformers blew and utility poles fell. Power during a storm was iffy. Would the voltage remain alive? Towel drying her hair, she tried to ignore the rumble of thunder and reentered the bedroom.

A streak of white heat zigzagged outside the French doors, and in concert, a loud thud rang through the hallway. She shoved her arms into a robe. A thumping noise came from the main level. Had someone broken a window and snuck into the house? Her internal urgency to locate the origin of the clatter warred with her desire to stay put until morning. She edged along the wall, toward the stairs with her knees threatening to fold. The door. She'd forgotten to prop it.

Her heart battered against her ribcage. At the edge of the staircase, the lights flashed off, cloaking her in total darkness. Quivers worked into stomach and throat. Outside the transom windows, lightning pierced the sky. To prevent exposure to an intruder, she pressed against the wall. Slow and easy, she took one step at a time down the stairs. Her breath caught. What if the spell had worked?

****

Through the pounding rain, Joe Reeves pushed his damn heavy, Harley close to the Greek revival house. Impressive and imposing the structure stood three stories high with six massive white columns supporting the veranda's roof.

Exhausted and cold from tugging the motorcycle for miles, he leaned the bike against the wide steps. Close enough to the porch to keep it out of the downpour. He lowered the kickstand, removed his gloves, and with numb fingers released the catch of the strap of his helmet. No lights shone in the windows.

Either no one was home or the storm had shut down the electricity.

Joe swiped rain from his coat and considered breaking and entering as he strode the stairs. He'd smoothed his wet hair, untied the scarf to hang inside his open leather jacket, and wished to hell he didn't have to ask for help. A wind, more like a cyclone, whipped over the porch. The gust slammed the heavy door against an interior wall.

****

Musky rain scented the hall. With jittery fingers, Ericka felt the wall to guide her way toward the thumping. A savage, bone-shaking crack of thunder vibrated through the foyer. Wind and rain sputtered, sprinkling the tile floor. Shivers rippled over her skin as each drop struck her toes. *Shut the door and ramrod it into place.* Inches away from the knob, she sensed something.

Ericka halted. The entry floorboards creaked. A man's shadowed form appeared. He, a well-formed he, stepped forward.

Long dark hair, plastered flat to his head, glimmered in the shock of light piercing the sky. Droplets fell to the collar of his open jacket, a white shirt underneath and a hint of red peeked from under his coat. The spell had worked.

She threw herself against her dream lover, wrapped her arms around his neck, and kissed him. His lips were cold, but perfect in form. At first, his mouth didn't move, but after a couple of seconds, he pressed into her. She flicked the tip of her tongue over his mouth, outlining the curves, and then slid it between his lips. His tongue played with hers. Sharp, decadent longing

14

powered through her.

Wait a minute, he didn't taste like she'd imagined. He tasted like mint and human. She touched whatever smooth cool skin she could find available between the coat and his neck and shoulders. Strong and virile hot body. She inhaled, taking in his scent; fragrant late fall wind and the odor of male sweat.

Sweat? Wet skin? She licked her lips, savoring the zest. A spear of lightning brightened the sky. Six foot three. Left ear piercing. Broad chest. Wrangler posture, with one knee bent.

Her heart thumped harder, pounding strong in her chest.

Whom had she kissed?

****

Joe supported her, keeping her in an upright position. Definitely a *her* as supple breasts snuggled tight against his chest. Her robe opened, and he fought the urge to remove his own garments to feel her warm body against his, flesh to flesh.

Lips tasting of wine connected with his, insistent and passionate. Six months ago, he embarked on his solo quest, but it hadn't been so long that he couldn't remember previous intimacies, and those encounters didn't compare to her lavish kisses. *Whew, hot,* he'd go with the flow for a little longer.

She jerked, and then shoved him away. Sadly, the kiss had been a mistake, and from the flash of surprise crossing her face, she'd realized it as well. The pale blue, almost white, towel came loose from her head. She snapped the cloth off. Sexy dark ringlets fell in twisted disarray to her shoulders.

Joe had been lucky enough to catch a joyful kiss

and snuggle. He'd delighted in the touch of her lips, the scent of her womanhood, and her wonderful nipples piercing into his thin, sodden shirt. Enjoying the mistake and resulting benefits, he grinned.

The gleam in her eyes went from surprise to anger. With a shaking hand, she wiped her luscious pink mouth.

He stood in a quandary and debated how to explain. Under the circumstances, she wouldn't accuse him of a forced entry.

"Sorry. No lights. I didn't hear a security system buzz. I would've shouted." He took a step. "Instead of coming inside."

She retreated.

Damn. He'd be sleeping in the rain after all.

Chapter Two

Shock and embarrassment paralyzed her, right there in her very own foyer. Ericka wanted her bare wet feet to move, but they were stuck to the cold marble floor. She took a few deep breaths, holding each for seconds to still her galloping heart. The wind tunnel whipped across her skin, sending shivers through her. Or jitters due to a flash of insanity.

Her spell hadn't created a dark-haired, tight-bodied supernatural lover. No, instead, she'd kissed a total stranger with tongue…and she'd liked it.

Venturing a peek into his dark eyes, the color of a stick of licorice, she witnessed curiosity and kindness. Her stomach muscles contracted in need. She couldn't shake free the ripples of what if. His scorching kiss imprinted. She wanted another. She tugged her robe to prevent such a move. "Who are you?"

"Joe, Joseph Reeves." He smiled and unlike the earlier grin, this one was lopsided, quirky and oh so sexy.

A funny feeling pulsated through her stomach. She wanted the pleasant sensation to continue. She took a deep breath and forced herself to retreat out of the rain instead of forward into the fire. His sexy heat pulled her toward him.

She knotted the robe's belt and repositioned the towel across her shoulder. "What do you want?"

His almost military posture and vivid expression changed from wide-eyed sexual interest to uncertainty. He walked deeper into the foyer, glanced along the hallway, into the library and parlor on the other side of the hall. Those fathomless dark eyes stared at her.

"My bike broke down." He nodded over his shoulder. Lightning illuminated the glossy, brown paint of a large motorcycle leaning against the porch. "Could you let me bunk down in your barn until the rain stops, and I can get it repaired?"

Even in the limited glow, the ride, a Harley, looked shiny and new. How often did a fresh-off-the-sales-lot cycle break down? At night during a rainstorm? The saddlebags appeared to be full. One T-bag hung on the backrest and remained flat against the bar. She looked at him, and as if channeled, a slash of lightning sharpened the background within seconds, highlighting the sharp angles of his face. The very image of her perfect lover.

She tightened her grip on the towel. Joe Reeves would be in the barn, about fifty feet from the house. Cautious, she hesitated. What harm could he do, other than rape, murder, and dismemberment?

With a critical stare, she evaluated his clothes. He wore leather pants, a designer jacket, and a tight, quality shirt. The tip of a red lamb's wool scarf looked like a streak of blood across his muscular chest. Her breasts ached to feel the pressure of his solid torso again. She wanted to press her hands all over his body-builder shoulders and biceps. *Good God, get your thoughts off his attributes.* She'd let biker Joe bunk in the barn.

"Ma'am?"

"Sorry. At least the rain has turned to a drizzle." She'd perfected evaluating people, in and out of the courtroom. Focused attention, missing very little, and now he held a relaxed stance. A slow southern intonation had slipped beneath his words. She had extended family in the Mississippi area, and they had a similar drawl. His boots were standard riding gear, and from her limited experience very expensive. The scent of leather, rain, and man drove tingles into her groin. Damn hormones. Damn spell.

After eight years as a practicing attorney, she could spot a deviant a block away. Sometimes, the good guys cloaked themselves in rough exteriors and vice versa, but Joe's honest demeanor, and her gut, made her trust him.

"Yes, you can use the barn. Want a cup of coffee to go?"

His face lit and that lopsided smile appeared again. Whew. Quivers exploded through her at the virility of this man. She stepped through the frigid puddles, splattered across the marble floor. She glanced at the collectible sword hanging in the parlor. Her deceased father's .38, in the library, and a 20-gauge shotgun, in the bedroom, provided backup weapons. Her brother had taught her how to use her fists, legs, and a head-butt as defense strategies. If for some reason her instincts were wrong, she'd fight. Somehow, she knew Joe was a good guy.

"Thank you. Anything warm. Coffee would be great." The door creaked as he tried to shut it. "The wood's warped. It'll continue to blow open unless it's planed."

"Yes. I'm expecting…my guy is coming by in a

while to fix it."

"Ah," he mumbled.

"Ah?" She opened a drawer in the Bombay table, gripped a flashlight, and handed it to him. She grabbed the top rail of a Mission-style chair and dragged it close to the entrance. Her brother's warning flashed through her mind. *"As an attorney, you are a target 'cause no one likes lawyers. You should question everyone. Don't be so damn trusting."*

Since she'd moved to Cyan, she'd relaxed, learned to trust people, strangers.

"Sorry, ma'am." Joe put the flashlight on the cabinet, pointing toward the door and rushed forward. He took the chair and wedged it under the doorknob. "Explains the kiss."

His deep voice sent a fresh wave of trembles through her. She wanted a visual of his facial expression. Would she see regret for kissing her?

She handed him the towel and grabbed a second long-handled flashlight stowed in the cabinet. The batteries were fresh and the beam provided a path into the kitchen. "Right. Come this way to the backdoor and lukewarm coffee."

In the kitchen, she laid the torch atop the counter top and moved some heavy glass jar candles to the center of the kitchen table. She located a lighter and within two flicks, vanilla scented candles lit the area. The aromas make her think of a bubble bath in the iron tub, one level above, with Joe working her loofah.

He must have dried his hair as he followed her, because strands stood-up in places and his forehead didn't have a glossy appearance. The towel circled his neck, touching those dark strands she craved to run her fingers through. He put his helmet on the tabletop. The clunk of hard plastic hitting against distressed wood table became the only sound in the room.

She'd placed mugs in front of the coffeemaker, ready for Griff when he arrived, no doubt at the crack of dawn, to fix the door.

She lifted a mug, but her focus continued to gravitate toward Joe's perfect body. In the jacket gap, his thin white shirt clung to each muscle, each valley, and each rippled part made her mouth-water. Christ, she needed male companionship.

"Electricity's out, so I can't start another pot of coffee. Want what's left in the carafe?"

He grinned as if she'd granted him a great gift. She filled a mug to the brim. "It doesn't appear to be steaming."

"Thank you, this is perfect." He accepted the cup, took a sip, and stared at her. Sharp, he had cop's prying eyes, missed nothing.

She leaned her side against the counter.

A random bead of rain slipped along his cheek. He wiped the wetness from his jaw with his shoulder.

She lowered her gaze. Lust was the devil's tool and this damn doppelganger threw her into a tizzy, complete with desire quakes between her thighs. Dabbling in magic, argh. She was over spell casting.

"Do you take cream or sugar?" A little late, but she embraced the mundane.

He shook his head, gripped the cup, and drank.

She nodded to the front of the house. "What happened to your Harley? It's a Road King, right?"

"Yes. Good eye. If I'm lucky, the problem's a spark plug. More than likely it's electrical. Do you ride?" He set the cup down, but continued to hold the handle.

"I don't own one, but I dated a collector. He had a garage filled with Harley Davidsons. I drove a Street Glide once. Nice ride."

He nodded, his direct look assessing her the same way she'd evaluate a key witness in a criminal case. "Once the bike is running I'll let you take a spin."

"Great. Your knuckles are a mess. Accident?"

He glanced at his hand. "No, just clumsy."

The scabs looked recent. She titled her head. "I have days like that. Where are you headed?"

"Cyan." His close-clipped fingernail tapped the handle of the mug. "How close is the town?"

Simply by the rhythm of his movements, he didn't appear to be clumsy. His intense gaze created a frenzy of renewed yearning. She had to keep the answer short and get him out the door before she did something stupid, like offer him a nice comfy bed upstairs. "Five miles to the southwest of here."

"If *your guy* doesn't come tonight, I'll fix your door in the morning before I go into town." He tilted the cup and glanced at the pot.

The carafe was drained and, even if she could make more coffee she wouldn't. Her heart continued its erratic beat, no doubt a result of his dark stare and close resemblance to the man of her dreams.

"You're a carpenter?" Instinct told her to trust him, but a dimwit would take a complete stranger at face value, even if he matched the image she'd used for the spell. Despite all of her conflicting thoughts, she snagged the black vessel and emptied the contents in his mug. Nothing but little flakes of dark remains and a smidgen of brown thick liquid occupied the bottom.

As if seeking warmth, even imaginary, he held the cup between both of his hands again. "I can be."

That's it? How cryptic. His soulful attitude presented deep-seated secrets, and she loved a good mystery.

"My guy will fix it. You can stay in the barn tonight. What are you going to do in Cyan? Job?"

He swiped a hand through brown hair, the color of fresh-turned soil. "No, I'm looking for a shaman who lives near the Healing Springs. White Wolf. Ever heard of him?"

She'd dealt with a multitude of strange characters in the past, but a dude looking for an Indian healer was something new and odd. "Shaman, as in Native American medicine man?"

"Yes."

"Not that I'm aware, but I've lived here less than a year. I can ask my guy when he comes." The battery operated clock indicated two A.M. Hyped-up by the surreal events of the night, desire continued to dance across her nerve endings. She had to get rid of the dead ringer before she acted on her funny feeling.

Joe stepped forward and placed the cup in the sink. He turned and his taut chest heaved, refreshing the memory of the raw and exciting kiss. She cleared her throat, tugged the collar of her robe closer to hide any exposed skin, and ambled to the door.

"The barn will be open. If you wouldn't mind going out the rear I won't have to re-jam the front." She held the backdoor open.

"I don't mind. You haven't told me your name." A helmet-sized wet spot marred the table. He took the edge of his shirt and swiped the table. His scarred knuckles created all sorts of diversions. How would his hands, caressing and stroking, feel on her skin?

"Ericka. Ericka Gilmore." She extended her arm. Their fingers touched and sparks flowed from the contact. She gave his hand a short sharp shake, but not enough to dispel the accidental link.

"Thank you, Ms. Gilmore." He bowed his head. "It's a pleasure to meet you." His smile and glimmering eyes gave her the impression he questioned why she'd greeted him with a passionate kiss and made him leave with a handshake. Despite their shared crappy coffee and an...oh-so-memorable hot kiss, he was a stranger.

Damn, Jacey was right; she needed to get out more. The Friday night date with the sheriff became more appealing. A real, solid man to hold hands with, and maybe a kiss to make her inner woman happy and to spur her pleasure zone. Umm, similarities between the two: ordinary Sheriff Caleb and Joe Biker. Average didn't begin to describe Joe—he was anything but ordinary. He and the kiss could transcend many barriers, earthly and unearthly.

The man, occupying her thoughts, positioned his helmet and took the offered flashlight, then rushed into the gloom. She shut and locked the door and blew out all but one candle. She carried the taper to the next room and peered through the window.

****

Thank God, the end was near, because shoving his bike through frigid rain and sludge had depleted his vital reserves. Joe sliced through the muck, tugged his bike, and kicked the stand to release the brace. The flashlight slipped between the strap of his saddlebag and the wet leather. He shoved the bike along the side of the house. He sensed her staring at him and glanced in the direction of the backdoor.

In a nearby window, Ericka was surrounded by soft candlelight. Her hair, the color of ripened walnuts, shimmered. She had an innocent and vulnerable appearance. The light extinguished.

Joe had evaluated her and the house. Details were important in determining the character of a person. She'd lacked a ring. Two cups had been set out in preparation. They didn't appear to be a morning ritual as only one placemat was set at the table. A woman living alone in a big house needed a high confidence level to invite a stranger inside. In Cotswold, Mississippi, where his roots had been planted at one time, this mansion would be worth two million, so she came from or had money.

From his limited view, all of the perfectionism, the well-staged furniture, cups aligned, attention to detail described Ericka Gilmore as SWFC, single-white-female-compulsive. There weren't obvious signs of a television. At first glance, it appeared her guy came to fix things and not watch sports.

He didn't buy her story. Something wasn't right with the details and the woman.

He rolled his bike toward the barn, kicked the stand down, and removed the flashlight from the saddlebag. The barn was a typical Midwest structure, antique red, not bright like a fire truck and not a maroon, but a worn, warm, muted scarlet. Despite the sludge in the tracks, the door slid to the side with ease. He flashed the light over the interior. Recent trim work created the fresh scent of pine and oak. A new set of stairs led to an untouched floored area, the size of a high school gymnasium. The hayloft didn't have an earthy grain scent. Eight stalls and an equipment room completed the ground level. Nice. Dry and warm-ish. Just what he needed for one night. Optimistically, he hoped his ride would be fixed tomorrow, and he'd continue his search.

In the meantime, he needed something to use for a barrier between the cold floor and his body. The south wall had a five-foot tall door with a rusted metal hook bolted to the thick wood. After a brief struggle, a strong wave of mustiness rolled out. Stashed inside were harnesses, so worn the white scars shone in the dim light. An odd assortment of equine gear cluttered the floor. He grabbed several horse blankets from a workbench and kicked the wooden entrance closed.

He dropped the woolens to the floor and shuffled into the hailstorm again. *Damn freaky mid-west weather. Sunny one minute, and dark and sleeting in the next.*

He shoved his boot on the kickstand. It slid. With the second attempt, the stand flipped, and he hauled the heavy Road King into the semi-warm, albeit dry, barn. Brace kicked into place, he secured his helmet to a hook and lifted the top of the saddlebag. He removed a black plastic tarp and laid the first layer of his makeshift bed. The horse blankets followed. He tugged a thick travel throw from the bike pouch and covered the odorous layers.

He tried to grasp the zipper at the bottom of his jacket, but his numb fingers challenged him. He shook the edges apart. Once removed, he attacked his drenched trousers, dragging them off his freezing legs. Under the gauze, his recent wound remained dry. He draped the damp leather over the stall wall. He wished for a hot woman to snuggle, to make him feel alive. Blah, he couldn't have a full time relationship, ever.

Exhausted, he pulled on a fresh pair of jeans and nested in his makeshift bed. He forced his muscles to relax, but his mind continued to spin. Ericka Gilmore haunted him. Her feisty shrewd demeanor drew him into the kiss. Her curves demanded exploration. He licked his dry lips. Her flawless mouth crushed his. A perfect fit.

Her snappy wit touched his core and yanked him out of his self-imposed isolation. At the impact of her body slamming into his, he'd lost his footing for a second, then her strong arms wrapped around his neck, drawing him closer, awakening a rampant desire. The demon inside him hadn't chased away his craving. He snuggled in a makeshift bed. Yes, he liked a quick-thinking woman with desirable curves.

The thinness of his shirt had paid off, as he'd felt her scantily veiled breasts pressed against his chest. He sighed. Her nipples peaked. *Don't think about her hot lips, or her magnolia-scented smooth skin.* He moaned, repositioned, and braced his head with an arm. She seemed surprised when he asked about the shaman.

Five miles away, the tiny town of Cyan, Indiana hosted a healing springs and a medicine man. Despite Ericka's lack of knowledge about the Indian, Joe could sense the shaman's presence. He pressed his eyes closed, as if denying the idea the spiritualist could be a myth.

Chapter Three

Rasp, hiss, rasp, hiss.

Ericka rolled to her side, gripped the heavy white and blue quilt, and covered her ear.

Rasp, hiss.

She pressed deeper into her feather pillow. The bothersome noise continued.

She shoved the covers aside and dropped her legs alongside the bed. Head spinning, she grabbed the edge of the headboard for balance.

All the furnishings in the master suite were bulky and dark, not to her taste, but they'd been a part of the house. Someday, when she didn't operate in the red, she'd update the furniture.

Sun poured through the arched bedroom windows. Squinting, she snatched her pale gold tattered robe from the end of the bed. She slid her arms into the sleeves, catching her right hand in a cuff hole. She tugged her finger free and stepped into her hard-soled slippers. *Slay the beast making the horrible racket.*

She snapped the thin belt together and stomped out of the master suite. At the top of the stairs she paused, daylight spilled into the foyer. She'd been robbed—— of a door.

She ran down the stairs and onto the veranda. Shadowed by a pillar, a man's muscled form bent over her door. Her toes bit into the top of her slippers as they

28

gripped the tile.

She squeezed her eyelids tight, waited a few seconds, then opened them in slow increments. *Still there.*

Joe Biker stood behind two sawhorses. Her source of annoyance had her door braced between the rises. He smoothed his fingers along the edge.

"What the hell do you think you're doing?"

Their gazes met, locked, once again making her aware of a spine-tingling connection to this stranger.

"Good morning. I'm fixing the door."

The surface of the sliced timber appeared smooth to her, so he must have some woodworking knowledge. But she'd rather it not be at…whatever frickin' time it was.

Slivers of fragrant timber adorned the top of his black motorcycle boots. She couldn't fathom how one became wedged between silver bars and the leather. A smattering of oak tendrils stuck to his form-fitting jeans. Curls of wood shavings held fast to the right side of his hard, well-defined muscled chest.

He swiped his forearm across his prominent cheekbones and smiled his lopsided grin. The smile she'd dreamed about most of the night. "As promised, I'm smoothing the wood so the door will close."

Sweat beaded his forehead and creased his thin muscle-revealing cotton shirt. He kinked his shoulders back and forward. She inhaled and tried to ease the frantic pummeling of her heart with each thrust and pull. She squelched the urge to rub those divine muscles. *Say something.*

She wiped the edge of her mouth. "Thanks. While I appreciate your help, I thought I explained my guy would take care of it."

He winked, a suave GQ move, and rubbed his hands across his jeans. Dust bits floated to his black leather jacket hanging over the porch railing. "Consider the repair my way of thanking you."

"No thanks necessary. Sorry for the attitude. I had a late night and the racket is giving me a splendid headache." She rubbed her forehead.

He couldn't have heard her lame excuse because Jacey's husband, Griff, drove along the lane in his loud, obnoxious, monster-sized red truck. Joe switched his glance from the vehicle to her, giving her a long slow sweep with those sexy dark eyes and making her acutely aware of the split of her threadbare robe. Her thighs heated, the tops of her breasts chilled.

She wished she'd taken time to put on lots of clothing, maybe pull a brush through her hair. No, she slept naked, and a biker gawking at her would not make her feel cheap. Shivers coursed through her thighs.

She didn't greet people dressed this way, but it would be rude and telling to scurry away. She brought as much dignity to the encounter as possible and unfolded the lapels of the robe, then wrapped the lower end over and retied the belt.

The white lettering of his business, "Carpenter Construction" gleamed. Griff climbed out of the cab. Mac, his golden retriever, followed stopping to sniff the ground at the base of the veranda. Joe put a hand out to the dog. Mac jumped onto the porch and sat near the tip of his boots. He rubbed the dog's ears and a canine moan transmitted through the air.

"Mornin', Ericka." Griff's blue-green eyes narrowed. He didn't miss a lick. He'd lived in Cyan all twenty-nine years and knew everyone, so a lecture about stranger danger would be forthcoming.

"Morning." She nodded toward Joe. "Joe Reeves, Griff Carpenter."

Griff sauntered forward. His lean frame was encased in work gear, chambray shirt, jeans, and those orange-yellow work boots. He extended his southpaw.

Joe grasped the hand, and they did the man-to-man evaluation thing men did. "Hi. How you doin'?" His sexy deep voice sounded loud in the awkward silence. "You must be her guy?"

Griff's light brown eyebrows lifted, and he glanced at her. She graced him with a hesitant smile.

The brilliant man, with his usual pleasant character, replied, "More like family. You are?" His focus shifted to the work in progress.

"Without transportation. My bike broke down a couple of miles out and Ericka offered to let me stay in the barn until I could get it repaired. Her front door didn't shut." He ran his hand over the wood. The rough swollen edges appeared to be splinter-free and, as promised, smooth.

Man sweat filtered through the light breeze. She stared at his trim form and the annoying tingle tripped. Okay, so he hadn't been a figment of her imagination or incantation and the now real attraction to him made her buzz with awareness. She'd think about something monotonous. In a flash, the memory of a speech to the High Technology Crime Investigation dampened the hunger, at least until Joe removed his tee and shook off the shavings. Six-pack abs led to a narrow waist. Sexy and quiet. Her dream guy.

An old bullet wound marring the right side of his

narrow waist begged for stroking and soothing. Something about him, besides his rockin' hot body, elicited a reaction and *what if* possibilities pitted her mind.

Griff coughed, one of those stop-what-you're-doing coughs he used sometimes with Jacey. She glanced at him. He smiled, large enough his white teeth stood out. Damn, he'd caught her lusting after a drifter.

"Well, if you'll excuse me. I need to..." She fluttered a hand toward the inside of the house.

Joe stared at her and grinned; a sly little upturned lip, as if he knew what bothered her. Nope. She had a case to prepare for and a handsome, clever, motorcycle rider was going to change her course. *Wasn't.* He *wasn't* going to detour her.

Confident she could pull off a nonchalant exit; she pivoted and slipped inside the house. She hurried into the kitchen, hoping the pre-set coffee maker had gone off as timed and hadn't reset due to the power outage. The coffee had brewed, so she poured a cup of java. A few sips later, she carried the mug to her room using the rear staircase.

She dressed in a dark blue business suit and appropriate sensible heels; high enough to make her calves look sexy, but not hooker-tall. She circled her neck with a strand of pearls. The end of the necklace fell in the grove of her azure cotton button-down. In order to keep their luster, pearls needed to touch skin, and fortunate for her, the pearls had plenty of sheen. Ready to go, she'd first check at the courthouse for plaintiff records.

At the top of the stairs, she crouched to see if Joe heartthrob was still shirtless. No guy and a snug entry door. She descended, snatched her purse and briefcase, and walked out. *No sign of him or Griff's truck.* She locked the door and peered around the corner. The barn. She hoisted her bag straps to her shoulder, tiptoed around the mud puddles, and shoved the barn door open. Joe's motorcycle shone in the shards of light, but the man didn't appear.

She shut the door, entered her garage, and slid behind the wheel of her Mercedes C-300. The old classic often needed repair, but as a gift from her late father, she'd hate to part with it. She'd need more clients before she could buy a more reliable car. No one had forced her to make this lifestyle change, so she'd deal with the resources available.

She drove along the country road, intending to check the progress of the new construction before going to Cyan. Jacey's antique store would have a rent-free office space, including a private entrance for Ericka's practice.

Three miles later, she parked on the gravel driveway. The grand opening, planned for the day before Christmas, fast approached. Open until midnight late customers would have the advantage of shopping when other stores had closed.

If luck were with them, the strong marketing strategy would allow Jacey to capture the all too common procrastinator shoppers. Once the building was finished, it'd be a rush to get the stock displayed.

Her car wasn't in the drive.

Ericka didn't have construction experience, but she'd return later and offer her painting or cleanup services. She checked the rearview mirror, threw the shift into reverse, and noticed Joe Reeves coming from inside, carrying a load of the deep brown floorboards. Was he working for Griff?

She approached the city of Cyan and curved onto Spell Avenue. As she drove past Dark Shadows, a bar and grill, she made a mental promise to return later. She needed a visit with her new friend and owner of the restaurant.

Ten minutes later, she parked in front of the stone-fronted courthouse. When she first came to Cyan, she had to wait an inordinate amount of time to get registered before she could serve and practice law. She longed for acceptance by the townspeople. What would it take to prove her worth and be a recognized member of the community?

An old man, wearing a cowboy hat and a leather jacket complete with fringe, held the ornate door open, and she passed through.

"Thanks," she murmured. She read the wall plaques of noted locals who'd become political. All males. Someday her portrait would decorate the wall of fame. She'd be the female pioneer to break through the conservative wall. First, she'd impress the mayor by getting his son's charges dropped or at least reduced to a lesser charge.

She ascended the stairs to the second floor, withdrew her name badge, and entered the office. She'd get the scoop about the badass her client had beaten to a bloody mess. The plaintiff didn't have priors, which didn't help her case. However, Mike had one arrest for assault almost a year to the day. He hadn't revealed the imprisonment.

Her contract with him warred with her oath to serve. Could she help a more-than-likely guilty client?

She rushed toward the records office. Her heels clacked on the slate surface of the hallway. What should her next strategic move be? A large hand grasped her arm. She yelped and turned.

"Sorry, Ericka." Caleb smiled. "I didn't mean to scare you."

She took a deep breath. Human guy, attractive, and wanting to be with her. She should at least engage in a conversation.

He tipped the bill of his dark beige hat, revealing a lock of blond hair plastered to his forehead.

"Hi, Caleb, how are you?" She ran her gaze over him. His big, round eyes glimmered with humor, but her attention fixated on his thick neck and broad shoulders. The brown of the sheriff's uniform didn't suit him despite the trimness of his waist. Nice guy, if a zing would tweak her core she'd consider him a viable dating partner.

"Better since we're doubling with Griff and Jacey." He rolled his hat between his fingers.

She wanted to run. However the conjure to get a lover hadn't worked and Caleb was alive and kicking. She should be happy to spend a few minutes in his presence instead of pining for something she couldn't have. Why did she feel a sense of betrayal to Joe? Get real. They'd had a moment and a kiss, a powerful sexy kiss. She shook her head. In a day or two he'd become a gypsy again.

"Sounds like fun." She moved back a step, just a comfortable space.

He frowned. She must have offended him. She'd like a friendship with him, but not with benefits, at least not at this time. "What did Jacey and Griff have in mind?"

"Dinner." His eyes twinkled.

The unintentional affront was forgotten. "Sounds great. Hey, could you check your database to scan for info about a Joe Reeves?"

Caleb's grin turned into a serious hard line. "Sure, come with me."

He captured her upper arm, and they climbed the wide staircase together. The backside of his hand rubbed against her breast. A probable mishap, but still no sizzle.

He guided her into the DA's office and indicated for her to sit on a gray leather chair. He whispered into the matron's ear, and her frown melted. She brushed a curl over her shoulder, pointed to a room off to her left side without breaking the intense stare.

"Thanks," Caleb murmured. He turned away without a backward glance. "Ericka." He beckoned.

She followed him inside the lavish office. The aroma of too much rose and gardenia perfume overpowered the space. She wanted to throw open a window to clear the air. Instead, she sank into the black faux leather sofa and breathed through her mouth.

Caleb slid his fingers over the keyboard and within seconds, his eyes opened wide.

She dropped her bags and rushed to stand behind him. "Probably the one from Mississippi. He has a certain intonation."

A click and Joe's photo, in dress blues, appeared across the monitor screen along with the essentials. They were the same age and astrological sign.

"It looks like he was a cop for the Picket, Mississippi police department. He quit a year ago."

So her intuition about his southern background and good character had proven to be true. "Good, thank you."

"Who is he?" Caleb shut down the computer and swung the chair to face her. He spread his legs. He appeared relaxed, but she knew him, he was alert and suspicious.

She didn't plan to lie, nor tell him the man camped out in her barn. "Griff's new employee." She'd assumed. "I'm making sure he doesn't have a record."

"Looks like the mischievous sort, huh?" His knees bumped hers making the assertive brush appear accidental. She didn't want his overt touching, at least not at this juncture.

"Just protecting my BFF." Her heart beat with a swift drum roar. Joe's old bullet wound flashed through her thoughts. What was the reason he quit the force at such a young age?

Caleb put his hand on her forearm. "If you're finished, I'll walk you to your car."

The courtroom glass ceiling had taken her several years to pierce. She refused to allow anyone to see her as anything but an assertive, honest, law provider. In contradiction, certain social situations had always been awkward for her, almost painful. She gave him a silent nod.

Caleb put his hand on her hip, reminding her what it felt like to be part of a couple. He nodded to the secretary. He kept his hand on her hip as they meandered along the hallway, down the stairs and out the door. She stopped, to allow her eyes to adjust to the light.

"Coffee?"

"I've research to do. Rain check?" She rummaged through her purse, squirming away from his touch without appearing rude, until she found her sunglasses. She twirled them, and then fit them on the bridge of her nose.

"He's guilty."

She stared at him. Did he mean Joe or her client? "That's to be determined."

He nodded, as if backing away from the subject. "I'll be at your place at six, okay?"

The automatic lock release for the car clicked. "Sure. I'll be ready." She lifted her head and caught his gaze. "Caleb, we've known each other since I rolled into town, and you gave me directions to Ames Mansion. Over the past few months we've become friends, right?"

"Yep." His short response and evaluative stare made her uneasy.

"I like you, but I'm not—"

"Ready for, ah, exclusivity." He crossed his arms. "Me either. It's just a date, Ericka."

****

For the past two years, Joe avoided confined spaces. He'd trapped himself inside a vehicle two times: by ambulance and in his sister's car when she took him home from the hospital. However, when good ol' Griff handed his truck keys over as if he'd known him for years instead of hours, he couldn't refuse. He took a deep breath, trying to acclimate. Behind the large steel engine, he searched for Pete's Parts, Vehicle and Otherwise. Griff had given him a shit-eating grin as he'd offered directions. Joe now understood why. The Broom Alley auto parts store had a western storefront.

The town had a population of twenty-five thousand. Cauldron's Brew, Toil and Boil, Magic Circle, and Spell Avenue, all annoying street names, however, yet perfect for the Victorian style buildings.

When his bike was repaired, he'd drive through the city and checkout each street name, if for no other reason than to get a good laugh.

Near the round a bout, he spotted Ericka's car parked in front of the courthouse, with her rear pasted to her car fender. She didn't look unhappy about the sheriff being a feather's length away.

The closer he got, Joe noted her back bowed. Her full backside touched her vehicle. Joe laughed at her let's-get-this-over-with expression. Badge or no badge, the cop wasn't getting anywhere with the lady.

Despite her obvious reluctance to the dude, a pinch of jealousy made its way into Joe's stomach. A physical connection existed between him and Ericka. Her kiss last night, even if by mistaken identity, had his entire being in a state of arousal. During those few unforgettable seconds, she'd made him feel normal again.

This rush of emotion and gut-clenching ache had to be a fluke. He should ignore his flash of faux humanization and go about his business.

He had to restrain the sensations and get the bike fixed, then get the hell away from her. He drove on Broom Alley and disregarded the next sign. Like a lovesick teenager, he circled the court and stopped the truck near the two turtledoves.

He knuckled the window button. *So much for overlooking emotions.* "Hey, Ericka, could you help me?"

Her face, as bright as a lightning bug on a summer's eve, struck his pulse into an intense rhythm.

The sheriff frowned and placed a hand at the top of his gun keeper. She nudged the man, scooted past him, and strode toward the truck. The cop acted as though he planned to walk with her. She glanced back. He stopped and assumed the position.

"Hi, Joe." She hoisted her bag's strap to her shoulder.

"Hope I'm not interrupting." He gave a head nod toward the law, validating the lie.

Different backdrop, but she was just as enticing. Beautiful chestnut brown curls swished across her shoulders as she shook her head. Last night, wet and shower fresh, her hair appeared darker. Today, red and blond highlights glinted from the thick strands. "Good, I'm looking for Pete's Parts. Am I close?"

The officer took a step toward the truck.

"Sure, it's just a couple of blocks from here." She lifted a slender hand and pointed toward the street he'd passed. In her sweet melodic voice, she gave him detailed directions.

He sighed. Little did she know, he'd already arrived at the place he hadn't been looking for, but he didn't want to leave.

He'd been curious about the color of her dark eyes. They reminded him of his favorite color and the amber tint of the shell on his bike engine case. Lured by her adorable mouth, he stared. She didn't need cosmetics to define those luscious lips. Would he get the chance to stroke his tongue across them and commit their shape to memory?

"Getting a spark plug?" She ran her tongue over

her lips, the very same path he'd fantasized about.

"Yes." To his own ears, his voice sounded hoarse. From a simple look, she had him tangled in thicket of nettles, stinging yet warm. Pain and pleasure.

"Ericka, need assistance?" The sheriff dropped a grabby hand to her hip. Joe's gut twisted.

"No, thank you. Caleb Knight, this is Joe Reeves. Joe, Caleb." She resituated her bag giving the impression she was ready to leave and put space between them.

Knight nodded in greeting. "Howdy. You're working for Griff Carpenter?" His scrutinizing stare evaluated Joe, and then traveled across the interior of the vehicle. *Very clever search, my man.* A few seconds passed. "You've got his truck."

He didn't want to like the guy, because of his possessiveness of Ericka, but Joe could tell the man was a thorough cop.

"Yes, I'm working with Griff doing carpentry work." He met the guy's stare. "Nice guy, to trust a first day employee with his truck." Defense would always be the best offense.

"Can I help you?" The officer's direct eye contact didn't falter. The man was sharp.

Joe glanced at Ericka's emotionless face. If she had some free time, he'd like to take her to Vegas. She'd win big time at poker.

"No, thank you. Ericka's taking care of me." He winked and cocked a grin.

Knight's fingers tightened, making the leather squeak. "We'll let you be on your way then."

"See you later, Joe." She stepped away from the truck.

"See ya," Caleb added. A man of few words.

"Nice to meet you, Sheriff. Ericka, see you at home." Joe drove forward, but kept the couple in sight. Words were exchanged between the two. Knight led her to her car. After putting her messenger bag in the trunk, she slid behind the driver's wheel. Her profile was as beautiful as full frontal. A fluttering of desire rushed through him. Although controlled, his imagination ran wild, flitting here and there, bouncing off the walls of the truck like a flea on a hound.

The deputy slapped the roof of her car. No kiss. There was hope.

****

Spark plug in hand, he stopped at Hank's Hardware. Joe purchased ordinary items; things he noticed were missing from the worksite that he'd need for the building process. Griff offered him a job through December with the possibility of a permanent spot with his construction team.

Joe would decline. Law enforcement flowed in his blue blood. But he couldn't get close to these people. He didn't want to see one of their deaths in a vision. Ever since the accident and the onset of his psychic abilities, he had a mere twenty-four to forty-eight hours to try to prevent the deaths. He didn't want to risk the tragedy of failure.

Unable to avoid people forever, he'd begun the quest to find someone to rid him of his ability. What if the shaman proved to be an urban legend? No, the healer of the unhealable had to be real. The shaman was his final hope to eliminate the precognition, the hellish gift of prophecy.

His stomach tightened. Family, friends, and even

an acquaintance had appeared in his death visions. So far, the dreams always came true. The first couple of times he didn't understand the meaning and ignored the forecast...until he got an image of a child. He didn't have enough experience to stop the child's death. Now, he paid attention to even the smallest details in the visions, and his successful saves increased. Bumps and bruises he could live with, but the death of a kid wasn't acceptable.

Townspeople might not confide in a stranger. Although Griff and Ericka seemed to have some clout, he wouldn't name drop. He'd refrain from asking questions, and stick to good ole' fashioned research. The next stop would be the local library, located straight across from the courthouse.

He parked in front of a window in order to keep the truck in sight. As he dropped from the cab, he shivered. A quick freeze followed the rain last night. The flap from his red scarf flipped and twisted. He tucked the cloth inside his leather coat. His thin southern blood hadn't adapted to the cool mid-western air. The barn would be very cold tonight. He'd check into a hotel and ask one of the guys if he could share a ride.

A half-moon-shaped window enhanced a portion of the library entrance. He walked inside the reception area and drew in the scent of new books mingled with old tomes. At the circular desk, a tiny gray-haired lady swiped a rod over a book cover. Behind her, five doors led to separate rooms. Above each doorway hung a sign: Fiction, Children, Biography, Audio-visual, and Non-fiction.

In spite of dedicating her attention to waving the electronic device, she'd noticed his entry. Her gnarled fingers flattened on top of the oak counter. The gray and black beaded threads attached to her glasses clinked as she moved. She didn't smell like an old lady. Rather pleasant floral scents wafted with her graceful movements. "May I help you?"

"Yes. I'm searching for information about an Indian, er—Native American who resides near Cyan. He's a shaman."

"That's folklore. Medicine men do not exist in Cyan today." With wrinkled hands, she pulled her dark blue cardigan tightly around her shoulders.

Was she kidding? He assumed librarians knew everything, doubted nothing. Wait. He said shaman, not medicine man. Was she keeping more than thin shoulders hidden beneath her sweater?

He kinked his neck and glanced out the window at the truck. No sign of disturbance. "Okay. Maybe something has been written about a Native American named Wolf in the area. Where could I find back issues of the local newspaper?"

"Audio-visual. The old newspapers are now on microfiche." She pointed, with her bent finger, to a room closest to the street.

"Thank you, ma'am." He crossed the threshold into the room labeled Biography and stopped. Ericka Gilmore's firm little derrière rested in the seat in front of one of the three computer terminals. She tapped one of her pointed toed shoes in a quick steady rhythm providing a nice tiled tune.

He stepped closer, until her magnolia scent infiltrated his personal space. With her focus and concentration directed on the screen, he took the opportunity to look over her shoulder. His name was splashed across the screen. What the hell? She was reading an article about him. Checking on him.

The Pandora Gazette, Arizona, headline depicted his *heroic save* of a boy. Like a bad movie, his mind flashed back to that day. After an instant bond, in part, because he missed his nephews and niece, he grew fonder of the kid. Then the nightmare came. Joe hadn't been able to prevent the previous three precognition deaths, but Sam—he had to save the kid. Shocked by his success, he told the boy's mother about the gift. A reporter got wind of the story and published. And yet again, he had to leave behind an adopted family. What good was the damn prophecy if he couldn't prevent a child from dying?

He avoided getting close to people. If he formed a friendship that resulted in a premonition, he could lose all the companionship, and perhaps the those in the visions would lose their lives. Act on the prophecy or walk away; either way he lost, defeated because if he saved the life or not, he'd be either hero or devil. And the flux would, sooner or later, kill him.

"Did you find everything you wanted to know about me?" he asked, letting the pissed tone slither through.

Ericka jumped. Her knees hit the bottom of the tabletop, jiggling her purse until it fell to the floor. Colorful female items spread out in a kaleidoscope on the wood planks.

"Sorry, didn't mean to scare you." Hunkering down, he lifted a lipstick and an elongated tube. A twist and a word appeared. *Tampon.* Red fingernails clasped the cylinder and a hiss of air flew past his ear.

He glanced into her face, noted the flushed cheeks,

and laughed. "Nothing to be embarrassed about. I have a sister."

She groaned and dumped the score of items into the bag. He stood and looked at the blank screen. Clever woman had powered down the computer.

She posed like a traffic cop directing a busy intersection and pointed toward the door. "Are you following me?"

"I wanted to get some information about the town. A better question would be why are you investigating me?" This time he kept the laughter inside, but let the irritability remain. Her guilt-ridden frown made him want to run as fast as possible out of the county and away from a woman who turned his insides to mush.

"I have to admit, I'm curious about you. Where you come from? Why you're a loner?"

He lifted an eyebrow. He was a loner, not by choice, and resented the woman he'd been fantasizing about for expressing the obvious. "Who says I'm a loner? Do you investigate everyone who stays overnight in your barn?"

Her foot stopped tapping and her face relaxed, making her more than stunning. "No. As a rule, I don't allow strangers to stay. It takes a strong person to travel alone across the country astride a bike. I didn't get to read all the articles, but the last one proclaimed you are a hero. Are you a savior, or are you running from something or someone?"

He'd ignore the barbs and focus on her kissable lips. Joe smiled, moved closer to her, and gripped the thick wood of her chair. *What are you doing?* He dropped his hand.

"I guess your search will determine the answer. I

need to get the truck back to Griff. Later." He stuffed his shaking hand into his pocket and strutted out of the library. She bugged him more than he cared to admit.

Chapter Four

Ericka took a deep breath, trying to sift through her conflicted emotions. She should follow Joe and say something. *Apologize*. She took a deep breath, inhaling the library's vintage book aroma and glanced at the computer screen. Why shouldn't she check him out? As a member of the community, she'd want to defend other citizens. Hell, she'd meticulously searched Griff before Jacey married him. Part of her nature was to protect her family.

Grabbing the printed documents, she left the library. She walked outside, but Griff's truck wasn't in the parking lot. She needed a drink and a burger. With a full stomach, she could better filter the information from the newspaper articles.

She tossed the papers into the car, climbed behind the wheel, and drove. Spell Avenue lacked appropriate parking, but she managed a space in front of her favorite restaurant. She liked the name of the establishment, Dark Shadows, and the owner presented a long list of international brews. Dark beers tasted of rich decadent yeasty goodness, reminding Ericka of home and her favorite bar in Indianapolis. A hundred-year-old oak tree blocked most of the front of Dark Shadows, making the three-story construction look like an elves' cottage instead of a major structure taking a good portion of the city block. The precise locations of the exterior lighting allowed the gothic-shaped branches to form obscure patterns across the lawn and walls. Wind added to the eeriness by moving and shaking the images into creepy shadow characters.

A businessman, in conversation with another suit, held the large oval door open. She waited for her eyes to adjust to the dim interior, and then moved toward the bar. A thin tall waitress swiped the top of a table, and a large pot-bellied bartender cleaned glasses. Mouthwatering scents made her stomach rumble. She could almost taste a greasy hamburger and full-bodied lager. She slid atop a stool and searched for Brandi.

"Hi, how's it going?" At five foot four, Brandi came into direct line with Ericka's chin. Large hazel eyes, set in a heart-shaped face, gave her an angelic look.

"Hi." She sighed and rubbed her forehead. "Not so good. I need a beer and a burger. Doable during off hours?"

"Sure, which one?" Brandi tossed her long black braid over her shoulder.

"What dark beers do you have?"

"Want a Belgian Dark?"

"Never had one, but sounds good. I'm all for trying something new." Ericka removed her cellphone and checked the messages, but nothing was in the queue.

Frosty mist billowed from the open refrigerator as Brandi extracted a brown container. She closed the door and the fog dissipated like ghost vapor. She twisted the brilliant blue label toward Ericka. *Chimays*. "Need a glass?"

"No thanks, you just finished tidying." She took the bottle and glanced at her phone, hoping she hadn't missed a call from Jacey. A good friend would be helping to organize stock, but the drink had more of a draw. Yeah, she could be a BFF after a couple of sips and a hamburger. She'd need the energy.

She plopped her bag on the counter. Her phone fell deeper inside, clinking against keys. She inserted a fingernail under the wire holder of the bottle.

"Let me." Brandi used a metal device and popped the cap of the *Chimays* and handed it to Ericka.

"Cheers." She lifted the container into the air.

"Here's to antioxidants found in good brew." Brandi raised her glass of water. "I want to thank you for helping me with the contract. I—"

"Brandi, I'm going out to get some paper goods," said the waitress who stood at the end of the bar.

"Okay," Brandi shouted. "BJ, you can take a break, too."

"You don't want me to stay and serve the ambulance chaser?" BJ asked.

Ericka frowned. *What a rude thing to say.*

"BJ," Brandi rumbled.

"Will she be posting signs indicating you don't serve attorneys? I seriously need a hamburger." Ericka let the remark pass.

A very unladylike honk came from Brandi's bow-shaped mouth. "No, she won't. I'll get you a burger."

"Whew, thank goodness. I was afraid you'd crack a lot of bad lawyer jokes." She hoisted the bottle, appreciating the repartee and trust they'd achieved in such a short time. She wouldn't trade the newfound camaraderie for a thousand ghosts.

Brandi laughed, a deep throaty chuckle, as she walked into the kitchen.

From the jukebox, a singer's high falsetto filled the empty room, telling people to take a good look at his face. Ericka took a sip of the thick and rich beer. The tipple rushed down her throat, filling her with an instant sense of euphoria. She didn't drink very often. Anxious about the store opening, her finances, and her houseguest made the beer very appealing. Joe created odd emotions in her. He made her want something she could never have.

"Hey, I'm sorry about the other night."

Ericka looked to her side as Jacey sat down. The milking stool creaked. "Okay."

"Look you're an attorney, not a Wiccan specialist. I'm surprised you even dabble in the occult. Not logical if you ask me. Okay, quit frowning, walk in my shoes and all that. I assume you didn't bring the dead back?"

She shook her head. "I wasn't trying to bring him back. I was trying to call forth a perfect lover, one with no strings. You're right, I don't have experience, and to be honest I'm afraid of magic. This obsession is impossible to explain. I just want to be happy and have a relationship I won't screw up." She placed the heavy bottle on the countertop. "You understand my fear of commitment which is why a conjured lover is perfect for me. Human frailty proves to be no problem with a supernatural."

"Yeah, I get it, but you need to stop trying to summon a lover and find a real one." She shook her head. "Stop magic altogether. Burn the books."

Ericka tipped the bottle toward her friend. "I'm not sure the spell would've worked anyway."

Jacey touched her arm. "You're very pretty and smart. You've been here long enough to start dating the locals. Let's find a live man for you to date."

"Jace, you're aware of my gene pool. All guys should run away instead of staying close." Ericka tapped her shoe against the barstool rung.

Jacey exhaled. "It doesn't have to be that way, Ericka. Marriage can be fulfilling and long lasting."

"I'm sorry; I didn't mean…your marriage will be forever." She pressed her fingertips to her forehead. "This man I've met has thrown me into a spin. I'm discovering emotions I've never had for a guy before, and his stay in Cyan will be short." She lowered her hand. "I'm not lovin' it."

"You've met a guy, and I'm just hearing about it?"

"We've both been busy, and I didn't want to interrupt your work with the store." Ericka's cheeks heated.

Her friend's back straightened. "Tell me more about him?"

"I think of him and imagine what if." She twirled a finger in the air. "He makes me want more."

"I get it." Jacey glanced at her phone. "I'll need more, but an auction is starting in a few minutes. I'll see you tomorrow? We'll sort stock and talk about this mystery guy?"

"Yes. At the store about nine?"

"Yep, works for me."

Brandi came through the door carrying a platter with a steaming hamburger and side order of fries. She placed the plate in front of Ericka and turned to Jacey.

"Can I get you something?"

"No thanks, I was just leaving." Jacey slid off the stool. "Ericka, embrace the possibility of love. Don't forget we have a double date this Friday."

"Friday? Oh, yeah, the Sheriff. Sure."

****

Ericka drove along the lane leading to her house. The nose of Griff's tomato red truck stuck out from the open barn doors. She parked the car, released the seat belt, and clasped her purse. She stepped from the vehicle, meandered toward the building and listened for voices. Going from sunlight into the barn, it took a moment for her eyes to adjust.

A couple of two-by-fours created a bridge to the edge of the truck. Joe stood to one side and wheeled the motorcycle, stopping when he connected with the flat metal surface of the truck bed. On the balls of his feet, Griff stood at the opposite side tying a red bungee cord to a stainless steel anchor.

"What's going on?" She crossed her arms at her middle.

"Taking the bike to the shop to get checked." Joe shoved the kickstand into place. "Then, I'll be out of your hair."

"Because of the football tournament the hotels are full. Joe's going to stay at my house," Griff spouted, as he wound the cable to the motorcycle and handed a hooked end to Joe.

She glanced at Joe. Crouched at the front of the bike he wove the cord through the metal pieces, and then his solemn stare pierced her. All of her self-erected walls quaked. He couldn't leave. He averted his gaze. With a graceful maneuver, he shifted to the rear of the motorcycle, secured a bungee, and handed the end to Griff.

Don't let Joe leave. "He can stay here." The opposite end of the bungee cord snapped into place.

Griff grimaced and slid the board atop the bed. "Ericka, it's too cold to stay in the barn."

"He can stay in the house," she shot back.

Joe jumped from the truck. With a languid poise, he snatched his overstuffed satchel from under the rear bumper, clutched the handles, and then snapped the gate into place. His stiff posture left her confused. Either he was pleased or angry about the discussion.

She glanced at Griff. His clamped mouth marked his disapproval. Her stomach muscles clutched.

"Joe?" he asked, his tone impersonal, edging toward uninterested, but his blue-green stare made her feel inferior.

"I'll stay." Joe tapped the line connecting his back tire to the truck. *Thong-pong* rang through the quiet as the ties snapped in place. "I need to go with Griff to deliver the bike to the repair shop. I'll be back in a little over an hour."

She bit her lip and nodded. What had she done? She wanted to spend time with Joe doppelganger. The hunk, so handsome he couldn't be unattached, but it didn't matter. Joe made her feel alive. Vibrant. Important.

The guys drove away, and she hurried to her car. She grabbed her briefcase from the trunk, secured the locks, and entered her house. The front door shut and locked with ease. The now flat surface was ripe with the fresh scent of maple.

She dropped her messenger bag and purse on top of the Bombay table. The reverberation of the thud filled the foyer as she searched through the drawer to find a spare house key. Had she made a mistake? Joe represented an upstanding man and being a detective for a few years gave him some credibility. According to a couple of newspaper articles, Joe and his partner had been broadsided during a bank robbery chase. His co-worker had been killed. Joe lapsed into a coma. How dreadful to lose a friend in such a way. If Jacey passed into the light, would Ericka aimlessly wander?

She climbed the staircase and strode into the guest suite. Had she made the right decision about letting him stay? No backtracking now. She opened the French doors. Fresh air whipped through the room as she obtained sheets from the armoire and made the bed. There, he'd have a nice warm place to sleep. She put clean towels in the adjoining bathroom, then sat on the edge of the bed.

Before Joe appeared at the library, she'd read two news articles. He'd become the hero and saved a boy from being struck by a stray baseball, flying with such a velocity he would have died right there. Joe had quit the detective's unit and the force; yet, he continued to perform acts of good will.

Joe Reeves had become stranded in Cyan, and his magnetism drew her. She stretched her neck, getting the kinks out. He made her think of something other than work and her nebulous bankrupt future for several hours.

She rose from the bed and straightened the wrinkles from the covers. A shower, then she'd make dinner and if possible find out Joe's version of the tabloid stories. Why didn't he go back to his police job instead of choosing a nomadic life style? Other than saving children, what had he been doing for the past several months?

She twisted the shower knobs. The old pipes

clanked and groaned as water poured. Stripping off the blue business suit and undergarments, she stood in the cool tiled room and devised a plan to introduce the subject. Showered and dressed in sweats and a long shirt, she hurried toward the kitchen.

The evening had turned cold and another bout of rain was predicted, so a thick hot chili would heat them. She'd already pictured Joe sitting across from her at the scarred kitchen table.

Serious concern for her mental health ran through her mind. One moment she'd adjusted to being alone forever, and the next, she pictured herself with him as a couple. Her southern charmer required further investigation, and she'd enjoy the research.

Why did the water pipes continue to rattle?

On stockinged feet, she tiptoed down the rear staircase and glanced into the utility room. Empty. She crept though the kitchen, into the hallway, and grabbed a tall metal-tipped umbrella from the canister at the front door. Umbrella in strike position, she slid toward the downstairs bathroom.

Inside her purse, her cellphone rang.

****

Joe's cellphone dinged. He turned off the water and tied a towel at his middle. He opened the glass door to allow the foggy mist to leak into the room. Out of the condensation a long sharp device appeared. He jumped and pressed the intruder against the slim bit of wall space between the toilet and shower. A quick twist of the arm and the weapon fell, pinging on the title floor. The fog cleared, and her gorgeous facial image solidified.

Ericka.

"Damn, sorry. For a second I thought you were an intruder." Powerful and vibrant, rapid breathing lifted her chest as he released her collarbone and neck. Magnolia scent drifted into his nostrils.

From every point of bodily contact, heat fused them. He glided his hands over her soft, thin shirt, learning the luscious hollows and hills of her figure, well worth exploration.

She gasped, but didn't back away. Good, he didn't want the contact to end. He attempted to rearrange strands of hair from her face. The fine strings stuck to his wet fingers like hot glue. He dipped his head to kiss her.

"Wet. Hard..." She coughed. "Griff let you—" She closed her eyes. "Please let go."

He dropped his hands. "Yes, he planned to wait, but his wife called and he had to leave." *Go slow. She's skittish.* He took a half step away from her fire, but close enough to keep the heat alive. "I hope you don't mind me using the shower."

"No, not at all. My house is yours and all that." She gave a tiny smile and licked her glossy lips, already plump from biting them. Little tendrils of her silky brown hair curled in the humidity. A small sound of want vibrated in her throat.

What was it with this woman? Questions didn't matter. In fact, what mattered stood in front of him, right now, right here. He should leave, at this instant, but couldn't because his nights had been death-dream free. His dreams were of Ericka.

He caressed her face, thinking the gentle action would slow her quick breaths. Instead, the rise and fall of her chest jetted to breakneck speed.

"Ericka," he murmured into her ear and followed it with a light brush of his mouth over hers, hoping she'd respond to his caress.

She broke the kiss. Instead of slapping his face, as he'd anticipated, her hips gravitated toward him as if seeking more heat. The woman was a total contradiction. She shifted her glance and looked over his shoulder. They'd formed an instant bond last night, although, the tether holding them might be short. Why did she avoid their obvious connection? Blatant naked desire stood between them and, from her body's response, she obviously wanted to satisfy the yearning.

Joe leaned into her, his mouth close to hers. She trekked her fingers from his chest to tuck around his neck, tugging him closer. Shiny pink lips tantalized him, and he wanted to enjoy the magic of their first real kiss…a kiss she intended for him.

She broke away from his grip, his touch. "I didn't invite you to stay here because I'm attracted to you. Griff and Jacey are newlyweds, living in a small house, and they don't need a stranger staying with them."

His stomach churned. Her words didn't match the burning embers in her eyes. Was he delusional, wanting her to desire him the way he did her? Didn't she feel the intense hotness connecting their two bodies?

"Ericka?" A high-pitched female voice echoed through the hallway, followed by hard-hitting footsteps.

Joe sighed at the lost opportunity and stepped away. The squeak of the door drew his attention. Ericka Gilmore threw herself in front of his near nakedness, backing her plump rear into him. The top of her head fit perfectly beneath his chin.

A red-haired, green-eyed spitfire stopped on her

toes in the doorway. The petite woman grinned, placed her hands at her hips, and cocked her head, evaluating them as a mother would a prospective date for her daughter. He liked her at first sight.

"Oops, sorry. I'm Jacey." She peered around Ericka and flung out a hand. "Jacey Carpenter."

What was protocol when standing behind a woman who shielded his engorgement?

Chapter Five

Ericka glanced between Jacey and Joe. The bathroom steam dissipated and the remaining dew fogging the mirror above the vanity faded. Tendrils of hair curled behind Joe's ears, highlighting his scrubbed face.

She took a hint from the elbow in her side and moved. He clutched the cotton ends of the daffodil tinted towel with one hand and thrust the other toward Jacey. "Hi, I'm Joe Reeves."

Ericka clutched her phone and flipped her hand toward the door.

Jacey didn't take the hint and gripped the doorframe. Her irises widened, an eyebrow arched, and then she sprouted a Cheshire smile.

Damn. Heat rushed to Ericka's face as she sidled around Joe and moved closer to the bathroom exit.

Jacey took a step back. Mischief zipped across her face. She oozed with confidence.

"Why don't we give Joe space to get dressed?" Ericka shoved her friend's shoulder.

Jacey craned her head, no doubt to get a good peek. "Nice to meet you, Joe."

He chuckled. "You too."

A second gentle nudge prompted Jacey, and she stepped into the hallway.

Ericka followed, pulling the door shut.

In the kitchen, Jacey leaned against the black granite countertop and tapped her chin. "He's gorgeous."

"Way to ogle. Did you forget you're married?"

Jacey winked. "He's perfect for you."

"Stop being a matchmaker. Come, help me make dinner." She sought refuge in the pantry, selecting beans, a jar of diced tomatoes, and a box of rigatoni noodles, putting the ingredients beside the stove. How could she explain her desire for Joe, who'd been in town a matter of days?

"You're kidding me right? He has all the makings of an Ericka fantasy man." Jacey opened the fridge door, and removed two bottles of water. "Obviously he'd just stepped from the shower, but what were you doing in the bathroom?"

"I thought someone had broken in." She put the heavy metal pan atop the stovetop and turned the dial to low. "No games, he's migratory. Now, how about chopping some onion?"

The dry skin of an onion crinkled as she removed one from the basket and handed it to Jacey. She placed it on a cutting board and slid a knife from the block.

Ericka nodded to the fresh load of fragrant yeasty goodness in a basket. "Thanks for the bread."

"You cannot continue to live your life using your genealogy chart as a map." Jacey straightened the cutting board. "And I'm really surprised you invited a *hu-man* to stay with you."

"Griff has a big mouth." Ericka removed ground turkey from the fridge, opened and dumped the mix into the pan. The sizzle of meat filtered into the space.

"Meaning you weren't going to tell me?" Jacey

passed the cutting board. "Maybe because he looks like your picture from the conjure ceremony."

"Of course I was going to tell you. Sunday night." Ericka dumped the contents into the pot and lowered the cutting board to the counter. "I think it'll be nice to have someone else in the house."

"Right."

While the ingredients sautéed, she opened a *Ball* jar and added the tomato juice to the pot. "When's Griff coming back?"

"Soon. He wanted to check the site for wiring blah, blah, blah and get the new birdhouses you were going to decorate for the store." After washing her hands, Jacey sliced a loaf of fresh baked bread.

"What can I do to help?" Joe's voice came from behind them.

"Ah…" Ericka stammered. Guilt made her heart tighten. She'd done nothing wrong, except maybe yearn for a guy she believed she'd conjured. Why did inviting him to stay feel like she was using him?

"Set the table, dishes in the cupboard to the right of the fridge, silverware to the left, in the drawer," Jacey ordered as she sliced the bread.

Ericka sneaked a look at him as he leaned over the table, placing blue and brown pottery bread plates and bowls atop the mats. His shirt pulled tight across his exquisite chest. *Damn lust.* She gripped the wooden spoon and gave the contents a hefty stir. Letting go of the spoon, she strode to the fridge.

"Need a drink?"

****

Joe glanced at red-cheeked Ericka. She had her back to the front of the fridge and returned his stare with an evaluating one of her own. She lowered her gaze, grabbed a pitcher of tea, and poured the liquid into four glasses. He pushed his hair behind his ears and contemplated how to ask about what a conjure ceremony entailed.

The kitchen door flung open. Griff, holding a large cardboard container, nudged the box against the wall with his knee. Joe set his tea on the table and rushed forward to hold the door from swinging back. Griff maneuvered the container through the opening. His golden retriever, Mac, heeled and then plopped on the floor. He shoved his muzzle into the air. Joe shut the door and rubbed the canine's head.

"Something smells terrific!" Griff situated the box close to the pantry and grabbed Jacey. He pressed his face near her neck.

A tingle of envy ran through Joe. He wanted a connection, someone to make jokes with and a love to have and to hold forever. Impossible. He wiped his mind free of any relationship ambitions, however vague, and sat at the table.

He met Ericka's gaze, and a spark of desire, strong and vibrant, stirred him, reminding him he was after all simply a man.

She turned, so fast she had to be dizzy. Steam rose in front of her, forcing tendrils of her light brown hair to kink at the edges of her face. He resisted the urge to smooth down those few strands touching her soft skin.

Like synchronized dancers, Ericka and Jacey finished preparing the meal. Jacey placed a basket of bread in the middle of the table. Her auburn hair swung across her shoulders as she turned. The expression in a person's eyes always cemented Joe's first impression.

He noticed details, body language, clothing style and color. Jacey's returning stare was filled with honesty, sincerity, and a touch of anxiousness. What could she be nervous about? Vigorous concise movements indicated she edged toward perfectionism. Her vibrant color choices placed her in the fun-to-spend-time-with category.

"How about outlaw chili?" Ericka's joking tone didn't bother him.

He snorted. Although they'd never discussed it, she'd read enough about him to know he wasn't an outlaw. However, he loved playing cops and robbers, so why not enjoy the sport?

"Is it okay if I show Joe the renovations to the library?" Griff took a sip of tea.

"Sure, the guest room's ready too. It's at the east end." Ericka continued to stir the chili. "House key's on the dresser."

He hoped she'd turn around so he could see her expression, but catching Ericka's attention was like attempting to capture quick silver, glittery and slippery. Guest room? She asked him to stay. Didn't she want to pursue the something-something, which sparked whenever their bodies touched?

"I'll get my stuff." Maybe she wanted him in a separate room for appearances. He grabbed his duffle bag out of the bathroom, and then followed Griff down the hallway to the front of the house.

"In addition to inheriting the house, Jacey's aunt left her a legacy. One she had to search for, a hidden fortune, the Ames Diamondhead sword. An arsonist set fire, hoping to scare her away before she found it." Griff smoothed his hand along the doorframe. "During her exploration she stirred up a hornet's nest of trouble."

Joe could smell the odor, a hint of burned wood. The average person wouldn't even notice the lingering smoke, but since the accident, his senses had been heightened and odors adhered like engravings. "I can't imagine Jacey took the assault sitting down."

"No, she didn't." Griff rolled his jaws, as if debating what to say.

"Did she find the treasure?"

"Yes, we found them. A couple of criminals tried to use one of the swords to kill Jacey. Ames spirit interfered and saved her."

An accident had changed Joe, made him believe in all kinds of things, so talk of ghosts didn't faze him. "There were two swords?"

"Yes, one with the Ames' crest. We found the Diamondhead sword under a building being demolished. The current site of the antique store. Come with me upstairs."

"So I keep the story straight in my head, Jacey inherited the house from an aunt, and Ericka bought the house from her."

"Right." The second floor had wide hallways with three doors positioned north and two on the south side. At the top of the stairs and at the end of the corridor, Griff shoved a wood panel. The portal's hinges squeaked. In the glimmer of light, from a high window, boxes and odd pieces of furniture collected dust.

"This is to the attic, and I assume in the past a room for a nanny. Children's furniture and toys occupy half the space." Griff shut the door and meandered toward the next entrance.

The room's high ceilings made the smaller space appear spacious. All the rich details of the room made the dark heavy pieces of furniture stand out. One thing was evident; the master suite didn't match the rest of the house. "Strange."

Griff chuckled. "Yeah, I feel the same way, not my taste either. Came with the house."

"Although hideous, I appreciate her wanting to keep the furniture in the same time period."

"I'll use that line the next time the subject comes up. Two additional guest bedrooms, a guest bath, and sitting room." Griff flung open a door. "And here's your room."

The space equaled his one-bedroom apartment when he'd lived as a normal person in Mississippi. He tossed his bag on the full-sized bed. The room, with detailed crown molding, was decorated with the simple elegance of furniture that appeared to have been purchased at an upscale boutique. His sister had dragged him to those stores often enough.

"A bathroom was added in the eighties and is in good condition. I figure the owners," Griff made air parentheses, "saw", he shoved his hands in his pockets as if embarrassed for the expression, "the ghost in the master suite, so they lived in this room. Maybe they feared retribution?"

"From the ghost?" His heart beat against his ribcage as hard as if he'd pushed his bike for miles. Joe had enough to deal with trying to prevent people from letting go of their ghosts without worrying about active paranormal.

"Don't worry, he's gone now. Kit Ames was murdered trying to locate the killer of his slain wife.

The apparition stayed and haunted, until he found and destroyed the reincarnated bitch who killed his wife." Griff lifted and lowered his eyebrows in a comical manner. "Revenge achieved, he disappeared in a cylinder of blue."

"If you're trying to scare me, it won't work. I've encountered my share of evil women and experienced so many unreal situations talk of a poltergeist doesn't faze me. Did he set the fire downstairs?" Joe slid his hands into his pockets. He had to change the topic.

His new friend shook his head. "I'd like to blame him for the fire, but he claimed to have contained the blaze, trying to save Jacey."

He chuckled, enjoying the story. "So he became the hero."

Griff's joyful humor shifted to pissed-off. Joe's stomach muscles clenched. His partner had a similar facial expression. He missed having a pal.

"On a couple of occasions, the arrogant ass wouldn't give in. He agitated me to no end, slammed doors, and moved furniture." Griff opened a set of French doors and walked outside to a balcony. "I'm glad he's gone."

Joe followed, leaned against the balcony railing, and inhaled. The panoramic view led from the driveway out to trees shrouding the road. Shadows heightened. A starless night set the scene for the story. He became lost in the vast loneliness of the world. "Don't you find it odd, two rational males talking about ghosts?"

Griff rubbed his ear. "Not until the Ames thing. I'm now a believer."

What about the people he couldn't save? Did they haunt the locations where they died? "Just so I'm up to speed, Ames stayed in this place until the spiral took him off to wherever."

Griff sighed. "Yeah."

Joe narrowed his eyes. "Ericka mistook me for someone else, acted like she'd seen a ghost." Was she waiting for her ghost to return?

"Yeah, strange." He crossed his arms and stared. "What's your story?"

Took him long enough to ask. If he were in a similar situation, had a friend allowing a stranger to share a residence in her home, he'd interrogate the hell out of the guy. Joe leaned against the wood of the banister. The cedar bit into his back. He slid his thumbs under his jean belt loops. "I was a police detective in Mississippi. We chased a bank robber. A truck broadsided our car. My friend died. I was in a coma for a few weeks, rehab for the next month, then I took to the road."

Griff met his gaze dead-on. "And?"

My best friend died, and when I came out of a coma, I saw people die. Unable to stop the visions I've been avoiding life and seeking a solution. Next on my list is a shaman noted to live in the hills of southern Indiana. "Not much else to say. Realizing how short our time on Earth is, I wanted to experience life as much as possible."

"As long as your experiences don't include using Ericka and then skipping town." Griff's voice was low-toned but as poisonous as the nightshade growing in the garden below the balcony.

"Don't worry. I'm not that kind of guy." Why, of all the women he chanced to meet, did he have to be attracted to one with a link to the paranormal world he shied away from?

Ericka and Jacey's voices rose from below the widow's walk. Joe turned to glance over the railing and pressed his elbows against the banister. A few seconds later, the women appeared within his line of vision. Their heads were tucked together, and their words scattered like dust particles.

Jacey shoved Ericka's arm. She stood her ground and laughed. They ambled to a garden plot to his left. After clipping off a bit of a sheltered long stemmed glossy plant, they disappeared on the other side of the pillar.

Griff tapped his shoulder. "I'm starving. Let's go eat."

****

"I'll cleanup," Joe said, as Ericka shut the door behind the Carpenters.

"Thanks. I'll help." She gathered glasses from the counter and carried them to the sink.

Joe merged leftovers in one container and stacked the now scraped dishes. "I like them both. Nice people. How long have you been friends?"

The dishwasher door dropped with a thud, the silverware in the catch rattled. He'd take a look at the loose dishwasher hinges tomorrow and tighten the screws.

"Jacey since college and Griff for about a year. She hired him to repair the place. They connected. I took a vacation from my firm and came to help her sell the house. What can I say; I fell in love and bought the estate."

He scraped excess food into the garbage disposal. "Where did you move from?"

"Indianapolis. I worked at Christ and Try Law Firm." Dishes loaded, she shut the dishwasher door and turned. "I spent all of my time in court or preparing cases. Life was passing me by, so I came here to find something different. Quiet. Simple."

He touched the back of her hand, imprinting her with his wet fingers. "I know what you mean; working in civil service can be twenty-four-seven."

She unfolded the dishtowel and handed it to him. "Yes, we have that in common. Are you going to return to law enforcement?"

Joe dried the copper pot, folded the cloth into a four square, and laid it on top of the dishwasher. "No plans. I appreciate your hospitality. I won't be here long."

Her face became a vivid crimson. "Stay as long as you need. I'm exhausted, so I'm heading to bed. Night, Joe."

She ascended the rear staircase at breakneck speed.

Great, he'd pissed her off. As his sister had claimed, more than once, his conversation skills needed polishing.

****

Joe couldn't sleep. Giving up, he slid into a pair of jeans and headed to the kitchen. A snack might help. Soft music came from the library. He braced against the doorframe, nonchalant like he didn't care if she kept baker's hours. There she was, climbing a five-foot ladder, diving for a book located at the top shelf. He rushed to her side. Her pink top drew away from her sweats and a tiny span of rosy skin glimmered in the desk lamp's illumination. He looked up, appreciating the gentle curve of her waist, the plumpness of her breasts, and the strength of her arms. He'd wanted sex before, but this feeling of quiet yearning, a vibrant desire for this one woman was new.

He didn't like it.

Ericka's forehead furrowed. "I'd rather you help me than ogle my boobs."

"I can't deny you have a fabulous rack. Now get down before you fall." He held out his hand, hoping she'd grab hold and create a diversion.

Their palms connected igniting a flame, stronger than the previous electrical charge. She dismounted. He held her gaze until she glanced to the top shelf. He took the hint, grabbed the eight-by-twelve-inch text, and lowered the book to her.

"Thank you," she whispered and grasped the hard cover.

Their fingers touched, giving him a double dose of longing. "About my comment earlier."

"No need to explain." Her grip tightened on the text. She walked to the desk and burrowed into the leather chair. "Thanks for getting the book for me."

She opened the dusty cracked hardback, as if dismissing him.

"Okay, well, good night." He strode toward the door, glancing in the mirror to see if he had toothpaste smeared on his face. He didn't understand why she distanced herself. Reflected in the mirror's background, she held her head between her hands.

He turned around. "Eri—"

She swiveled her chair around, presenting her back to him.

Showered and snug between the crisp clean sheets he willed himself to fall asleep. Deep breath in, long nose exhale. The breathing didn't help achieve a mindless haze. He rolled over to look out the window. Half moon and knockout stars, yet deep sleep eluded him. Why?

He tossed the covers and dropped to the floor. One hundred reps later, he'd exhausted his muscles and climbed into bed. Varied rapid thoughts followed until he counted the proverbial sheep. They worked. He finally relaxed, and his mind went blank.

The vision came in black and white instead of color. Joe stood outside the car parts store, holding a new lock for his saddlebag. Roaring of a large motor vehicle sounded close, and he glanced in the direction of the noise. An older luxury car with the typical sleek lines and double horseshoe motif reminded him of aviator wings. Under the streetlight, the car's shiny frame glimmered. A gray-haired woman surged from a bent position. Her fear-filled face made the sense of urgency stronger. He got a clear view of the librarian with her eyeglass holder beads swinging as she looked right and left. The squeal of tires drew his attention. The roar of a large motored vehicle drew closer. Her car bulleted out of the parking lot and into the street.

Jolted awake, he clutched the covers as his heart pounded in his throat. A semi-truck hurtled into the car tossing it into the air as if it were a balloon.

****

The following night, Joe stood inside the auto parts store. His vigilance would pay off, and knowing the librarian would show, he stalled at the register. The clerk had started hovering in the past twenty minutes. In the dream, the librarian parked her car in the lot, but he hadn't seen her in the store. He selected a lock, wanting the incident to be as real as possible and paid for it, then he walked outside. He glanced to the half-moon hanging in place. The librarian's car wasn't in the lot, and he didn't hear the roar of a semi-truck motor.

He tucked the lock into his pocket and jogged to a fence, concealing the trash bin at the east side. He peered through a crack. No sign of her. He rushed to the store's entrance. Bingo, she'd parked at a diagonal with the motor running. Her fluffy gray hair pressed against the window. The rumble of a semi's massive engine drew closer.

His heart thumped faster. He had mere seconds to get her attention. He ran to the car and pounded on the driver's window. She didn't look in his direction, but her hands gripped the steering wheel. He knocked a second time. His throat grew drier as the booming engine became louder, closer. "Miss, please talk to me."

She didn't respond. Her head continued to hug the window.

He grabbed the door latch. Locked. He couldn't catch a break. "Miss. Librarian. Unlock the door."

She moved, a fraction, and soon after became alert. The door clicked, giving him a moment of relief. He clutched the door handle. The car propelled backward. Her wide eyes were red-rimmed and filled with panic.

"Move," he shouted and opened the door.

Her jaw dropped open, and she fell against the backrest. The car rolled backward. He jumped, grabbed the doorframe, and hit his knee against the casing as he crawled inside. The car's speed increased. He put his leg aside hers and hit the brake. Joe tugged the safety brake jarring the vehicle to a stop. Horn blaring, the semi-truck swerved around the long car.

Joe climbed from her lap and stumbled to the pavement. The salesclerk shouted something from nearby.

"Call 911," Joe yelled. Heaving deep breaths, he reached inside the car, shut off the motor, and hit the emergency flashers. The librarian attempted to move her mouth. He tapped her arm. "Don't worry. You're safe. The EMT's will be here soon."

He turned away, but a tug stretched his sleeve. He glanced at her. Her glazy-eyed stare begged.

"Don't worry; I'll stay with you until they arrive."

His stomach muscles clenched as a tear slid along her bruised cheek.

Chapter Six

"Hi!"

Ericka glanced away from the program playing on her laptop. Joe leaned against the doorframe of her upstairs parlor. "Hi yourself."

He looked edgy with one foot inside the room, one in the hallway. His skin sparkled with that just scrubbed and buffed to a gorgeous bronze sheen. His thin white shirt showed dark areas where it clung to his chest absorbing any leftover condensation.

Ericka sucked in a breath and shifted her glance back to the computer monitor. The medium talked to an invisible spirit.

Phffft! Ericka disagreed with the ghost whisperer; ghosts do not morph from a decayed corpse to a fully clothed, normal-appearing person. However, the story seemed accurate, even if some of the scenes were for entertainment purposes.

As a rule, she didn't watch recorded programs, not even on a rainy afternoon, but Jacey had tacked a note to the antique store door stating she'd gone to an auction with Griff. No doubt, the very reason her sexy biker hung halfway inside the room, work must have been canceled for the afternoon.

"I'm surprised your nose isn't pressed between the books." He nodded toward her legal texts. "You watch TV? I haven't seen one in the house."

"There's a TV in a cabinet downstairs, but I don't want to pay for cable or satellite service." Her pissy mood continued. She'd had a couple of bad interactions with court clerks, and now she shared her irritation with Joe. Maybe due to his persistent, charming, wit and *supercali-fabulous* smile, tingles bounced in her stomach. She didn't want the smoldering desire to linger, so she shot him a snarly get-away-from-me frown.

"All right then." He tapped the doorframe and turned to leave.

Guilt rushed through her. Several people in town had conveyed the tale of Joe saving the librarian. He was a good guy, and she'd treated him like crap.

"Wait. Joe, I'm sorry. I seem to be saying all the wrong things today. Please come and join me. We'll stream a sitcom, or I'll play some DVD's if you're interested." She tossed the pillow she'd been hugging and sat forward. Stored inside the steamer trunk, used as a coffee table, was a stash of classic and current movies.

"Relax. You seem so uptight." Joe laid his hand on her forearm. He snatched his hand back, but not before the twinges went through her.

"No, I'm not."

He sighed. "Whatever you're watching is fine. I hadn't realized how much I missed television. Who knew I'd crave escapism through make-believe in high def?"

Ericka grabbed the dark blue and cream striped pillow, pressed the soft fluff to her chest, and folded her legs under her. He lowered to the sofa and their hips bumped.

"Behind the dart board is a high definition and a sizable wide screen."

He slid his hand along the arm of the couch. His fingers brushed against her neck. "Ah, explains why the furniture is positioned in a half-circle facing the dart board. I thought you held tournaments or something."

She laughed her no-holds-barred laugh. Most men were repulsed by her larger than life chuckles. They always expected some sort of dainty, groomed, princess to be present, but in real-life, perfect didn't happen.

His jaw dropped. Humor glimmered in his eyes. "God, you have a sexy laugh."

Ericka shook her head, absorbing his words and resisting his male essence. "Thanks, not something most guys would say." She pointed to the books, "I should be preparing for a case, and instead I'm watching a show."

"I'm curious. Do you carry your law books everywhere, or is there a duplicate stack downstairs?" The man cut to the core.

"My life revolves around work, so I carry them everywhere." She chuckled, but the sound came out as a nervous little twitter. "I consider them cardio. I carved out some time to help Jacey organize stock, but she baled, so here I am." She nodded toward the computer. "You?"

"Paint's drying." Blue jean fabric swished as he crossed his ankles. New jeans, he must have found the mall. No socks. His hairless toes pressed against the metal band decorating the trunk, then lowered his feet. The shiny dark silver metal had heat imprints.

Christ, even viewing his perfect toes sent sparks of want through her system. A comfy mission style bed was a mere five or so feet away. She swallowed. "No doubt a good plan. Do you want to watch something else?"

He focus went to the screen. "No, this is fine. Bring me up to speed."

"This guy, part-owner of an Asian restaurant, had a fire, and he died. His spirit remained on earth, because he blamed his partner who is now married to the ghost's wife. Melinda, who sees and talks to ghosts, is trying to help him resolve his issues so he can go into the light."

"He doesn't? He thinks his partner set the fire and was having an affair with the wife?"

"Yes. You catch on quick." She leaned forward and pressed the volume button to increase the level, then sat back again.

"Why does she think she can help him?"

"Because she's the whisperer." She leaned forward. The piece of hair she'd snipped earlier waved and distorted her vision. "It's all for show. For a happy ending she helps them find their way into the light."

"The premise isn't logical." He rubbed his knee.

"Maybe supernatural healing is possible. You ask good questions, not surprising considering you were a detective."

Joe moved his arm and it nestled with hers. "Yep, very little gets past me."

From working with wood his skin texture was rough, but nothing could compare to the rush of having this hot guy touch her, however innocent. They watched the show in silence while the whisperer got the human and ghost together to talk.

"I heard you saved the librarian last night."

A slight red rash spread across his neck. If she

hadn't memorized every pore of his skin, she wouldn't have noticed. She had and she wanted to kiss away the heat.

"I was there when she needed help. It was nothing. How did you hear about it?"

"It's all over town." The Internet connection allowed them to watch the show, but it also included commercials. A popular detergent promised clean clothing.

His muscles tightened. "Is she going to be okay?"

"Yes. Mild stroke. She'll recover. People talk, so you need to get used to your new hero status." She moved her hand a fraction, reconnecting their arms from wrist to elbow.

He pressed his shoulder against hers. She curbed the temptation to push the intimacy.

The commercial ended and too soon, the actress helped her lost spirit resolve his issues and walk into the magical light. Did the ghost call forth the aurora or was it always in the background waiting until the spirit departed?

"It looks like it's going to rain," Joe murmured.

She glanced out the windows. Dark cloud formations merged, becoming darker in some areas and lighter at the outside. "You sound disappointed."

"I am. One of Griff's clients paid him in beef, and I was going to grill a couple of steaks." He repositioned his fingers close to hers. Their pinkie fingers touched, brief, but sparks charged through her. The earlier shock had been real and not static electricity.

She closed the laptop. "Umm, barbeque sounds good."

****

Joe had witnessed a hint of desire in her gaze. Perhaps over dinner he could experience a rarity, freedom to enjoy the company of a beautiful woman. He left his hand against hers and dragged his other across his chin stubble. "If we work together, I think we can get the meat glazed before the downpour. Are you down with it?"

Her finger slipped between his last two digits. "I am. Let's go."

God, a grown man, in his mid-thirties with a commendable sexual history, and his current unsophisticated state of arousal became ludicrous. What was wrong with him?

"We can heat the coals, get a little grill flavor, and then pop them in the oven to finish." Her eyes lit with the flare of joy, freeing his illogical assumption. "I've been craving Southern style barbeque for such a long time."

He swallowed. His mind kept repeating heat, flavor, juices, crave, sweet Mississippi biker. Not what she'd said, but oh, how he wanted the idea of her wanting him to be true. "Yes, I'm already tasting them."

Ericka stood. She hefted the textbooks and handed them to him. "Coming?"

"Yep. Can't wait." He stood, holding the stack in front of his belt buckle. "I need to get shoes."

She braced her hand against the doorframe. "I'll see you downstairs. I can already smell the fire, and hear popping bits of fat."

"Yep, popping bits."

The thump of her naked heels striking the staircase planks echoed through the hall. He tugged the shirt away, separating the cotton from his moist skin. The woman would kill him.

Chapter Seven

Ericka craved more shared glances and subtle touching from Joe. Each moment they spent together increased the strength of their odd connection. Despite the attraction, he was a self-proclaimed wanderer and not a contender for a romance. He'd leave soon enough. She had to get over the zing.

She evaluated her outfit in the full-length mirror. Her date with the sheriff tonight might be a good thing. Except, her image reflected an anxious woman on the verge of a very big mistake.

Rays from the setting sun glittered off her gold hair clip. She rubbed her scalp beneath the claw. A sophisticated up-do came with spiked pain.

She smoothed the sides of the shiny emerald A-line dress. Her diamond necklace dangled, creating a pink cast to match the bright pink bra peeking from the V of the outfit. A sharp tug and the material hid the undergarment. She should change, because the dress might give the wrong impression. She glanced at her second best evening dress, solid black with a turtleneck. She'd regret the high neck. Maybe—

Dong, ding, dong.

No time. She'd have to be vigilant. She grabbed her evening bag, rushed out of the bedroom, and started down the stairs.

Joe stood at the entry door, grasping the doorknob.

"Damn," she mumbled.

Joe's feet were planted to the floor, as he flung the door open. Casual-like he braced one arm against the doorframe and eased a thumb through a loop of his worn hip-skimming jeans.

"Hi, Sheriff Do-Good," Joe drawled, sounding hickish and defiant.

"Knight. It's Sheriff Knight." Caleb's face remained cop-wise immobile. "You're here fixing the crapper?"

What? Her toilet was broken?

"Yep, that's me, fix-it man dealing with a load of shit." Joe moved his hand from his belt loop, and into the pocket. He acted calm, but his back muscles bunched under his thin shirt.

Her heart knocked into her ribs. Caleb tightened his fingers into a fist. Double damn, she couldn't have a respected and well-liked local cop insulted in her foyer.

"Hi, Caleb, I'm ready to go." Moving past Joe, she bumped him with her hip. He didn't budge an inch. She turned to apologize and include a warning glare. "Night, Joe."

Joe's hot gaze made her green dress seem smaller, the V lower, the heels higher.

"Think you might need a coat, its cold." Embedded in the words of advice was sarcasm, as thick as the southern drawl he'd revealed their first night together.

"Oh, right. Just a second, Caleb." She turned toward the hallway closet, snagged Joe's arm at the crook and dragged him along.

"What do you think you're doing?" she whispered. Her voice came out like sandpaper scraping metal. Part of her rejoiced in the idea he might care about her date with another man. A far-fetched notion, but oh so lovely.

"I'm acting as your man-servant." His stare hadn't left the area just below her shoulders.

She shoved her index finger under his chin and lifted. Their gazes leveled. "Don't. If I want you to service me in anyway, I'll ask. In the meantime, don't call an officer of the law a load of dung."

Like wind over a calm lake, a hint of laughter rippled across his beautiful eyes before he narrowed them. She shook off the goose bumps sprinkling her arms and suppressed the tingling in her stomach. She removed her black, cotton-wool blend coat from the closet.

Joe took her coat and held it out. "Do you mind if I use your computer, in the library, while you're out with the pretty-boy in brown?"

She stifled the chuckle and slid her arms through the coat sleeves. Caleb wore brown, not the light wood tint of his uniform, rather a coffee bean brown suit jacket and lighter mocha shirt underneath.

"Ericka?" Joe whispered, his voice sexy low.

Hot air, near her ear, whipped short strands of hair against her neck. His corded bulk jarred her side. He smoothed the overcoat across her back, making her breasts feel heavy. Her want became more intense.

"Ericka?" Caleb called, his voice sharpened to an edge. His large shadow stained the tile floor.

"Coming," she answered. She wiped her sweating palms across the soft wool. She turned, bumping into Joe again. She met his glance. His irises darkened. Her lips quivered. Did her eyes advertise her mix of emotions? "Yes, use my computer. The password is…"

He lowered his head. The thump of heels sounded near.

"K-I-T," she whispered and lightly brushed his ear, and the soft skin between his cheek and lobe, with her mouth. Her heart struck her rib cage. She regretted touching his hot, sandalwood-scented skin. A swipe of her palms on her coat again, and she gazed into his widened eyes.

Joe's glance slid to the portrait in the parlor.

"Ready?" Caleb snaked his arm through hers.

"Yes, where are we going?" She switched her purse to her non-dominant hand and buttoned a couple of the coat's pearl disks. *Joe knows about the ghost who'd occupied her house.*

"Yacht Club. We're meeting Griff and Jacey."

"Bye," Ericka said over her shoulder.

Caleb left the door open and escorted her to a...clown car. Smoke filtered out the tailpipe. A creased front fender bent outward with rust speckles adding color. Her steps faltered.

He tugged her toward the death trap.

"Sorry about the car. My kid brother needed safe transportation to drive to Chicago. Griff couldn't get all of us into his truck, so we're using old Peter here." A chagrined smile spread across his face.

"That's nice of you." She smiled in understanding. "Is he going to Chicago for a job, school, or fun?"

Caleb opened the car door, and she sank into the seat. A spring poked her. She shifted a little to the right.

"He went to visit a university." He tucked her coat inside and a second later climbed behind the steering wheel. With a confident grin, he strapped in and shifted into reverse.

The rattles vibrating beneath the floorboard bothered her. "It's a long ride to the other side of Cyan."

"Don't worry. We'll make it on time." Gears shifted into second, then he placed his hand in front of the fans. "Are you warm enough?"

"Plenty warm. I'm glad you helped your brother. Is he looking at the U of I?"

"No. Just Chicago."

As Caleb made accolades about his brother, she turned to glance at the house. Joe stood at the end of the veranda, watching.

****

Outside, Joe leaned against a pillar as the sheriff hauled Ericka to his car. Hauled was a little harsh, he escorted her. Jealous, Joe didn't have the right to interfere. Granted he and Ericka shared a few moments of intense-something.

He dangled his foot off the porch. Anticipating the need to hero-up when the rust bucket broke down, he sauntered to the end of the veranda. He had to get closer to the driveway. A simple backward glance from her and warmed his stomach.

Let it go. She's not for you. Find the shaman; get the pre-cog to go away. Until then, you're a loner traveling the country. Tomorrow he'd have to tell Griff he wasn't taking the permanent job offer.

He'd invested the settlement from his accident and the funds multiplied. The motorcycle took very little gas, so he'd taken odd jobs as a means for quick cash. He didn't want to use the death money. After meeting some of the townspeople and getting acquainted with the layout of the town, he could imagine settling down and creating a home in Cyan. He'd open a detective agency, and along with consulting, he'd sell security equipment. He shook off the illogical idea of ever remaining in one place.

Joe told himself Ericka's date couldn't have come at a better time. His focus should be to find the mysterious shaman. He strolled into the library, booted the computer, and typed in K-I-T. Had the ghost held Ericka's mind captive? He didn't have a lot of experience with spirits, but she didn't appear to be the sort who'd allow a phantom to dominate her home. Of course, you don't know a person until you've lived with her or him.

Absent-mindedly, he typed in real estate for Cyan, Indiana. The main street had a couple of old-world styled buildings, as if New England shops had relocated to the Midwest. Own or lease. He did like corbels. He envisioned being on location most of the time, so he just needed a front for the security business. Before Joe could question himself, he sent off a query about the price.

He flipped a piece of paper to jot an address and the scent of magnolias infiltrated the air, tempting and teasing him to lift the scrap to his nose. Precise script, Ericka's notes were organized with headers and footnotes. Unable to resist snooping, he evaluated the rest of her desk; an aged document, clasped by an enormous clip, a photograph of Griff and Jacey's wedding. Ericka had been dressed in a sleek bronze dress. Her eyes sparkled and fine lines creased the corners. Kissable dimples appeared at each side of her pink lips.

A set of scales of justice, smaller than the seven-inch frame, perched near the edge of the desk. The gold chains glimmered under the gooseneck lamp. He shifted and the leather desk chair squeaked. She'd left bits of her scented personality everywhere.

He moved the cursor to the top of the computer monitor to 'favorites', to discover her Internet life. She accessed *Spells*.com, conjuring and resurrections, *Ghost Hunters*.com, and she downloaded a book, *The Tarot Card*. In addition, a couple of legal reference sites were bookmarked. The woman's preoccupation with the supernatural worried him.

Joe clicked the newspaper reference, taking him to an article dated eight months ago, *Ames Mystery Solved by Local Resident*. He read through the story. Two locals were sentenced to prison terms as a result of theft, vandalism, and attempted murder. Ericka Gilmore, attorney and new resident of the Ames Mansion, provided legal counsel for Jacey Hewson. The story gave additional details, but Joe concentrated on the reported sighting of the ghost of Christopher 'Kit' Ames. *The spirit sparkled and liquefied in a blue light*. A quote by Jacey Hewson.

The grandfather clock in the corner bonged nine times sparking his empty stomach to rumble. Joe closed the piece and typed into the search box, map of Cyan's foothills. He scrolled the list and selected the best option. As it loaded, he wandered into the kitchen.

His motorcycle had a short circuit in the electrical and a new part had to be ordered. The bike wouldn't be repaired for another week and a solid three to five inches of a snowfall was predicted to arrive in the same time frame. He'd need to consider an alternative method of finding the healer. He couldn't grow more attached to Ericka and the Carpenters.

Hunger gnawed a hole in his stomach. He opened the fridge and removed a chunk of Colby-Jack and ham. Jacey had been forcing him to take leftovers and the ham looked delicious. With the oven set to heat, he sliced the cheese and stacked a sandwich coating the outside of the bread with butter.

A cookie sheet had been stored inside the range. Using a dishtowel, he removed the heavy pan and slipped the sandwich on the tin. He shoved the unit into the oven and stood from the bent position, noticing a stiff joint for the first time in several days. He strained to hear anything that would reveal her premature return. Nothing.

Bootleg jeans allowed him the freedom to roll the material above his knee and he evaluated the incision and sutures near his lower right thigh. The stitches needed to come out, should have been removed a few days ago. Red frayed the three inches of scattered points of needle entry and exit, but the flesh wasn't swollen. Why hadn't the puncture sites itched?

The future scar, and from the cragged stitches he'd have one, would be a sign of regeneration. Joe had suffered, but he'd recovered. Would he, again and again? Every time he took a risk, to stop an accident, he put his own life on the line. He sighed. Deep down, part of him got a rush from trying to save the person. As a cop, he dealt with life and death on a daily basis, but now, he had a greater appreciation for life's fragility.

He tugged the jeans in place, grabbed the towel, and opened the oven door. Spatula in hand, he flipped the sandwich. While waiting the last few minutes for his dinner to toast, he searched through the fridge for a beer. Not one good ol' American tipple in sight. A bottle opener had been tacked to the side of the fridge, so he popped off the gold cap of the international brew and took a swig.

Smooth, a touch of citrus, the beer had a cool and refreshing flavor. Not bad. He placed the open container on the counter, turned off the oven, and removed the cookie sheet. After slapping the sandwich on a paper towel, he grabbed his bottle. Back in the desk chair, he glanced at the computer screen. The map of Indiana had loaded. He clicked the webpage suggestion for the best route to the Native American village near Cyan. A variety of choices populated the page. He opted for the first one and a plot loaded with detailed directions.

The route depicted led straight up a county road, with one detour to the west. Easy enough. When the street ended, he'd hoof it to the shaman's home.

Joe sat firm against the back of the chair, lifted the sandwich, nibbled, and looked for pitfalls in the map. Griff wasn't aware of a shaman in the village. Joe would inquire about the spiritualist when he arrived in the Native American community. So far, the search process seemed simple, albeit not one Cyan citizen claimed to know of a medicine man. He'd expected to wait in line to have the shaman cure him. Could the medicine man's abilities be a red herring?

Did the man exist?

He finished the sandwich, dropped the paper towel to the stack of documents, and brushed crumbs from his hands. *Ten o'clock, not too late.* He removed the cell from his pocket and pressed the contact. "Hi, how's life?"

"Depends on if you're calling to tell me you dreamed about me," Tess shot back.

"Not yet." Nor did he plan too. He couldn't handle having a vision of his sister's death. He'd stay away from Tess, and her family, as long as necessary regardless of how much it hurt. "Is Brett there?"

"Yeah, he's putting the kids to bed. Reading them grisly stories," Tess hissed.

He chuckled. "Considering you've chosen a husband who happens to be a psychology professor and paranormal researcher, I'd think you'd appreciate your kids recognizing the unusual. People like me, a f—"

"Don't you dare call yourself a freak! I swear Joseph, I'll track you down—"

"Chill, littl' bit." He smothered a laugh. He was a freak. Soon, though, he'd get back to normal.

Air whispered through the phone, as if she'd exhaled. "You haven't called me by my childhood nickname in over eighteen months. Have the visions stopped? Are you ready to come home?"

"No, sorry sis, still got the power. Besides, home isn't in Pennsylvania." His knee itched. He wished he hadn't touched the wound. Now it bothered him. He rubbed the area, deciding to clip the stitches himself. "How are my niece and nephews?"

"Good. Great. They miss you. Where are you?" Her voice cracked. "Just a second."

Scratches and dead air came through the receiver. "Tess?" he deepened his tone.

"Hey, man. How's it going?" His brother-in-law's calm deep vocals echoed through the line.

"Speaker phone," Tess said.

"Kids are trying to sleep." Brett's voice became

clear. "Where are you now?"

"Cyan, Indiana." Joe flung open the desk drawers looking for scissors.

"You're close to Penn, why don't you stop in and see us?" Brett's voice boomed.

His stomach knotted, and his heart beat faster. He'd like nothing more than to be with his family. "I miss you guys, but I can't put you at risk."

"Have you found him?" The sound of papers being flipped came across the line.

"Not yet, I have a couple of leads. No one seems to have any idea of a shaman in the area. A guy, I'm doing construction for, said the best place to look is in a village somewhere along the side of a mountain. Native Americans hold most of the land, not a reservation, but sole ownership of thousands of acres. That's where I'm going." Joe grabbed a pair of tiny scissors about two inches in length. What did she cut with such small clippers?

"I wish I would have been able to find out his legal name, White Wolf of the Coterie Nation, doesn't provide a lot of results."

"Brett, do you think your source could have been mistaken? The library doesn't have a reference for a great icon who heals people and the locals aren't talking." Sorting through the desk, he found a small bottle of antiseptic hand rub. He soaked a tissue and cleaned the metal pieces, then swung the scissors, the silver handle of the clippers pinged against the edge of the desk.

"I trust my source. Spiritual leaders are sometimes reclusive, not wanting the public to bombard them. Their medicine is through harmonious relationships, combining religion, spirituality, herbal remedies, and rituals. In addition, Indians tend to keep to themselves so if your community is primarily white ethnicity, then you'll not get good data." Brett's voice tapered off. "Facts validate an Indian tribe is nearby Cyan. A library without references to them is strange."

"Don't they prefer the PC term, Native American?" Joe stuck his fingers in the tiny holes of the handle and scissor cut the air.

"No, most of the nations prefer the term Indian." Brett paused. "When are you going to search for him?"

"You can't come. You need to protect Tess and the kids. Besides, my bike's in the shop. I'm going to try to borrow a truck. I'm going to leave in the next day or two, because a snowstorm should arrive within seven days." He held the phone between his ear and shoulder and rolled his pant leg to his knee.

"If you're welcomed into the village by the elders, be prepared to go into a sweat lodge. You don't have any injuries do you? Open wounds? The *scratches* from saving the kid have healed over right?" His insistent voice didn't bother Joe. Brett, more brother than brother-in-law, would worry.

He glanced at the stitches. "Yes, scratches are gone. It's all good."

"Take a token of appreciation. Rituals have been in place for over 40,000 years and tobacco is a component. You don't want to make a mistake at the get-go. Historically…" Brett expounded.

While Brett lectured, Joe snipped the knotted end of a thread and tugged. A bead of blood appeared as he jerked the stitch free from his skin.

"Joe?"

"I'll take the pouch of tobacco you recommended that I buy in Kentucky. I need him to help me. I don't want to look cheap. Should I take something else?" Joe winced as the blood seeped faster.

The library door squeaked. He glanced upward, jerking the scissors and snagging the next thread. Ericka.

She opened her mouth and inhaled a strong vibrant rattling breath. Ericka put her hands at her hips. Her necklace bounced, making the diamond facets glimmer. "What the hell do you think you're doing?"

"Brett, call me when you have a suggestion."

"Joe, wait—" Brett's sharp command ended as Joe snapped the cellphone shut.

"Good evening, Ericka." He glanced at the clock in the corner of the computer monitor. Ten twenty. Her date must not have worked out.

"You're bleeding on my desk chair!" She grabbed his paper towel. Bread remnants flew over her desk. She crumbled the napkin in her fist.

He stood and snagged the paper towel from her clutched hand. "Sorry, didn't think the pinpoint would run quite so much." He stuck the wadded napkin to the tiny stream of blood, then glanced at her.

A red blush covered her cheeks. She shifted her focus to the bits of brown soaking into the antique-looking documents scattered across her desk.

"I'll clean the mess." He nodded to the papers. "Sorry. Didn't think, I guess. You're home early, date didn't go as expected?"

Her right eyelid twitched, and her lips straight-lined. Stroke? Other than call 911, what did one do when a stroke happened?

"I'll get it. Leave please." She pointed toward the door.

He tugged his jeans, to hold the paper towel in place, and then used one hand to swipe the crumbs off the desktop. "Sorry, I'll just..."

Cheese-oil soaked breadcrumbs rubbed deeper into the brittle paper. The words *dark magick* smeared. A magnetic force stopped his hands from scraping more from the page. Ready for the shit to hit the fan, he blew out a breath and glanced at her. The twitch disappeared, and her lips pursed.

"I'll clean this up later." He flipped the scissors into his palm and limped toward the door.

"Please leave the Scherenschnitte scissors."

The temperature had dropped at least ten degrees. Indeed, her date hadn't gone well. What, no suck-face in the back seat of the Pinto? Pure curiosity made him halt instead of continuing his stumble across the threshold. He pivoted. "Shear and snit what?"

Her lips twitched and a hint of laughter bubbled out. "The scissors, they're for paper cutting, not medicinal use."

"Oh, sorry." What the hell? He'd faced perps and murderers for fifteen years and within seconds she'd made him feel like he'd been caught going through her underwear drawer. Refusing to limp, he took two steps and laid the scissors on the edge of the desk, then sauntered from the room.

Chapter Eight

Ericka sat in the leather desk chair, slumped forward and finger-tapped the desktop. Joe had asked permission to use her computer. An unsuccessful date didn't give her the right to treat a houseguest in such a horrible way. Besides, she'd been relieved when Caleb got an urgent call to investigate a body found in a lake near Edgewood. After he left, she enjoyed her meal.

Pent-up sexual frustration, financial problems, and late nights trying to prepare for her case had transformed her into a spiteful wicked *biotch*.

She closed her eyes. Joe should always cover his abs. His coppery skin, visible mid-chest, created an instant fantasy of ripping his clothes from his body and ravishing him. When had defensive tactics become her method of dealing with her weakness?

She'd become someone she didn't understand. Since Joe arrived at her door, her attention to facts and details had scattered like pollen. Financial survival should be her priority. Living in a new community, she should be building relationships, associations and making new friends instead of fantasizing about a nomad biker.

She shrugged off her coat and let it fall to the back of the chair. A quick glance through the library indicated her houseguest hadn't disturbed anything, or at least nothing appeared changed.

She kicked the trashcan in front of the desk. A couple of deep breaths later she lifted the precious documents describing black magick spells. Fear of the entire world of dark magick made goose bumps skitter across her arms. The priceless aged documents had grease smudges, blurring many of the words. Could she still sell them?

Despite the dread of touching the worn and fragile paper, she shook the documents sending the greasy crumbs into the garbage can. She tilted the lampshade. The light illuminated the words. "Love spell."

She let the documents fall to the desktop. The mouse scooted a couple of inches, the screen brightened and a map of Cyan appeared. What had he said the first night when she'd met him? He was looking for someone. She clicked the history and other than the sites she'd visited, a map site was listed.

"Treat others, as you would want to be treated." Her forehead hit the edge of the desk. "Ericka Gilmore, you're a cantankerous old maid, and you've taken your disappointments out on an injured man."

She rose from the chair, strode into the kitchen, and got her emergency medical kit from the cupboard above the refrigerator. She prepared her apology speech with each stair step and stood at his door. Three raps later, she overheard unsteady shuffling movements drawing closer. "Joe?"

The door flew back.

She exhaled.

He wore a pair of black knit boxers. The tight cotton hugged his muscular thighs.

"Yes?" Chagrin undulated through his voice.

"I'm..." She swallowed and looked away. "Sorry."

"What?" The gruffness of his voice made her more aware of how childish she'd acted.

He had every right to be angry.

She coughed, clearing her throat. "I'm sorry for my bad humor. Please let me help you with your..." The contents inside medical box clanked as she pointed toward his knee.

His fingers tightened around the edge of the door, and it moved a fraction of an inch. Was he going to shut her out? Just as suddenly, his stance relaxed. "Thank you. I don't have the proper tools, and I could use a steady hand."

"The bathroom has the best light," she said and walked into the room.

"Okay."

Her heart beat double time when he hobbled into the bathroom and grabbed a wrinkled blue towel from the rack. He sat on the toilet and draped a cotton towel on his lap.

Good, good, he'd covered the main parts.

He rested his heel at the edge of the shower-tub and stared. She placed the med-kit on the countertop and grabbed the stool from under the counter. *Okay, pretend he's one of your nephews with a boo-boo.*

One of his gorgeous thigh muscles popped and twitched. Images of Joe's leg muscles, toned from riding his bike, and his sun-bronzed rough arms taut from push-ups took center stage in her mind. She'd peered through the open bedroom door. At 7:30 A.M. sharp, he pumped. Every day. Slow and precise rises and falls of sinewy delight. Nope, Joe wasn't a child, not related to her. *Focus.*

She used her thumb and index finger to pry the lid

open, selected tweezers and scissors and placed them beside the sink. With a sharp turn, she snagged two towels from the linen closet. She flipped the faucet, squirted soap in her palm, and scrubbed each finger. Hands dried, she tipped the rubbing alcohol dousing one of the cloths and wiped down the instruments. Step-by-step processes always relaxed her.

"You look like you've experience. You've done this before." He nodded toward the alcohol-soaked towel.

"Yes, older brother, several nieces and nephews, in addition to being somewhat of a tomboy in my pre-adolescent years." In the reflection of the silver scissors, the lace of her pink bra showed under the top. She resisted the urge to yank her dress together and went to the next step: Clean the instruments.

"I'm surprised," he mumbled.

She glanced into his eyes.

His gaze shot toward the floor.

"Surprised?" She tugged the dress and sat on the stool. The stitches were ugly.

"That you were a tomboy."

She tried to ignore his repetition. Men presumed she was a cold-hearted princess. Success in her field meant she had to adhere to some male affectations and distancing people was one of them. She doused a second clean towel with rubbing alcohol and placed it in his hand. "How did this happen?"

He wiped down the upper thigh area, without a peep. Clotted blood removed, fresh liquid sprung from the site. Once washed, she used the tweezers and removed a section of black thread. The skin had adhered to the suture and pulled taut.

"Fell. I was supposed to see a doctor in Cyan yesterday, but I got distracted." *Thunk, thunk, thunk* of the toilet paper dispenser sounded through the small room as he ripped off a few pieces. She manipulated the stitches far better in the middle. He dabbed at the bits of blood beading at the separation of skin.

"What were you doing?" She took the scissors, tugged a piece of the knotted thread, and snipped. *Four down, two to go.*

"Just crossing the street." He held out the alcohol-soaked towel, and she wiped the suture on a rag.

"Hum, the injury isn't jagged enough to be a fall, more like a straight cut." She extracted the last section of black string and lifted it from his skin without impairment. A quick dab with the clean cloth, and his blood clotted.

"A simple clumsy attempt to run." His downcast glance negated the nonchalance of the words.

Okay, he hid something. Instruments pinged against the ceramic sink as she dropped them. She opened a tiny brown bottle of peroxide and soaked a cotton swab. "The wound will heal faster if you leave it uncovered tonight."

"Got it."

She swiped the clean side of the alcohol-laden cloth to the outer edges of the wound. "This might sting a little."

She dotted a swab with peroxide and with a light touch pressed the gauze to absorb the excess blood. The burning bubbles got inside the open areas. "Who did the stitches? Frankenstein?"

"That's what I thought."

The liquid bubbled around the wound. Other than

the hiss and a muttered ouch, he didn't whine about the discomfort. She removed the swab and shook her head in admiration of his strength and pain endurance. The towel slipped, revealing his tight jersey underwear complete with a manhole. Could she see what she'd been fantasizing about? She shouldn't have looked. What she detected bumping against her weeks ago was all man. Unaware of how his body affected her, his concentration remained on his leg. The blood oozed. He flexed his knee and dabbed at the renewed leakage with a towel.

The silence could have been cut with the Scherenschnitte scissors.

His dark gaze pierced her.

"Sorry…for staring." She stood. In the pretense of cleaning her tweezers, and scissors, slid her glance to the numerous scars located on his outer thigh. A bullet had slipped through his side, leaving a marring of his beautiful skin. In addition, he had a knife wound on his upper left shoulder. A cop would've been engaged in a violent lifestyle, but he'd been away from the force for a while. What about the recent wound? "Here is antibiotic ointment for when the bleeding stops."

He took the tube. "Got it."

"Tell me about your family. You're from Mississippi?" She used the steaming water to wipe the instruments. Leaving a few Band-Aids out, in case the sites continued to ooze, she repacked the kit and closed it.

He hesitated.

As an attorney, part of her success was due to her ability to read people, their body language, and subliminal clues. Priests and honest citizens were easy to interpret, but corrupt people, those who led a life of deception, were more difficult to decipher.

"Yes, Cotswold. I've one little sister who's married to a psychology professor. They live in Pennsylvania and have three children. Mischievous little angels and perhaps candidates for Ritalin, but they're mine. I love 'em and wouldn't trade them for all the bullion in the treasury," he paused, "or put their lives at risk."

No blinking, no aberrant eye, mouth or cheek movements, and not one muscle twitch, at all. The man could win big time in Atlantic City. Except for the last part, *put their lives at risk*, what did he mean? Okay, so she'd introduce the topic. "Pennsylvania is nearby, are you going to visit them?"

"Can't."

Odd answer. He said he loved his family and from his intonation, he did, so why wouldn't he travel a couple of hours across the state line to see them? "Why did you quit the force?"

The bleeder from the first stitch removal continued to seep. She plucked a sticky-note-sized adhesive bandage from the counter top and jerked off the first layer of the wrapping.

He took the bandage and removed the tabs. "Since you work in the field, you might expect me to say burn out. Not really the reason. I don't plan to reenter the troops in blue, but I might become a P.I., after I fix a problem."

She applied the adhesive bandage to the red-rimmed wound. He stood and wrapped the towel around his waist and hid temptation from her sight. Her wishes had been answered.

"What's your problem? Maybe I can help you."

She held the box in front of her, as a miniature shield. Her heart had a slow leak, making her susceptible to this strange biker and the possibility of love.

"Ericka." His mournful tone of voice made her heart seep all the more. No bandage could hold it together if she let him in. Resist!

The deep gong of the doorbell broke the moment, clotting her heart just in time. Joe receded into the background and her wants and desires were once again hidden.

"I should see who's at the door." With heated cheeks, she ran into the hallway.

"Ericka, wait."

****

Joe dropped the towel, grabbed his jeans from the end of the bed, and scrambled into them. Bloody spots would show on his lower thigh, but she should not answer the door at this hour.

What should he say to make her halt? Eleven at night, a guy with bad news stood on the other side of the entrance. Granted, he'd rejoiced Ericka hadn't held back when he stood outside her door. But now he feared something dangerous would be coming through the portal. Besides occasional surliness, impulsiveness might be one of her few weaknesses.

Heart beating as fast as the pistons pumped on his Harley, he hesitated at the top of the stairs to zip his pants and listen. A male shouted. Joe flew down the stairs, missing every other step. He cringed as his tender leg jolted with pain.

"What the fuck do you think you're doing? I'm not going to jail. Get me off," the squeaky voice had a dangerous merge of effeminate and thug.

She didn't respond. Could she answer? He braced the doorframe. His heart, already pumping strong, jumped to Mach speed. Barely visible behind a massive bulk, she dug her fingernails into a man's thick ski coat. He raced forward.

Over the brute's shoulder, Joe met her glance. Her pupils darkened and shifted to the right then left. One-armed, he circled the enemy's neck, and then grabbed the guy's arm pinning her, and twisted it. The fast action and the element of surprise worked in his favor.

Ericka massaged her neck and gasped for breath.

The goon switched positions and kicked, tassels flipped as his shoe hit Joe's injured thigh. Pain rushed through his leg.

Joe dragged him farther away from her. "Not going to happen, jackass."

Ericka bent, placed her hands against her thighs, and sucked great gulps of air.

Joe knee-kicked the guy in the lower back and took him to the floor.

"Joe, let him go," Ericka puffed out, yet her gaze held fear.

"What?" He tightened his hold, constricting the man's airflow. The guy's face reddened. Joe glanced at her, hoping the order was a mistake. "Assault, pure and simple. He should be hauled off to jail."

She gave a deep cough and strode forward. "Thank you, for your help. Mike Ward is a client."

Stunned for a moment, he looked at her then released the guy from the stronghold, allowing him to breathe. Joe's muscles remained taut, in fight mode, ready to pounce. He hoped he'd get the opportunity.

Ward circled and threw a punch toward Joe's head.

Anger and aggression he'd been storing, since Adam died in the accident, erupted. Perhaps because Ward had Adam's build, looked a little like him. Joe ducked and struck his right arm into Ward's left kidney. Ward bounced back a step. Joe prepared to throw another hit. Ericka slipped between them.

"Move," he snarled. He fisted his hand and drew his arm back, wanting to act.

"Can't," she replied, voice catching. She placed her hand against his chest. Finger imprints singed his skin.

Joe unclenched his fist and shook it, trying to get the blood flowing. He mentally kicked himself. The day of the car accident, if he'd driven like usual, his friend would be alive today. *Ward isn't the one who deserves your anger.*

Ward heaved sharp intakes of air and glared.

Ericka shoved her fist into Ward's chest, a hard wallop, and he fell onto a short stepstool. "What the hell do you think you're doing?"

He nodded approval of her assertive stance, even more when she used one of her sharp-nailed-fingers to tilt Ward's face level with her own. He liked her this way. Was he getting a glimpse of the true Ericka?

"I'm your sole support here, Mike. Even your father is wavering. The townspeople are running when you get close. Your friends don't want to give testimony in your favor. You'll get jail time if you keep punching people."

Joe released the tightness of his muscles. "Apologize to her."

"Sorry." Ward wheezed. Fear and the putrid odor of booze-laden sweat reeked from his deflated form.

"I've been thinking, to help you change your

attitude, you need to go to counseling." She jerked her sharp claws across his jaw and lowered the hand to the desk. "Anger management." She sat in the desk chair and drew the computer out of sleep mode. "Do you agree to go?"

"No," he barked. White marks imprinted his chin.

"Prison it is then." She met Joe's glance.

"Great. I'll phone in the assault." The slightest affirmation and the man would find his ass nailed to a chair, awaiting the law.

"I guess if it'll keep me out of jail." The pitiful whine seeped from Ward's lying lips.

As she keyed, Joe stepped closer to Ward and whispered, "You raise a hand to her, ever again, and you're a dead man."

Ward sniffed.

Joe crossed his arms at his chest and leaned against the bookcases. Her client acted like a child and no doubt would provide another opportunity to be taken down. He could wait. Since the accident, he had a wealth of patience.

She typed. The keys on her computer clicked, creating a mini-musical of sorts.

Her delicate white teeth tugged the center of her lips. Released, the plump lip flesh reshaped.

Joe evaluated the red rash marring her neck, ugly crimson dots inflicted by Ward's arm. He frowned. Instead of wariness in her gaze, he witnessed determination. Why would she aid this man? Ward needed prison time or at the very least hospitalized in a psych ward. He switched his stare to the guy.

His Adam's apple slid up and down his throat like a carnival game. He unzipped his jacket and with shaking thick fingers rubbed his side. Joe didn't have any regrets. He wanted the man to feel pain for days.

"Ah, ha." She grabbed her cellphone from the top of desk and dialed. "Dr. Bash, I'm sorry to be calling so late at night. I need to get a client into your anger management counseling session."

"No. It's not an emergency, but—"

"Yes, I do appreciate a full schedule, but the patient is Mike Ward." She stared at Ward and like a bug under a microscope. "Yes, his trial is in four weeks."

She snapped a piece of paper, grabbed a pen, and scratched words across the page. "I'm sure the mayor is aware of your community service, and I'll convey your need for assistance." Ericka glanced at Joe, held his stare, understanding passed between them. *You scratch my back, and I'll scratch yours.* Most deals were made outside the courtroom.

The sound of a pencil scratching paper created an annoying noise in the room. "Yes, sir, thank you. Again, I'm sorry for the late hour. Tomorrow, at two in the afternoon, will be fine. Thank you."

She pressed her thumb to disconnect, gripped the paper, and rose. Joe forced his muscles to appear in relaxed mode and slid his hands into his jean pockets to prevent any mishap.

"Mike, Dr. Bash will see you tomorrow at two o'clock at this address." She held out the note.

Ward snatched the paper. "What does my father have to pay the nutcracker in order to have a good report go before the judge? Your strategy is to have my head shrunk so you can declare I'm on the path of rehabilitation?"

"As your attorney I'm trying to defend you in whatever way possible." She marched to the front door and opened it. "If you ever come into my house uninvited or touch me again, I will press charges."

Tonight Joe had learned something new about her personality and values. He yearned for her. He stared at Ward and nodded toward the door. "Move."

Red-faced, Ward skulked through the opening like a two-year-old after a scolding. Joe and Ericka followed and stood at the threshold of the front door as the criminal dropped into his cherry sports car and sped away. Cold wind chilled Joe's shirtless skin, but he refused to leave her side.

She sighed and walked inside. He followed, shut and locked the door. He wet his lips. She'd turn into him and in appreciation, or to fulfill that emotion sparking in her eyes, he'd get a kiss.

The V of her sleek emerald dress drew open and the pink perfection, he'd caught a glimpse of earlier, was exposed. Perhaps he'd wrap his arms around her, while receiving the thank you kiss.

"Joe." She pressed her back against the wall and into the ghost residue of Ames Mansion. Her chest heaved, making her cleavage lift and lower.

He switched his gaze to her eyes. Lost in the anticipation of what was to come he'd missed the anger igniting them. They'd changed from amber to molten gold fire. Shit, once again he'd misjudged her.

"Thank you for helping me, but I could have handled him."

"It didn't look like it—"

"While I appreciate your ah…chivalry, if you ever interfere when I'm with a client, you'll be out on your ass faster than you can spin a tire on your ride." Her hands rested at her hips, drawing the fabric even farther apart exposing the tip of a nipple.

Was she serious? The sheer force of will kept his arms at his sides, and his gaze glued to hers. "I witnessed a guy attacking you. My code, as a man and former law enforcement official, is to protect you, the innocent. Client or not, I wouldn't have done anything different." Enunciating each word should have worked in his favor, because he wanted to glance south.

"Assume I'm not innocent." Arms stiff at her side, she hurried toward the parlor across from the library.

"Assumption made," he shouted, grabbing her arm to prevent her passing. He kissed those very lips he'd imagined thanking him a few minutes before. Anger subdued, her mouth softened under his, and her tongue lit into him like cayenne pepper. He consumed, taking as much as he needed to give.

Chapter Nine

Ericka leaned into Joe. The parlor walls of Ames Mansion closed in on her. He stretched his arm across her shoulders as if he'd never let her go. The notion he came to her rescue gave her a rush. She inhaled, hoping for something. Reckless, she wanted more. *Stop!* She didn't want to hurt him, and she destroyed relationships.

Vanilla candle scent warred with Joe's sandalwood fragrant skin. She wished more lights were ignited, so she could see beyond her want. Darkness always encouraged sex, and she battled with the urge to flip on the light switch biting into her right shoulder blade.

Stop him. He interfered with your business, and he'll be leaving in a few days.

He defended you.

She remained single at the age of thirty, partly due to power issues. A man would never control her. After all, like daughter like mother.

She should not tolerate Joe's Machiavellian action. Yet, her hips ground into his, seeking the source that would extinguish her misery. His warm lips tantalized. The man knew how to kiss, and she wanted more.

Dark strands of his hair blew with each breath she exhaled. A damn moan escaped her lips as his hot mouth found her neck. Working his way south, he nuzzled her breast. He bent and lifted her, fitting their bodies together. She wrapped her legs around his waist. God, he felt so good, like coming home to comforting arms at the end of a long trip.

She wanted what the man offered, satisfaction to the need growing inside her at warp speed. She dug her fingers into the muscles of his tense neck, and tightened her legs, anchoring their bodies. He carried her across the room. A timed candle flickered on, creating a dimly lit romantic setting.

Joe propped her higher against the wall, and she fell into his hot gaze. He unlatched her front closure bra. His gentle strokes heated her core. The silken material of her dress and bra lowered. Her skin tingled, and her stomach muscles quivered in anticipation.

The sharp snap of a zipper pierced the air. Their soft breathing increased to a faster rate, becoming a background symphony. She trembled. She needed this union.

His lips caressed the soft skin around her breasts. Calloused, workingman fingers lifted the skirt of her dress.

Just a hook-up, her future didn't include love. She had to make the liaison clear.

His fingers tucked in her panties, stroked her vagina, then slid the lacey fabric over her buttocks. The luscious softness of his mouth continued its pursuit along the side of her breasts.

Considering Joe may want more than sex, sent a seed of doubt through her mind.

She moaned, turned her head into his neck, and took a deep breath. She trailed her mouth along his jaw, sucking the tender skin.

Elastic snapped against her leg. His fingers

caressed her inner thighs. A slight breeze rose, cooling her fiery skin, but not easing the tremors below her waist.

"*Please don't stop*", her mind insisted, but the words, "We're going to just have sex, right?" spewed from her stupid pie hole.

She held tight, kissed his cheek, and waited for his next move. He didn't stroke. A chilled draft of air whipped across her mouth. She sought his gaze.

"A one-night stand," she whispered.

"If that is what you want." The sharpness of his tone and narrow-eyed glance made her uneasy.

A one-night stand. Joe didn't want to consider her question. From what he'd overheard and read, she'd want something more than an interlude. Why did she deny the real mojo that existed between them?

All women expected some form of promise.

Stomach acid rose to his throat. Damn, her words pierced his heart. He wanted to take her, enjoy what she offered, the sex, and walk away in a few days. Why did her non-committal offer piss him off?

She provided a nice arrangement. He wanted this fascinating, tempting woman. Yet, underneath all of his layers, he was a family man kind of guy and needed a sense of togetherness, a future. He couldn't do a one nighter—not with Ericka.

Through sore lips, he exhaled. He bent, lifted her panties, and then took a step away. He zipped his jeans.

If he connected his gaze with hers, would he see remorse? Would this woman, his heartbreaker, resent his unwillingness? It took a great amount of determination to step away. He stared into her eyes. Confusion had replaced desire. He cupped her chin, drew her forward, and kissed those perfect pink lips.

He ambled from the room, leaving her clutching the wall.

Certain Ericka would assume he'd brushed her off. In reality, Joe experienced a bond with her. When he was with her, he was capable of relaxing without worrying about who would die next.

His heart thumped against his ribcage. A vision hadn't occurred since he'd saved the librarian several days ago. Ericka Gilmore became vital to his peace of mind, and he wanted her today, tomorrow, and maybe for always. Never for just one night.

****

The next day, Joe climbed in on the passenger seat of Griff's truck, anticipating a distasteful conversation, or at the least a freeze out, but Griff acted as if everything was status quo.

Silence appeared to be the mode of the day. At the worksite, Griff gave him a two-fingered wave and went inside the store. Joe slipped on a tool belt and gathered treated lumber. He'd prepared the base structure for the disabled access ramp yesterday. Today, he'd lay the wood and finish the entrance.

He couldn't have asked for a more appropriate outlet for his pent-up angst. The power tool wound the wood screws into the lumber, allowing his mind to replay the time he'd spent with Ericka.

Two nights ago, they sat snug together on the sofa in the living room and watched an action-comedy on her laptop. As before, her enormous law books stacked on the coffee table provided the perfect height for viewing a program. Hell, she even let him prop his stocking feet beside the volumes. Their gazes met over the shared bowl of popcorn, and he experienced a draw, a tie he'd never encountered with another woman. Peacefulness, dare he think love, surrounded him. He didn't want to lose the tranquility they shared or his closeness to Ericka.

He had to leave.

His muscles heated with the use of excess energy. He could abandon his vow to rid himself of the prophecy and remain with her. Could he live with the constant fear he'd see her life end in a vision? His heart thumped, matching the speed of the motorized screwdriver. What if he couldn't stop the incident from happening and she died?

Had he entered some alternative universe in Cyan, Indiana? A place where the illogical occurred? He'd never wanted a permanent connection, but knowing this woman for a few weeks made him want the impossible, a relationship. Granted, his parent's marriage had been tight, and they'd been perfect role models. His stomach muscles tightened as he experienced the pain of their loss. Tess, his sister, had a solid relationship with her husband, Brett, a forever-type marriage with honest communication. He snickered. Brett told Tess to wait. No one told Tess to do anything she didn't want to do. They trusted each other, enough they felt free to say whatever they wanted. Trust and consideration was something he wanted in a marriage.

God, why did he feel the need to substantiate a relationship? Because, Ericka Gilmore had bewitched his heart. Joe weighed the possibilities of settling in one place and romancing her. He shook his head. He couldn't think about any type of permanence, at least not until the forecasts stopped.

"Hey, Joe, time for lunch. Jacey's made soup. Come inside," Griff shouted.

He lifted his gaze. Griff stood in front of the door, holding a cup with steam rising from the contents.

"I'll be right there," Joe shouted.

A wave of cold air draped him, reminding him why none of the others had volunteered to work outside today. A bitter forecast prepared the inhabitants for the late winter storm due to arrive. Heated because of the effect Ericka had on him, he'd maintained a fast working pace.

He swiped a hand across his sweating forehead, feeling the roughness of the glove, then rose from his crouched position. Sharp pains ripped through his sore leg. Shaking it off, he grabbed the cordless impact driver and strode toward the building.

As he entered, a blast of warm air hit him. He tucked the driver under his arm and removed his gloves. He shoved them into his pockets and noted the progress. The painted walls had dried and half of the oak floor planks had been laid. Soft light came through the south-facing arched window, providing a comfortable serene milieu in the main area of the shop.

Jacey came out of the storeroom with compacted corrugated boxes in hand. An elfin smile spread across her face, making her appear mischievous. "Hi, Joe. How are you today?"

"I'm fine. How's the unpacking going?" She didn't look at him with repugnance or hate. Maybe she hadn't been told about the incident with Ericka.

With an exaggerated sigh, she stuffed the flattened boxes into a larger open container. "It'll be better once I have some storage solutions in place. When you get time, can you hang shelves for me?"

"Sure will." He strode toward the tiny kitchen, at the back of the shop, glancing at the door in the hallway as he passed. White lettering, Ericka Gilmore, Attorney at Law, etched in the glass drew his attention.

Griff sat at a small table while he held a spoon of aromatic reddish liquid close to his mouth. "Help yourself to vegetable soup."

"Where's everyone?" He set the power tool on a piece of cardboard on the counter and removed his coat, then nudged the imitation farmhouse nozzle and water flowed.

"They ate earlier. Tyler drove to the Waymakers to give an estimate on fencing. The others are at Dark Shadows putting the finishing touches on the upstairs renovations."

After washing his hands, Joe ladled a scoop of soup into a ceramic bowl, grabbed a spoon, and set them on the table.

Griff nodded. "Water's in the fridge."

"You didn't want me to go?" Joe opened the fridge, snatched a bottle of water, and lowered to a chair. He stirred the broth, allowing the steam to scatter and tantalize his senses.

"No, it looked like you were fighting demons the way you knocked out the ramp. What do you have left to do?" Griff's mouth hovered above the lip of his cup.

Did he have any demons left? Hell, yeah. He couldn't wait to get rid of it. He stared at Griff. "I've four boards and the border. Jacey asked me to make shelves. Do you want help with the planks first?"

"Yeah, that'd be great. A couple of hours and the floors will be done." Griff sat the cup down, then lifted his soupspoon, and blew.

"Okay. Twenty minutes and I'm all yours."

"Bread?" Griff pointed to a half-eaten loaf. "Some of my finest brew has been sacrificed for this batch, and I want to make sure it doesn't go to waste."

He snorted and sliced a piece of bread. "Sure. Speaking of beer, I need a night out. Where do you recommend I go for a drink and entertainment?"

Instead of a wide-ass grin, questions rippled across Griff's eyes. Would he voice the thoughts already etched on his face? He nodded. "Brewhouse on Cauldron Street."

"Is Saturday still a popular night at bars?"

Griff shrugged. "As far as I know."

"Since you brought it up, can I borrow the truck in a couple of days? I need to find the Coterie Village somewhere on the mountain?"

Griff lifted his cup. "Did you find where the shaman's located?"

Joe twirled the butter knife, and then scored a pad of butter. "Not an exact location, just Black Mountain. I thought I'd ask at the local hangout."

"Sometimes the citizens of Cyan don't share with strangers. If you can wait until later I'll go with you." Griff nodded toward the hallway. "Besides Saturday is Jacey and Ericka's designated BFF time."

"I'd appreciate your company." He dug into his soup with gusto, in a hurry to get the ramp finished and help inside. The quicker he got a true location for the shaman, the sooner he'd get away from the spellbinding Ericka.

****

"Hey, sorry I'm late. Got busy researching a case."

Ericka stood in the hallway of the antique store and sniffed. "If I'd known you'd cooked, I wouldn't have eaten left-over chicken."

Jacey's head popped from under a box. "That was for Joe."

"Yeah, well, since he crumbled greasy ham sandwich bits all over my spell book, I don't trust him with food." Ericka peered into the box. Empty. She folded it into a tidy recyclable package. Discovering a packing peanut stuck to the corner, she tossed the plastic into a tub of packing materials.

Jacey aligned reproduction 18th century Wedgewood candlesticks on a shelf. The blue jasper sat with white Pegasus on one side and Helen of Troy on the other side. A pink Hathaway Rose pattern sat next to the terra cotta.

"Will you keep aside a set of the blue candlesticks for me? They'd be perfect for Joe."

Jacey pivoted so fast the boxes, near her foot, rattled. "What?"

She pointed to the candlesticks. "The imitation Wedgewoods. I'd like a blue set. They'll be perfect in the guest bedroom."

Jacey's hands landed on the sides of the boxes holding them steady. Her mouth opened and closed like a goldfish seeking fresh air. Finally, she let her words roll. "Sure you don't want the Sheringham green which is a younger, contemporary candlestick or the Dynasty, boasting ancient symbolism and a flatter base?"

What? Was this her roundabout way of asking if she was sleeping with Joe? Her preconceived responses coming from her friend continued to elude her. "I don't have a clue what you're talking about. Are you high on the shellac Griff is putting on the salesroom floor?"

Jacey swayed back and forth. "No, just trying to figure out what you want. If Joe represented the blue candlesticks, the sheriff green and the pink candlestick was your imaginary lover, which one would you select?"

Ericka shoved her to the first rung of a stepstool and crouched. "You're pale and not making sense. I'm afraid you're working too hard. Don't worry. We'll get it done. The store will open on time."

"I'm not worried." She ran her fingers through her hair. "I think everything will work out."

"Sorry to interrupt. Here are the last of the boxes to be unpacked. You want me to leave them in the hallway?" Joe asked.

Ericka rose, hating the popping of her knees. Establish a workout routine added to her mental list of things to do. She wet her lips and turned to look at Joe. "Hello, Mr. Reeves."

His smile stretched from a grin to showing all of his pearly whites. *What, no second thoughts about hooking-up? Fine, so be it.* She could get over him…maybe.

"Ericka, you're looking ravishing today."

Sweet words, but she sported a black jogging suit. The baiting battle would continue. She bent her head, trying to get the kinks out.

"Ah, Joe, please put the boxes in the hall, and we'll get them when we have more room."

"Yes, ma'am." His glittering brown gaze didn't leave Ericka as he answered Jacey.

Tingles jetted through Ericka's lower belly.

The man had a considerate nature. From the

moment she kissed him on the threshold of her house, she'd maintained a constant tug and push of emotional conflict. The spell had worked because she'd conjured the devil, and he'd created a multitude of romantic notions.

"Ericka?"

"Yes." *Hot.* She had to get out of the jacket and sit, or she'd faint.

Jacey's mischievous smile indicated something was amiss. "Tonight we're going shopping for an outfit for your Cyan criminal court debut, right?"

The zipper flew down. One arm became stuck in the sleeve of the jacket, and she couldn't move. "What?"

"Clothes shopping later?" Chuckles erupted from her friend. Good, at least her color looked better.

Joe separated the zipper and slid the jacket from Ericka's arm. His gaze glided to her face. His stare held that dark sadness again.

Not hearing anything but "shopping" she jerked the coat from his hand and held it in front of her. "Yes, later."

"Well, you ladies have a fine time. If you need anything, call." He ran through the hall and a moment later the rear entrance slammed shut.

"Yep, I'm confident you prefer the blue candlesticks."

"What are you talking about? I'm not even familiar with the green or whatever the other thing you mentioned." She glanced into Jacey's impish sparkling eyes. "Forget the schemes. I'm not playing." She tossed her jacket on top of the recycled packing peanuts and proceeded to open the next box. "Let's get busy."

Jacey lifted an item wrapped in brown paper. "Right. You can deny Joe all you want." Her voice turned to singsong. "Love is in the air."

"Oh, oh, oh no," Ericka sang along. Forever love was an illusion, and she wouldn't foolishly believe in forever.

Chapter Ten

Joe glanced into the mirror, for a final look, before leaving the room. His fresh washed jeans, last clean white shirt, and best-punched belt all looked good in the reflection. He tilted his head to comb a stray strand of hair. Ericka's quiet house made him wish for a stereo system of some sort. He hummed a catchy tune, as he debated the gift for the shaman.

His brother-in-law's rare plant idea would have been great if he'd had time to search for one. Special herbs didn't pan out because the local garden centers were seasonal. When he asked for wolfsbane, the drugstore pharmacist stared at him as if he spoke in tongues. A rare book could have been ordered, if he'd had an opportunity to use Ericka's Internet again. Griff offered his workshop, so Joe would use good ole' American creativity and craft a cauldron. If he could remember his grandfather's welding instructions, a fire pit container with portable braces might be the perfect gift for an outdoorsman.

In a few minutes, he'd go with Griff to the local bar and maybe together they'd gather information about the shaman. Joe descended the stairs and strolled along the hallway. He glanced in the library, expecting to see Ericka. Although she wasn't there, her magnolia scent still infused the area and revived his interest in touching her soft fragrant skin.

"Where are you going dressed like a movie star?" She stood in the doorway of the parlor or sanctified space as he considered the room. He'd witnessed her lighting candles and murmuring lyrics. His skin prickled, like a ripple of jealous emotion. She wasted her time. Nothing good would come from casting spells.

"Griff and I are going to the Brewhouse."

"Well, enjoy yourself." A scowl tarnished her face as she marched across the hall and plopped on her desk chair.

Griff's truck horn sounded. Joe stood at the entrance of the library, planning to tell Ericka he wouldn't be in until late. Something must have caused her insensitive mood, so he'd talk to her later. She never went to bed at a decent hour. He'd located her twice leaning over a volume by Fisher, *Evidence,* and *Fisher's Federal Rule* at the cock's crow. He had plenty of time to chat and come clean about his reason for not having sex with her.

She'd understand. He was a loner after all.

****

Joe staggered into Ames Mansion, a little past midnight, stomach-sloshing full of Brewhouse's homemade beer. Blurry-eyed, he peered into the library. Ericka sat hunched over her stacks of literature investigating her client or magic. The perfect man didn't exist, so why try to find one?

"Honey, I'm home." He didn't reign in the illogical jealousy, but bee-lined to the side of the desk and propped his hind quarters on the edge. "Did you miss me?"

"You're an insufferable drunken ass. Get off my

desk." She shoved her dagger-pointed red fingernails into his leg. If he could feel pain, the pierce would've hurt.

He stroked the inside of her wrist resting on the desktop. "Not until you answer my question. I'm curious." He tapped her arm.

She met his stare, but held a finger on a line of her lawyer bible. "You invited me to stay, but not in your room. I felt your hands caressing me as you hid my nakedness from your friend. I try to play nice, and you shove me away. You can't tell me announcing *only sex* wasn't a ploy to stop me, to tease me. What is it you want from me, Ericka?"

"I want you to leave this office." She jerked her hand from under his and stood.

Should he punish himself and enjoy the end of the evening? Already bedeviled, he'd at least feel alive. He slid from the desk, closed in on her, leaned into her curves. The light brown circles pulsed around the black centers of her eyes. Pheromones surrounded him, trailed into his nostrils tantalizing him, sending him further into an alternate reality. He became the beast he abhorred. His attempt to shed the darkness was lost. "Before or after a kiss?"

A shadow of a smile appeared. "I'll forgive this transgression, Joe, because you've been tapping the keg." Her grumpy voice and quick full-fledged smile enticed his groin to life.

He quirked an eyebrow, at least he thought he lifted the right side of his face. "Drinking or an attempt at a kiss? I don't have a drinking problem. I might take a sip at weddings and New Year's. However, the hot waitress kept our glasses full. And thoughts of…"

"Leave."

Her pissed expression made him stumble back a step. Was she angry because he'd caught her lusting for him? On second thought, he'd always been good at puzzles and could anticipate the criminal's next move. He'd apply his skills to this delectable, fierce, magnolia-scented woman. Amending his approach, he took a bow. "Your wish is my command, my sweet."

She hurled the book. He bent, doing a deep knee bend, and missed being crowned by the thick volume. Perhaps it would have been wiser to wait, until she got over her mad about the sex play, to poke.

He grinned. No, his prodding had proven his suspicion. Strong emotions were a sign of love. *Yes siree, love drenched the air.* Joe whistled a tune as he sauntered out of the room. Sleep came very easy with dreams of Ericka and her multi-faceted personality.

Chapter Eleven

Joe kept busy and two days passed without a peep from Ericka. Either she was repulsed by his behavior, or she'd been busy preparing her case. *Good*, they'd needed a separation.

Before the Brewhouse incident, he'd been too involved with her. They had shared stories regarding the legal system. She'd sat hip-to-hip with him while they watched a reality TV program. She'd jiggled her leg when she laughed. Her sexy chuckles had about killed him.

A flashback of their simultaneous comment regarding the fashionista contestant who backstabbed an opponent ran through his mind. She'd tittered and followed with, "We have the same sense of humor."

"I was thinking the same thing, one of several things we seem to share."

"Tell me about some of your cases, and we'll compare." She'd bent her legs, hiding her feet under her thighs.

Their comfortable night's activities had drawn them into a cozy togetherness. He had to create a distance and run as fast as possible from Ames Mansion and its stimulating owner before he did something stupid like sleep with her.

He double-checked his suite. He'd made his bed with military corners. All of his personal items were loaded in his bag. Stalling, he strolled through the room. After the shaman got rid of the *gift*, Joe would return and pursue a relationship with Ericka.

He tugged on his one nice shirt, covering the tee Tess had given him. He wrapped the scarf around his neck and wedged his leather coat between the handles of his bag. Griff had given him the truck and a couple of days off to find the shaman. Tomorrow, an early snow would blanket most of the southern area of Indiana. Today, he would find White Wolf of the Coterie Nation.

Clutching the duffle in one hand, he secured a thick oilskin bag holding the greeting gift. *Shake it off, Reeves, and get on the road.* The predicted overcast sky would make the atmosphere darker than normal. Regardless, he'd climb the side of a mountain to reach the guy. The possibility of change excited and scared him.

He stopped in front of Ericka's bedroom door, wanting to enter, but unable to commit to a future he might not have. He recalled her tossing the book at him, a woman wanting a man could react with such passion. Instead of knocking, he continued down the stairs. He peeked inside the library. She had her nose shoved into a law book. Dim lights cast a romantic glow over her. He put his palm flat against the doorframe. Could he transcend all human and non-human barriers to reach her?

He wanted to say something, make her aware of his interest. Due to a nebulous future, he couldn't make any promises. He hurried along the hallway, until he stood on the portico. Sharp cold air woke him from his brief illusion of happiness. His shiny motorcycle and the shaman called him.

****

Ericka finished the paragraph, put down the reference book and glanced at the doorway. She expected to see him propped against the doorframe, like usual. Empty. Thoughts of Joe destroyed her concentration. She rose from the chair and strode from the room. Embarrassed she'd let two days pass since she'd tossed *Evidence* at him. While forming an apology, she dashed to the second floor.

The bedroom door was open. Something seemed out of place, she flipped on the switch to the overhead light. His personal items were missing from the dresser top. She rushed into the bathroom, also free of grooming products. He'd left, without saying good-bye.

Her heart thumped hard against her ribcage. He was gone. Fine. She had a case anyway. Curiosity about his ambiguous past, and what he continued to hide, plagued her. She'd failed to ask him about the search for the medicine man. *That's it.*

She hurried downstairs and rushed into the library. As she typed shaman, Cyan, Indiana, into the computer browser her phone rang. She didn't glance away from the screen as she reached for her cellphone and hit her hand on the corner of the desk. She shook her fingers and grabbed her cellphone with her other hand. "Ericka Gilmore, Attorney at Law."

"Hey, I'm swamped and Joe's going to take our truck, so Griff has to use my car to go to a new worksite. Can we postpone selecting wallpaper?" Jacey exuberance rippled through the telephone line. Her enthusiasm didn't make Ericka happy. She didn't want to be alone tonight.

"Please come over, we'll use my new facial mask." Ericka hated the begging tone in her voice. In the intense silence, as a mid-town girl, she was reminded of the noise of city life. The quiet gloomy atmosphere, and her best friend bailing on her twice in a matter of days sparked her need for activity, for excitement.

"As tempting as that sounds, I'm going to have to ask for a rain check."

Ericka dropped and kicked a bag filled with matches and candles into the trashcan. "Why is Joe borrowing your truck?"

"He's going to see an old Indian. To give you something to do, you might want to go with him. Have a new adventure. Just a second and I'll ask." Jacey screamed Joe's name. "I'll call you right back."

"Wait—" The phone connection ended.

****

The Harley roared to life as Joe shifted and drove into Griff's driveway. Joe parked beside the garage. Reluctant to abandon his sense of freedom the bike gave him, he glanced at the truck. He'd do what he had to do.

Griff came through the backdoor of his house. A set of keys dangled from his fingers. "Here you go, buddy."

Joe took the offering and handed him the motorcycle key in return. "Thanks. I might need the truck for a couple of days."

"Sure. Keep it as long as you need. Good luck with the shaman. Jacey's flagging me. Drive safe." Griff turned and strode toward his wife.

Joe climbed into the cab of the shiny vermilion truck and exhaled. The tight quarters closed in, bringing back the memory of the car accident ending Adam's existence and altering his own. He exhaled and turned the ignition, starting the motor. The radio blasted the final notes of his favorite song about a stormy night and full moon. Nervous excitement riffled through his gut. He'd get rid of the gift of death prophecy.

Knuckling the button to lower the window, he glanced at the overcast sky. He breathed in deep, inhaling the scent of condensation. The wintery blast would be coming sooner than the forecaster had predicted.

Headlights shot a beam, brightening a gloomy day, and exposing Griff and Jacey in a heated conversation. Joe checked the rear view mirror in preparation to back out of the driveway.

Anxious to get started, he thrust his arm out the window and gave a wave. He put the truck into reverse and turned to check the traffic. At the shout, he turned. The lyric "...she's there to find me" proved to be true. She was.

Ericka.

She slid from her car, leaving it running and the door open. This couldn't be good. Joe's heart sank. He lowered the passenger window flush with the casing.

"Hey, Jacey cut my call off." She nodded to the immobile couple, standing toe-to-toe. Their voices rose. "What's going on?"

"I'm not sure."

Griff ran to the truck. "Sorry man." He rubbed his ear, making a pink spot. A bright flush brightened his cheeks. He shot a glance to Ericka. "Jacey suggested Ericka go with you."

"What are you talking about?" Ericka belted out.

"Why?" Joe asked.

Jacey, having arrived, stood between Griff and Ericka. "She's interested in the occult."

"He's a healer not a warlock." Joe clutched the steering wheel with both hands. He sent a silent prayer to make this conversation end. He wanted to visit the shaman alone, no interference. Worse yet, none of these people realized they kept company with a freak, someone who could predict their demise.

"The shaman," Ericka said. Her voice was soft, but the air carried the hope to his ears.

Damn.

"I don't think we should interfere with Joe's plans. He came to Cyan specifically—" Griff, the pillar of reason, drew his wife off to the side. Her mouth, so often smiling, became a tight, firm line.

Double damn.

Despite Jacey's elevated voice, he'd heard Ericka.

"I'd like to go with you." The intonation of her words made him think he misunderstood her plea.

Her happiness was important to him. Bottom line, he wanted to be with her and to shield her from the evil in the world. He also needed to see the shaman before the snow fell to ensure Ericka wouldn't be a part of his death dreams.

Chapter Twelve

To avoid a pothole, the size of the barn door, Joe jerked the steering wheel to the right. Stones bounced and pinged off the underside of the truck. He guessed another mile, and they'd see the entrance to the village.

An annoying cellphone chime interrupted the silence. Ericka whisked the device out of her bag and growled, "Hello." A long breath of air whistled through the cab. "Great. I'm not available for the next day or two. Stay clean and don't worry overmuch about who says what."

Joe waited until she met his stare. Mr. Personality, suited for prison life, occupied the other end of the conversation.

She switched the phone to her other ear and took an intense interest in the scenery. "Mr. Ward, your case is sensitive and you should not discuss the details with anyone outside your therapist and immediate family."

"When I return we'll meet." Her tone rose, but not to eardrum piercing level. Her knuckles whitened in direct contrast to the black phone. "Threats are not a way to get you out of an assault charge. Are you going to see the doctor for continued counseling?"

Tap, tap, tap, a white-tipped fingernail hit the shell of the cell. "Listen to me; you need help with anger management. You do have rage issues."

The phone dropped to her lap, squeaky shouting

rang through the interior. She snatched the device and held it near her ear.

"Mr. Ward, just a head's up, don't ever threaten your attorney. I'll be back in a day or so, and we'll discuss your situation." She clicked the end button, shutting off the cellphone and her client.

A strong urge to tell her to dump the guy battled with none of your business. No doubt she had a long list of clients; why keep an abusive one?

Joe felt her stare. *Don't look at her.*

Sweet floral scents hung in the air as she leaned toward him. "You haven't said one word to me. It'll be a long ride if you're going to be mad for the rest of the night."

Joe ignored the warning in his mind and followed his instinct. "Why don't you dump the asshole?"

Her eyes shimmered, and her jaw hardened. She tilted her head, and then rolled her neck. A few clicks later, she pressed her cheek against the leather seat. Razor sharp glares bore holes into him. "Long and involved story."

Okay, he could pry the details out of the woman-child or let go. She could spend the rest of the trip stewing. He could tell her all of his issues, but then she'd feel sympathetic. He didn't want pity. No, it'd be better, safer, to keep her at a distance. "Other than Jacey recommending you tag along, why did you want to come?"

She sucked in her cheeks and pursed her lips. His first impression of her having a poker face flew out the window. "I'm...I think meeting a shaman might be interesting."

Why did he expect her to say she wanted to spend

time alone with him? Their brief romantic interludes could have been a tickle and slap situation. She couldn't know about his hellish gift. His drive for absolution remained a secret. *Except.* "I heard you saw a ghost go into the light?"

She snapped upright. Her stiff shoulders thrust her breasts out. "He was there, we connected, and then he wasn't. Strange and wonderful at the same time."

"I see." He didn't. "Your first time seeing a ghost?"

"Yes, and apparently my last."

Why couldn't she understand, messing with the mystical caused grief and sadness? "Let's change the subject. How about you come clean. Why don't you dump Ward?"

"I don't have any other clients." Her eyes were closed. "I'm scared I'll fail and lose my house. My funds are running out." She exhaled.

"I've a marketing degree, along with the criminal justice. I'll help you create a plan when we return." Why did he make an offer he might not be able to keep?

"Thanks, I'd like that." She stroked her diamond necklace. "And the reason you're going to visit with the shaman?"

The silence grew uncomfortable. Should he reveal his ability slash problem?

"I have the gift of prophecy. I want to get rid of it and resume a normal life." Once the words left his mouth, the simple and somewhat odd answer didn't sit well with him.

She frowned, bit her lip, and then bent to lift her backpack purse. The brown leather created a nice contrast to the gold letters. She withdrew a lipstick, removed the top, screwed the ruby rod beyond the silver, and outlined her plump lips. No response? He anticipated a hundred successive questions rippling off her rubicund lips.

"I can't claim to understand. Have you had this ability all of your life?" Ericka rotated the glossy stick down.

"No. For the past year." He justified her calmness as a result of her cold, detached, fact-gathering, attorney persona. Should he tell her his new talent resulted from a car accident, the one she'd researched? Given they drove along a seedy road, under gray skies, which turned to over washed black, the setting would be too unsettling.

She turned in the seat and tugged the seatbelt, then clicked the latch and released the strap. "Why do you believe the shaman can eliminate your ability?"

"Research. Put your seatbelt back on," he growled.

"I can't find my scarf. It's freezing in here. Lift the window please."

"Can't. The car accident, which killed my partner, the one you read about, damaged me. I feel trapped in a vehicle, so the open window helps. There are blankets behind the seat." He took a deep breath.

"Oh, okay." She crossed her arms. "Tell me about the shaman."

"White Wolf is a healer or shaman. But for some reason the majority of Cyan citizens don't seem to have a clue. If it wasn't for a drunken mountain man getting inebriated at the Brewhouse, I wouldn't have this much of a lead."

The road narrowed into a lane, so he reduced his speed. Thick green shrubs and bare branched thickets closed in, almost touching the sides of the truck. Wind whispered through the crack of his window. The truck headlights flickered off something metal.

He stopped in front of an old-fashioned wooden gate with massive iron spikes shooting from the top, similar to what forts in the past used to prevent attacks from intruders. He braked and shifted into park. Large Pinyon pine trees lined the sides and created a backdrop and additional obstacles. Thorny bushes used the fence posts as growing stakes.

Green moss had wrapped around the iron hinges. So the fence wasn't frequently used. Either Joe had gone in the wrong direction, or the residents used a different entrance. No, the gate latch looked shiny and new, but no lock. Was the gate a diversion?

Private Property. No Trespassing. The sign didn't intimate him.

Ericka nodded toward the six-inch opening of the window. "Do you care if I raise the window while you're out?"

He understood her need for heat. "Sure. Get the blanket behind the seat." He pressed the lever lifting the window. As he stepped from the truck and jogged to the entrance, the scent of pine and the rough-hued cedar overrode the aroma of cold, musty condensation.

The gate latch appeared to be made of ordinary forged iron. Granted the tips had sharper points than most. He stroked the edge. The hitch had been filed to a razor's edge. From the position of the hitch, it had been manually altered. Someone went to a lot of trouble to make it offensive. He glanced along the fencerow, searching for cameras. Nothing obvious.

Summers at his cousin's home in the woods had

given him a firm foundation of wildlife awareness and not one creature scurried in fear. Night birds didn't fly overhead or perch on the bare branched trees. He unlatched the clasp and shoved the thick iron bar. Despite the squeal of metal against metal, the gate swung as if well oiled.

He jogged forward and in the distance, a smattering of flickering lights and house shapes came into view. He ran to the truck, climbed inside, and closed the door. A blast of forceful heat fluttered the sleeve of his jacket. In deference to Ericka, he lowered the window an inch and turned the vents toward her. The cool breeze gave him relief from the combination hot interior and claustrophobia.

"Well?" Ericka peered through the windshield.

"I think I saw the outline of houses and streetlights." Joe drove the truck through the opening and stopped at the other side of the gate. "I'll be right back."

He dropped low to the ground, ran to the gate, and latched the iron bar. Settled behind the steering wheel, he glanced at Ericka. "Don't you find it odd the village has a massive fence with no end in sight, but doesn't have some type of contemporary security measures?"

She shrugged. "Maybe they do and we're not aware of it, yet."

Doubtful, he would have detected an electronic system. Their defense might exist in another form. Reaching inside his jacket pocket, he verified his faithful Glock 26 remained snug inside the worn shoulder harness. "We'll find out."

He approached the village and slowed to twenty-five miles per hour. Entering the center of town, the road's condition vastly improved. The structures had large rectangle solar panels built into the roofs.

Likewise, the streetlights appeared to be solar-powered as they created diffused shadows. Storefronts had signs marking a pharmacy, general store, and bank. He noted other businesses with old-fashioned clapboard exteriors.

"The place resembles something out of a fairytale book." She released her seatbelt. "Kind of fake."

He put the gear into park in front of the Village Bar. Beneath the neon light, figures were outlined inside the building. A heavy male and pear-shaped female moved beyond the frost-laden window.

"Yeah, surreal." Uneasy, he evaluated the perimeter. "It's safer inside the truck. Lock the doors. I'll find out where the shaman's place is located. Need anything?" He raised the window.

"I'm more of a local than you, let me go with you." The lever clicked, and the door unlocked.

"Ericka, please stay in the vehicle." He stepped to the ground and slammed the truck door.

His scarf snapped in the wind, flapping against his leather jacket. He grabbed the ends and stuffed the material inside his coat. Ready to enter, he twisted his earring. *Adapt and blend.* He drew open the door. A blast of warm air curled the fine hairs on his neck. The pungent scent of beer mingled with lemon sage rode the heat wave.

As luck would have it, five people were inside, two men in close conversation at a small stainless steel table near the exit and a guy at the bar. The server held a tray of empty glasses. She hovered near a tall dark-haired broad-shouldered man who guarded the till, counting bills. At the click-clack of the entrance shutting the bartender, wearing a black shirt with red lettering, closed a sleek new cash register drawer and glanced upward. His dark hair had a peak pointing downward to his eyes. His dark stare held a hint of sadness, a lot of weariness, but mainly suspicion.

Joe evaluated each of the patrons. None of them appeared to be an immediate threat. He ambled to the counter. Music filtered throughout, but not loud enough to drown out the clink of glass hitting glass.

The bartender lifted a bottle of tequila from a line of colorful liquids. Joe noted the guy's evaluating glance in the mirror.

The brute schooled his expression and turned about. "What can I get you?"

"I'm looking for the White Wolf. Is his house still east of here?"

"Buddy, I'll offer you a beer, tequila, or whiskey, but I ain't mixin' a white wolf." The bartender crossed his beefy arms showing off his intimidating pectoral muscles and a post-card-sized crow tat.

"A beer is fine."

The entrance opened and smacked shut. Heels tapped on the sticky hardwood floor. He recognized Ericka's scent. Damn.

"Do you have a restroom?" Ericka asked.

"Go right," the bartender replied.

A stocky, mesomorph-body-shaped, guy from the end of the bar slithered around the edge and stared at Joe. The server scurried to a table near the windows. Her bleached-blonde hair covered most of the deep wrinkles near her mouth as she whispered to a rough-looking bearded man. Shaggy, marked by a multitude of hand scars, stared straight ahead. The lack of emotion was typical and ominous.

He'd keep an eye on the short dude and Shaggy. He'd arrested a large percentage of undersized round men with bad attitudes. If anyone in the room caused an incident, it would be the guy at the end of the bar.

At the squeal of a chair being tugged, Joe glanced into the mirror. Ericka took a seat at one of the empty tables instead of beside him. Her hair caressed the side of her face as she lowered her coat to the chair back. She smiled at Shaggy.

Sweat coated Joe's neck. He tapped his leg, wishing he could simply toss her over his shoulder and carry her to the truck. A room full of strangers. Why would she put herself at risk? He lowered his glance. He'd get directions before something happened, and get her the hell outta here.

A chair moved.

Ericka chuckled, her loud toneless, nervous laugh.

Joe glanced into the mirror. The dark-haired, shaggy brute rested his arm around Ericka's shoulder and whispered into her ear.

Jealousy ripped Joe's stomach to pieces. He crossed his arms in an attempt to shield the annoyance pricking his skin.

Like a seasoned bartender, the guy flipped a short glass and then drizzled a finger full of clear liquid filling the container near the top. He slid the crystal across the scarred surface to the server, then jerked a tumbler from a rack of like containers and held it under the tap. A few moments later, the yeasty brew flowed over the side of the mug and covered the coaster, tainting the counter in front of Joe.

He drew his arms back and let the foam dissipate. Joe should leave her snuggling against a stranger. No, he liked the idea of tossing her over his shoulder and rushing to the exit. He gripped the handle of the beer mug and took a sip. The tang of the thick ale tantalized his taste buds, while her chatter burned him.

Liquor sloshed and glasses clinked as the shots were lined along the bar. In an attempt to get the bill, he waved his hand. Ericka bantered with her captive audience, including the bartender.

She'd left her sweater coat in place. *Thank God.* The V-cut black knit blouse would expose the shiny gold bra he knew lay beneath.

He left a ten spot on the counter, slid off the stool, and glanced in her direction. She nodded and proceeded to sip a cream and red liquid shot.

The nod he took to mean she'd be okay left alone. He walked outside and cold air hit him, shocking him into reality. A few steps and his stride faltered. He couldn't climb into the cab of the truck without her. Near the frosted window he'd be somewhat hidden by the frame and support pole, so he assumed the position. He watched her and wiggled the phone from his coat pocket. A quick glance at his contact list, and he selected the person he trusted.

"Brett, I'm sorry for the late hour, but I need a clue."

"Shoot."

"I'm at the village. The locals are holding tight. Tell me, from your anthropological viewpoint, what type of home would a shaman live in?" Joe kept his gaze on her. "Like in the center of town or secluded in a woods?"

"Indians were nomadic, creating and living in homes designed for their specific environment."

"So, I need to find a forest?" He glanced at the houses in the village, newer, and permanent. Urbanized natives. The towers indicated they maintained an efficient energy source by wind power, very fore thinking.

Brett, in professor mode, described the difference between the woodland and plains natives.

Come on, Ericka. Through the foggy window, she rose and kissed Shaggy's cheek. Shoulders back and head held high, she wobbled toward the exit. Shaggy, sans overcoat, held her arm. Joe rushed to the door just as it opened, and she stepped out.

"Unlock the doors, please," Ericka said. She tilted her head and smiled a wide, sappy drunken smile.

"Brett, just a sec." Joe pressed the electric lock.

Click, click snapped through the thick quiet. The guy hauled the door open.

"Thanks, Tom. Night." Ericka tilted to the left as she tugged the handle. She stepped on the running board.

The man stuck his hand to her rear and gave her a boost. Annoyed, Joe rushed forward and nudged Shaggy aside. Ericka, settled in the seat, grinned. Still holding the phone to his ear, Joe shut the door then ran to the front of the truck and climbed behind the wheel. He locked the door, shutting Shaggy out.

She fumbled while trying to snap the seatbelt into place. "Had to suck-it-up and join the fellas in a drink or two, but I got the address." She winked.

"Did you hear?" he asked Brett.

"Yes. I want details about your visit," Brett

responded.

"Got it. Thanks." He disconnected the call.

Ericka's neck hit the headrest of the seat and a long alcohol-scented breath left her glossy lips. He had to give her credit; she knew how to work the locals. Yep, Ericka Gilmore was good, a damn good investigator. He had the strongest urge to kiss her.

Instead, he started the engine.

****

The truck jolted to a start. Not accustomed to hard liquor, the liquid sloshed making her empty stomach burn. Ericka hoped the cocktail stayed put.

Joe talked on the phone. His voice, far different from usual, held the saccharine warmth she'd experienced at one time. She wanted him to speak to her in that tone again.

She diverted her thoughts to the incident inside the bar. Her leg tangled in a chair, and she tumbled. Tom, Wolfe's brother, caught her inches from the floor and lifted her upright. He chuckled and mumbled an indecent offer.

Being accepted by the locals gave her a rush and not even the sour bile caught in her throat dispelled her happiness at getting the coveted information Joe sought.

She shook her head, swallowed the noxious phlegm, and strapped the seatbelt across her parka. From the corner of her eye, she spotted his relaxed posture. Joe's legs didn't jiggle like they did when he talked on the phone. A knot twisted in her stomach. Could he be talking to a girlfriend?

Joe scratched his head, then smoothed the hairs he'd ruffled. His earring glowed in the dash lights. The jewelry seemed out of character. How would his six-o'clock facial hair look come the morning? Unable to hold her heavy head upright, she rested her face against the tan leather of the seat and continued her Joe accolade list. His intelligent walnut-tinted gaze delved deep into her soul and always ignited a fire. A heat she wanted Joe to extinguish.

"I wanted to get the address for you," she repeated. He sent her an odd expression, not the soul-snatching one.

He frowned. No smile. No banter? No congratulations or well done?

"Okay, so I didn't stay put like a trained monkey, but I did get the directions."

"You could have been...in all sorts of trouble."

"Sorry."

"Are you going to tell me which way to go?"

He'd stood guard outside the bar, proving he cared about her. She embraced the tidbit. "Yes, siree. At the corner, turn right. Thirteen miles along Spring Pass, and you'll see William Wolf's house."

"William Wolf aka, White Wolf the shaman?" He drove along the main street.

"The one and only." It took some effort to keep her eyes open and sarcasm harnessed. In the dim streetlights, a very prosperous Native American village passed. "He's expecting us."

Chapter Thirteen

The interior of the truck had a chill and not from the open window. Ericka used her teeth to remove a glove and shoved a cold finger on the button to generate more hot air. Despite the freezing air, her insides burned with the heat of spirited adventure. "Why don't you ask what I meant by White Wolf is expecting us?"

A smile tugged at his lips, before he set his granite jaw. "I asked you to stay in the truck. You could've been drugged or taken hostage."

"I told you, I could handle myself. Besides, Tom's the shaman's blood brother. Wolf instructed him to provide directions to me."

"Who's Tom?"

"The guy who walked me to the truck." She peered out the window. "What a beautiful night." She sighed. "Neither of us planned to travel together today, so don't you find it odd Wolf thought I'd be at the bar?"

"Maybe Shaggy just wanted to get close to you and coax a kiss." He stared at her lips. "I would."

Yeah, let's pursue the idea. "The key to success is leaving nothing to chance." She smiled. "I don't believe stealing a kiss motived him. Granted I have limited paranormal experience, but I believe in the supernatural. Wolf is expecting us."

"Yeah."

The scenery changed. Modern buildings faded to

145

the background. Red bramble roofed barns had large security lights filtering over the land. White and brown cows lingered by hay mounds.

Joe raised the window, leaving an inch for air. She closed her eyes, listening to the whistle of the wind and the fan rolling heat from the vents.

The truck curved to the left, then a sharp right. The seat strap bit into her skin. She tugged the belt and glanced at Joe.

"Sorry, a critter ran across the road."

"That's okay. Look, there's another one." A rabbit hopped from the street into the snow-covered brush.

Less than five miles to go, guessing by the distance markers, and they'd meet the shaman. She considered how to discuss Joe's problem, which had drawn him to the medicine man. Other than the third eye and claustrophobia, what did he hope the shaman would help him cure?

He kept his emotions and secrets close to his heart. She'd bet analytical Joe had been an excellent detective. Obviously, his nomadic lifestyle hadn't provided him peace.

"When we see the shaman, I believe you should present your request and not hold anything back."

"Will do." His fingers gripped the steering wheel in a chokehold.

Why couldn't she ever say the right thing? He'd say potato, and she'd say patato. The possibility of them as a couple flew out the window, along with the heat.

"Sorry. You got saddled with me and from what I can tell, you're enduring my presence." She turned the radio dial and scanned until she came across a soft rock station.

He turned off the radio. "I just don't like you taking chances. You could've been hurt."

Her heart melted, just like the large billows of diamond shaped snowflakes swaying in the sky. They created a glittering blanket before disappearing. Would Joe disappear from her life after he got what he wanted from the Wolf?

Miles passed as slow as a morning line at the local coffee shop. The shadowy outline of a building came into sight.

"According to the lettering on the mailbox, we've found William Wolf."

Joe maneuvered the truck, gravel crunched under the tires as he parked. The ranch-styled house had multiple lights beaming from the windows.

"I expected a hut, or at least a one room log cabin." His voice grated like a rusty chain, and disappointment rippled in each word. A massive wind tower stood at the west side of the house. In the background, pine trees appeared to go for miles.

A wealth of sympathy for him came over her. His burden was so great he was forced to travel across the country, alone.

Be positive. "It's made of roughhewn logs. Look, smoke and sparks are shooting out of a chimney. The house is beautiful."

Joe turned off the engine. An outside light flashed on and illuminated the wraparound porch. He opened his door, lowered to the ground, and secured his bag from behind the seat. Ericka unsnapped her seatbelt, placed the strap of her purse over her shoulder, and glanced at the building.

She questioned if any one person could accomplish eradicating a paranormal ability. It'd been a year since her friend told her about inheriting the haunted Ames estate. She'd always been levelheaded and a follow-the-rules kind of gal. Other than connecting with the Ames ghost and trying to work a spell, she didn't have true magical abilities and remained a borderline skeptic of the supernatural.

Her stomach twisted. How could Wolf's ancient power help Joe?

Joe opened the passenger door and extended his hand. Even in the cold, when their fingers touched, fire ignited. The spark reassured her of their mystical connection. The first night their shared contact caused a similar shockwave.

She took a breath and hoped for a miracle. For him. For them.

She glanced into his face. Just for a second a flash of hot desire sparked his saddle-worn brown irises. He must have experienced the awakening of lust. Yes, a shared attraction, but the trepidation of true romance stole to the deep depths of her heart.

She lowered from the high seat of the vehicle, and bumped into him. She clutched his strong shoulders, seeking support. Her breasts smashed against his hard chest. She slid, slowing the drop by clinging to his jacket. Through the worn jean material, his thigh muscles tightened. To her disappointment, within seconds her feet touched the ground.

He took a long breath.

Steady, she locked her gaze with his.

A hint of a smile appeared in his eyes.

His mouth captured hers. *Wow!* Her lips warmed

under his. Hot steamy emotions rippled through her, heating her blood. A pool of warmth flooded her lower region. She couldn't catch a breath.

He pulled away.

"Welcome." A man's voice sounded aged, with a quality of wisdom few souls possessed.

She glanced at William Wolf. His silver hair sparkled under the porch light. He wore a sweater, jeans, and fluffy gray slippers.

"I'm glad you arrived safe and sound. Please come inside." Wolf's gaze held hers.

Reason returned. Wrong place. Wrong time. She'd need to pursue that zing later.

Joe rubbed his hands against his thighs and bit-by-bit exhaled foggy puffs of air.

She slid past him.

"Please, come inside and warm yourselves." Their host turned and disappeared inside the house.

Joe shut the truck door.

Shaking off the remorse of what could have been and stifling the need for more, she walked toward the house. Flakes swirled, hazing her route. Under the shelter of the veranda, she waited for Joe.

He got a large duffle bag from the back and joined her on the porch. She gazed into his eyes. A dark cloudiness overrode the previous hunger. Could he be nervous?

She subdued her own quivering nerves, removed her jacket, and gave it a shake before crossing the threshold. Wolf maintained a crooked grin as she slid past him and entered the house. Joe walked into the foyer with the contents of his bag clanking.

She draped her coat over her arm and held out her

free hand to Wolf. "Hi, I'm Ericka Gilmore and this is Joe Reeves."

White Wolf gave it a pump and then shook Joe's extended hand.

"William Wolf. Welcome. Please, hang your coats by the door." The healer nodded to a row of iron wolf-shaped hooks.

"Would you like some tea?"

"Yes, thank you," Ericka said and glanced at Joe.

Wolf walked a few steps to the kitchen and ignited a gas-stove burner.

An open concept, cathedral ceilings and no walls between the two main rooms, gave the impression of spaciousness. Rustic rough-hewn logs had been used to frame the structure and provided supports between the kitchen and the main living area.

She hooked her purse and coat on one of the large hooks. Her face burned...a result of a windburn or from Joe's chin whiskers? She pressed her cool palms to them, trying to reduce the heat.

****

Joe hung his jacket beside hers, getting a whiff of her scent from her coat. He removed a pouch of tobacco from his pocket and as usual scanned the home to check for exit points. Rust-hued Indian pottery with ancient symbols and woven materials in brilliant blues, greens, and oranges had been placed strategically around the living room. A shiny log table, complete with benches and placemats set for three, served as a dining table. Set for three? Their host poured water into a teapot with two tags hanging outside the brown pottery.

"Let's get comfortable in the living room." Wolf placed the tray holding three cups, scones, cream, and sugar on an antique trunk converted into a coffee table. He hustled to a cupboard and removed a bottle of liquor, the same color as the trunk.

What the hell? Joe had foolishly romanced the idea of the medicine man living in a hut and going into a cave to brave out the winter. When in reality the guy lived in a house, nicer than Joe's last apartment, and served tea and cookies.

"Come, have a seat." Wolf patted the back of the sofa. Instead of knobbed wrinkled clumps for knuckles, his unlined fingers narrowed to smooth pale nails.

Ericka's stare followed their host. "I have to tell you, I expected a crusty old man. Your face is unwrinkled in contrast to your white hair. How old are you?" She sat in a large leather chair by the fireplace and accepted the teacup.

Joe shot her a glare.

She pursed her lips and blew into the steaming brew.

"I'm forty-two, and on a cold winter's day I can be rather crusty." His blue eyes glittered with amusement. "Sugar and or cream?"

Joe shook his head and sat on the sofa. "Black is fine." He placed the pouch of tobacco on the trunk and took the cup. "I'm rather surprised you're so young. I thought all professional shamans gathered wisdom from life experiences."

Wolf sipped his tea and settled against the seat. "I'm not a shaman, but a medicine man."

"Forgive me. Please explain the difference." Joe set his cup on the table. He may have made a mistake coming all this way if the healer couldn't help him.

"A shaman is prehistoric, someone who has pure

and simplistic beliefs with a strong spiritual base. The shaman goes into a deep meditative state, crossing into a different reality to obtain knowledge and power. A guardian spirit will transport him or her." Wolf stared into the firelight. "Not a ghost, but a spirit guide. The guide could be a dog, eagle, bear, or other being."

"No healing powers?" Ericka asked.

"Depends." He shrugged. "If you were to go into an Indian's camp and spout about seeking a shaman for healing you might be ostracized." He lifted his elongated nose a slight pinch. His already tapered eyes almost disappeared behind high cheekbones. "Practitioners of controlled or summoned spirits are intermediaries between the natural and supernatural realms and are not considered a shaman. However, the great spirit is sometimes sought to heal disease."

Joe needed to hear the words *I can heal you.*

"My abilities are varied, and as you could tell, our people tend to be reluctant to discuss issues about medicine." Wolf smiled, as if contemplating the next question.

"What about communicating with spirits?" Ericka asked. The ceramic cup clicked against the metal bands of the table as she put it down. Tears shimmered in her eyes. She shoved a strand of hair behind an ear, and then crossed her arms at her middle. A smidgen of pity ran through him. What had she expected from the medicine man?

"I wonder if you're referring to a lost soul in the spirit world. Lost spirits or missing parts of souls go into another realm. If those spirits are willing, I assist them in continuing their journey." He lifted his hand in a stop motion. "Either into the great white or help them by discovering and dispelling the trauma which is the reason for their gravity." His steady hand touched Ericka's. "Tell me, my dear, who are you seeking?"

Her head shot upward, so fast the snap of her dangling star earrings flashed. Brilliant colors of the fire, yellow, blue, and orange of her diamond necklace glimmered with firelight. "No one. Joe is the person you should help."

"She said a spell, and I showed up instead." He watched Wolf for the slightest indication of repulsion.

Ericka licked her lips. "I was trying." She glanced at Joe. "To conjure a supernatural, ah, mate."

The amount of angst in her voice made his heart sink. Even if he lost the devil taking over his soul, he didn't have any hope of attaining her affection. Without her brightness, his world looked bleak and full of loneliness.

Wolf's sharp glance shot to Joe. Damn, the man could read minds. Did he glimpse Joe's infatuation with Ericka? What could he think about, or use, to divert the attention from his exposed heart?

"We brought you a token of appreciation for welcoming us into your home." Joe rose from the sofa and went to the front door. A moment later, he carried the bag, and the clanging of iron-to-iron added to the cadence of snapping fireplace logs. He'd hope for the best, because if he didn't have hope, what was left?

Within minutes, Wolf had created a presumably safe environment, where he and Ericka felt compelled to spill all of their secrets. Did she regret coming? What had they walked into?

"Thank you." Wolf tugged the brace and the metal pot out of the bag. "Well done. This will help me tremendously during a walkabout in the summer. My gratitude to you both."

"Walkabout?" Ericka asked.

"Yes, each summer I wander, walk through nature, and absorb knowledge. I find internal peace. The journey allows me time to contemplate how to help others."

Wolf went to the fireplace mantel, removed a small wooden puzzle box from inside, and withdrew a sachet. He carried the packet and pot to the kitchen, and filled the cauldron with water. Without a second's thought, he toted the kettle to the blue and white embers and slid the handle on a hook. He plunged his hand into his pocket and eased out a pouch. He dropped the second packet inside the pot and hung the kettle on a hook over the fire.

Joe hoped the container conformed to its potential. Griff had provided guidance, so the cauldron should hold steady. Joe didn't want to disappoint the healer.

Wolf knelt in front of Ericka. Her doe-eyed gaze didn't leave the healer. He clasped her hands.

Joe's heightened senses caught the sweet scent of sage, rosemary, and underneath the faint hint of frankincense. Thanksgiving meets Sunday mass invaded his personal space. He drew in a deeper whiff. There was one aroma he couldn't identify.

Wolf turned toward him. "Myrrh, a symbol of death and suffering is the underlying ingredient, Joe." He sneezed. "My goal is to promote harmony between man and woman and between man and nature."

Damn, he did read minds.

"What are you talking about?" She flipped her glance between them.

"Incense and my goal for you two. Let's talk about souls. A soul departs and is unable or unwilling to be held back. Most of all it is foolhardy to conjure a spirit to become a mortal's lover. A conjured soul might be malicious. We all seek balance. Balance within us, our neighbors, the universe, most of all nature. It is unnatural, unbalanced, for a soul to return to Earth once the being has connected with the great above. If part of the soul of the one you tried to conjure is present, it would be signified by existing close to your heart chakra." Wolf lifted the clear stone dangling from the silver chain. "If you tried to conjure a soul, for any reason, that humanity might be contained in your necklace, waiting for the opportunity to expose itself."

The healer's fingers grazed her skin.

Malicious? The book he'd seen in her library contained dark spells.

His heart pounded hard and fast, making him choke and gasp for breath. He prayed, a small plea, not to let any part of a soul or evil exist in the diamond. Selfish, but true.

Ericka's pupils were dilated and glassy. Her fingers gripped Wolf's free hand as if the man possessed her reason to live. "I don't need to know. I'd rather not know."

"Could there be another in your life, one who gives you pleasure? Someone you could love or already do love?" Wolf kept his hand entwined with hers. Did he give her comfort? He flipped the crystal over and over.

She looked at Joe, their gazes met and held. He resisted the urge to grab at his chest and slow his pounding heart. Did she care for him? If so, they'd have a chance, a future together. "She needs to be aware of what chaos magic can create."

"Please. Just help Joe."

Wolf dropped the necklace and her hand, but remained on his haunches in front of her. "Your choice. Do I look into the crystal and see if you brought forth something, other than Joe?"

Chapter Fourteen

Joe couldn't reveal his true desires right here in White Wolf's living room, because Ericka needed peace from whatever had her wired. Joe held tight to the belief spirits exist in the great above, or down below, and would not have occupied the diamond.

As Wolf recited lyrics, a light spicy layer of herbal smoke clouded the house and obscured Joe's logical thought process. He needed to open a window, before he succumbed to the incense. Maybe the fresh air would revive him. Ericka's dizzy grin collapsed. White-hot anger replaced the twinge of jealousy jetting through his belly. *Release the rage, the envy. Tell her of your feelings. Make her understand how much she matters. And how she makes you feel whole and human.*

Wolf leaned forward. She tilted her head, as if to catch the precious words the medicine man had to impart. The leather of her seat screeched as she shifted her weight. Uncomfortable with the silence and the intense connection between the two, Joe reached for his mug. He wrapped his fingers through the teacup handle.

"Do you always wear that jewel?" Wolf asked. How long could the man remain in a crouched position? Joe's knees would have turned to jelly by now.

She nodded. Joe found it odd not a single syllable came from her pretty lips. She always had something to comment. He lowered the cold brew to the table, then propped his elbows against his knees.

"I understand you've a tenderness for someone other than the one you hoped to conjure, but considering you cast a spell, it would be wise to confirm no spirit rests within the jewel. Sometimes, when a person loves with such passion, they refuse to pass into the nether world. The spirit will find a home, occupying a token, furniture, or pet. Any item which will allow or keep the soul close to the object of his or her true desire. The essence might simply want to remain Earthbound. With your permission, I'd like to see if any spirit resides inside the diamond. You'll not be harmed, but I'll need to touch the necklace and your body at the same time. May I?" Wolf's softly spoken words traveled across the room. The cadence of his intonation subsisted and became mesmerizing.

"Two times I tried to cast a spell, and I believe I've failed. But, yes, please see if I've made an error in judgment and conjured something I shouldn't have."

In a mellow state, perhaps due to the scent of steaming herbs flooding the room, Joe dug his elbows into his knees wanting to feel the pain and remain alert. He worried a hangnail on his middle finger. Near to bleeding, he gripped the edge of the sofa seat.

Wolf nodded and plucked the possible spirit vessel from its resting place against her chest. He drew her face to the side of his cheek and chanted in liquid sounds, the words similar to what Joe had overheard when watching an old black and white western movie.

"We live in a parallel universe with other spirits. It's possible to pull them into our time and space," Wolf murmured.

Christ, was the man about to produce a ghost right

here, on the spot? Was a conjured soul inside the necklace nestled between her breasts?

As Wolf's incantation gathered force, he increased the speed of the words and his shoulders rotated swaying to the left and right, all the while keeping the necklace between his fingers. He stopped wavering and placed his free hand over her heart.

Sparks shot from under the pot in the fireplace. Disregarding hot bits of ash, floating to his woven carpet, Wolf focused on the prisms in the glass. He held the crystal aloft, puckered his lips, and blew against the stone.

Nothing happened.

Joe sat deeper into the sofa. Mentally, he whistled in relief, believing himself the consequence of Ericka's dabbing with magic. Fate was a magical element, wasn't it?

The jewel fell to rest between her breasts. Her deep breaths became harsh and frequent, lifting and lowering the pendant.

Wolf shifted, putting several inches between him and Ericka. His quads had to be giving him grief, yet he maintained his crouched position. He grabbed both of her hands, holding tight.

She inhaled. Her knuckles became as white as the snowflakes coating the earth outside.

Joe started forward, but stopped when Wolf sent him a pointed look. His eyes had darkened to indigo.

"Some spirits travel to the inner arc, especially if they exist in a blue plane. Their souls spin until being welcomed into their new realm. Your loved ones will be waiting for you, when you grow old and are ready to enter the nether world. However, people seek peace and contentment, as should you. Look deep into your center to find the people who make you happy, who provide you with peace. Harmony will exist if the sun, moon, and stars are aligned. Look for serenity in them." Wolf paused. "And love, Ericka. Love cannot be conjured. Love is magical and should be found under the stars if you side with your sun." He halted and stared at Joe. "Although—"

"My sun?" she whispered. "Forever?"

"Yes, the female is represented by the moon and a male by the sun."

"And the stars?"

Wolf's attention returned to Ericka. "The stars represent all of nature, Earth, Water, Fire, and Air. All things exist under the stars...including the love you seek."

"Love?" she murmured, followed by whimpers deep in her throat.

Joe settled against the sofa cushion. Hope continued to exist. He wanted to shout, "Look at me. See me. Love me." Christ, what had he admitted? Did he love her? An instant vision of them holding a dark-haired baby flooded his mind. His heart exploded with longing.

Wolf's upper body undulated for several minutes and then stopped. No movement—not one twitch. "No spirit has transmitted to your medallion." He turned to Joe. "Your loved ones stay in transcending mode before going to our sky father. If he is in the nebulous band between afterlife and earth, there's a method to find out."

The odd comment squelched Joe's temporary joy. "What? I'm not looking for a ghost."

Wolf dropped Ericka's hand. Balancing on the tips of his toes, he stood. He extracted a clean square piece of cotton from his back pocket and extended the scrap. His keen dark gaze returned to Joe. "No, you're not looking, but you'll see a spirit and the encounter is necessary for your goal, to find solace for your gift of prophecy."

He grabbed his cup and strode to the kitchen. Joe admired the man. He didn't rub his thighs. With the grace of a seasoned ballet dancer, he sat on the sofa. With steady hands, Wolf lifted the bottle of whisky and poured a dollop into his teacup.

Joe glanced between the two. Ericka stared at the fire bursting into multi-colored flames. Instead of remaining quiet, shouldn't she have asked for an explanation?

Wolf's face appeared pale, brilliant, and glowing. The pearl-essence quality didn't distract from his frown.

From what Brett had told him, a ceremony should be holistic in nature. Expressions of the participants would reflect and respond to the universe. Chants are ceremonial. Also prayers, dances, and smoking pipe. How did raising consciousness come into play?

"She breathes. Her emotions are clear. Her thoughts have been voiced and her heartbeat is in sync with her words, all the elements becoming one cadenced whole." Serenity circled Wolf like an invisible cloak. "Besides, you are the one in pain. Your aura glitters, and your internal angst…it bursts through your skin."

Wolf's answer to the unspoken questions gave Joe a moment of pause. Thank God, the medicine man was occupied when Joe's love for Ericka broke free, a revelation he'd rather keep private for now.

The encounters of the last two years should have immured him to surprise, but this man's showmanship and abilities impressed him.

Wolf lifted the pouch of tobacco. "We use pipes for certain ceremonies. Thanks for the tobacco though." He unfolded the foil and sniffed. "Fresh."

Joe nodded through the wooziness. "So the other, the dance, the percussive instruments, expressions, and movements are just for show?"

Wolf added a second smidgen of whisky to his cup. The strange glow continued to emit from his gaze. He lifted the mug to his lips, hiding a grin. After taking a sip, he held the vessel between his hands. "Not always. Two key devices are used for any healing situation, one psychic and one magical. Both are tied to rhythmic patterns. In formal tributes, ceremony and participation from members is assumed. Contribution is not of activity, but rather interest and repetition."

Joe exhaled. The teakettle bubbled and boiled, scenting the room with strong herbal fragrances. "Are you going to finish? What is the method? Why do I have to go to catch a spirit in order to find solace?"

"He wants to get rid of his visions." Ericka fell forward, her necklace dangling in front of her.

"I understand. Joe, people need to grasp their role in the universe to achieve harmony. Any deviation, such as the loss of identity, memory, or drastic change and the response will always be rage. The person may not have adjusted to his new reality. He might become out of sync with his balance. Regardless, harmony must exist." He closed his eyes, sealing off the strange glistening light shooting from the orbs. "Your balance isn't in harmony."

"What if the person can't find harmony and doesn't want the new reality to exist?" Joe glanced at Ericka. She lifted her chin, waiting. What would happen next in this odd play?

"Have you ever read any of James Welch's books, *Winter in the Blood* or *House Made of Dawn*?" Wolf's black pupils, mere pinpoints. Had the potpourri simmering on the fireplace drugged him?

Joe shook his head.

"Ericka?" Wolf invited her into the conversation.

"Nope, I don't know him." Cup in hand, she rose from her chair.

"In *Winter of the Blood*, Welch writes about vision-questing. The seeker hopes to have a vision, a rite of passage for most individuals. To be considered an adult by the community he must obtain his vision."

Ericka went into the kitchen. A few minutes later, she refreshed their drinks. She placed the pot on the table and sat down. "What is that scent?"

"Herbs to help us with our communal vision quest," Wolf gushed. "Rituals are very important in our culture and must be adhered too."

Joe had a sinking feeling he didn't want to hear the next comments. Would Wolf deny him harmony, to rid himself of his new reality? Was Joe wasting his time? The dreams had to stop.

"Individual experiences are not always isolated. They provide personal empowerment and shape directions to the person's destiny, his or her route in life. The network of human and nonhuman life is replicated in oral traditions, storytelling if you will."

Wolf drew out a small leather pouch, the strap caught on the button of his cotton shirt. He pressed the bag against his chest. "Vision quests will heal unbalanced souls, restore harmony, and make clear paths for future seekers. Meaning is obtained. Life is given. In whatever form, once the vision quest has been achieved, then water, the Earth Mother, will cleanse the person's soul and reunite him or her with his or her true destiny."

"I'm not thirteen and seeking to leave my mother's house. I don't believe a vision quest will assist me. Death prophecy visions are my problem." Joe fisted his hands. "I need you to help me get rid of my ability. I want to be normal. Have peace and harmony. I want to see my family again."

Ericka gasped.

No going back, he was what he was. If she didn't like it, the kiss by the truck might be the last time he'd have intimate contact with her.

"Joe, look closely to your spirit. You have the power to see, to understand, to discern the future. You have the ability to destroy by not acting on your visions or to nurture life. You could prevent the casualties." Wolf tapped Joe's arm. "Yes?"

He scooted his arm from under Wolf's hand. "It's a power I don't want. Are you able to help me?"

His brow furrowed, giving him the appearance of an actual Wolf. Joe refused to give an inch. He'd been searching for months for hope, and the journey might end here.

"No evilness surrounds you. Your vision of prophecy, is it immediate, the near or distant future?"

"Yes, immediate." Joe shook his head, trying to sharpen his dulled senses.

Wolf grabbed his wrist, pressed his index finger into the pulse point. "I assume by your strong reaction, your visions are of your family and friends?"

The pressure went through the haze barrier and hurt. Joe tugged his arm free. "Yes, and the people surrounding me. I see their deaths. Through trial and error, I've found there is a twenty-four to forty-eight hour window to play out the prophecy. Or they die." He glanced at Ericka. She bit her bottom lip, and unshed tears shimmered, tears of empathy or fear?

"My record for saving people isn't great."

"You had a vision of the librarian?" Ericka whispered.

He nodded.

"You saved her life."

Joe stared at the floor. He wanted to save all of them.

Wolf rose, clasped his hands behind his back, and paced in front of the fireplace. "In our culture the woman is the heart and rule. She is able to produce life. A ritual means changing something from one state to another, and the condition is inherent in the process of mothering. Women are primary peacemakers. Appreciating harmony and cooperation, they strive for health and prosperity. Females are an organism of thought and practice. This woman," he pointed to Ericka, "she has the power to create and transform."

"Where are you going with this line of reasoning?" He sounded a little strangled, unintentional but there it was. A vague excitement centered in his chest. Ericka would be part of the process. He'd have another chance to...what?

"Women weave existence, even from the

supernatural planes, into being." Wolf blew out a short breath. His dark gaze pierced him. "Joe, your quest for the understanding of yourself, your faith, your life, and your new ability has led you away from your community. A human, alone and separated from society, will not survive."

Joe's self-induced isolation had been difficult. His sister had a baby, and he'd yet to hold the infant. He wanted to be with his family, needed them to be a consistent part of his life. The loneliness got to him, made him crave human contact despite the possible consequences of such an association. And the very reason he took the job with Griff and lived with Ericka.

He grabbed his aching knee. The bruise was a token of saving the librarian. He glanced at Ericka. He would not put her in danger. Due to the vision, he became responsible for the impending peril. His gut clutched. He'd already put her in danger.

"You might feel you don't have control, but you do. The visions are valuable. To understand the meaning of this gift, answers to your questions, you must go on a vision quest. I'll provide a ritual, a rebirthing, using a purification ceremony. If you do not get resolution during the journey."

"Purification like walking in hot coals or dunking in cold water?" He could take the hot coals better than being enclosed in a watery confined space.

Wolf chuckled. "A sweat lodge is the common method. Working with spiritual energies is a sanctified and potent course of action when executed for the right reason. If a ceremony isn't performed correctly it becomes dangerous." He moved between them, holding his arms out like Jesus gathering the flock.

Ericka took a deep breath and leaned forward. What was she thinking?

"You'll need strength because a sacrifice is warranted. Women have the power to weave, they can also undo the binding...disrupt. Ericka, you'll need to come to terms with your self-esteem and fear of the future to obtain purification. At the full moon, both of you will go on this spirit quest."

"What?" Joe asked. He'd like nothing more, but as Wolf paired them, his heart rebelled. He didn't want her on the deathwatch any longer.

"Why?" Ericka said in a loud voice.

They'd shared a passionate kiss, so her quick response shocked him. Did she fear him?

"Strong and capable of radiant movement, you travel in and out of Joe's mind. Your destiny is with him, entwined souls." Wolf's words intensified. He stared at Ericka. "You, my dear, have intelligence and the spirit to understand the universe. You will be his salvation."

She opened her mouth, and then snapped it shut.

"I don't want Ericka involved in this. Don't you see? The longer I'm near her, and others I care about, the more I risk seeing their deaths. What if I can't prevent the casualty?" Joe dug his fingers into his scalp, trying to get the sting of his increased blood pressure to reduce.

"She is the heart. The moon. She has the power of creation. She will be your protector and salvation." Wolf whispered the words, but they echoed off the walls as if the utterance had been shouted.

Ericka's eyes widened. "Joe, let me help you."

He hesitated.

She bit her lower lip. Already pink, it'd be red if she kept biting the soft skin.

Why didn't she want to avoid him? She could die.

"Time is of the essence. There is a slim interval in which you can awaken a departed spirit, and the limited time is near an end. Based on the information you've provided, and what is forecast by the alignment of the stars, I'd guess two or three days are left to connect with your spirit guide before he crosses into the afterlife, if he hasn't already. Joe, if you want to obtain absolution, both of you will need to go to the nearest ley line. Find the bridge to the other realm. There you will find the answers you seek, if your guide remains in transcending mode." He tented his fingers. "You have a difficult choice to make, because the spiritual place will intensify your already outstanding gift. Your visions will be tenfold there."

"What spirit?" Joe asked.

Wolf leaped to his feet. "It's late. Tomorrow, you'll begin your journey at sunrise. I'll outfit you both in proper gear and provide a food sack. You'll make your way to the sacred place and there, Ericka, you'll discover what you seek. Go to Old Stone Fort in Tennessee, I'll give you directions. You have questions, but they must wait. Come, I'll show you to your room or would you prefer two rooms?"

Joe's pulse continued to zing at a high rate. Would Ericka run for the exit? The truck keys poked out of his jacket in plain sight. She rose from the chair and followed Wolf.

Joe exhaled. Should he continue to deal with the visions or seek this spirit guide? What bridge?

What realm?

Chapter Fifteen

"Joe?" Ericka winced as her voice boomed through the bedroom. He didn't answer. The dim light coming from the window outlined his shape. His chest rose and fell in a light steady rhythm.

"Joe."

"Yeah," he mumbled.

She shuffled to the other side of the bed and dropped the blanket from her shoulders. As chambers go, this one duplicated hers, but the white bead-board walls and barn siding decorating the twelve-foot ceiling made the space appear bigger, fresh and pure.

Chilled, under her gold bra, her nipples hardened. She lifted the covers. For the last two hours she'd imagined nothing but easing the ache deep inside, eating away at her heart. She threw aside her values and climbed under the sheet to spoon him. His skin smelled like the spicy cinnamon-based cologne he used, and his hair had an overpowering aroma of the sweet herbs stewed in the pot. The roughness of his hands excited her, but the old puckered circular scar marking his stomach made her want to weep.

Maybe a combination of the herbs and splaying her issues out in the open gave her *c'est la vie* attitude. Mellowness created from the idea of a typical man-woman future. Did the possibility exist?

Weave. She didn't weave anything together except

words to get people out of a jail sentence. Why had she been named the "one" to help Joe?

Her toes tingled at the idea of being so important to him. As an individual, she'd always wanted to do things her own way and thumbed her nose at the guys who refused to acknowledge a woman could be as competent as a man. After all, people aren't born with hard edges. They develop sharpness over time. In her work world, she had to adapt, jagged edges and all.

She focused on the ceiling fan. The reversed blades kept a flow of warm air near them. Thanks to Griff, she had a head full of useless carpentry information to keep her mind busy. Wolf's declaration managed to overrode how to measure a board. She and Joe had to go together. Maybe in this mystic place her genetic make-up would be altered, and she could have a normal long-term relationship with Joe. She pressed her eyes closed, wishing for such happiness.

While the medicine man talked to Joe, she forced herself to admit her time with him might be short. Was she benevolent? She'd driven human males away for years. Could she smooth her rough edges and provide solace to Joe? Wolf had thrown out a final lifeline, work together. She moved closer to Joe.

Unable to resist, she ran her hand along his scarred back, into the curve of his slim waist and down his hip. He could provide her the joy of a physical connection, moon to sun.

"I can't sleep."

"Why not?" He didn't tense.

She was surprised when he flipped to his side and faced her. He caressed her face, gentle strokes. His long slow caresses soothed her mixed emotions.

She gazed into his eyes. Lust. Pure and simple lust radiated from the black irises. "From what Wolf said, we were meant to be together."

"I'm not the perfect guy you tried to spell cast." Joe's harsh tone conflicted with his movements as he shifted her loose hair to rest against the pillow.

"He said you're my present. And God willing, my future." She kissed his mouth, running her tongue over his upper lip, learning the shape and the texture.

Joe didn't ask about tomorrow, as she'd anticipated he would. Considering he predicted death dates for his friends, he'd avoid conversations of the future.

She leaned forward, and he slid his arm around her shoulders. "Are you okay going with me to the ley line?"

His caresses had moved to her shoulder. A sensitive spot. She released the suppressed air. "Yes. I want to help you."

"Thank you." He sighed and stroked his fingers over the crests of her breasts. "I don't want to need you."

She pressed her palm against his chest. "I understand. I feel the same way."

The barrier between them had to be removed. Her tongue circled the diamond stud, as she sucked his earlobe.

She slid her hand around his neck and urged him onward, to touch where the liquid pooled between her thighs. She shifted her hips closer. The time had arrived. She'd get relief from this angst of desire for the man who'd kissed her during a violent storm and little by little created a spot in her heart.

Her nose fit into the groove between his jaw and

collarbone, a lover's nook from the start of time. She exhaled, ruffling the silky stray dark hairs along the side of his head.

A deep, low, sexy chuckle erupted from his perfect lips. His stomach muscles barely moved, but his chest surged against her breasts.

"Wolf was right," he said, and then bit the edge of her chin.

"About?" She bumped her chin against his firm obstinate jaw.

"Strong and capable of radiant movement," he kissed her lips. "You constantly travel through my... mind."

She rolled over and straddled him. Their parts fit together like pieces of a puzzle. "Let's see how radiant I am."

His hand pressed low on her stomach. By the simple contact, ripples of pleasure rushed through her.

"No." He lowered his hand. "I can't be your stand-in-lover. When you want me and only me, let me know."

His strained voice shocked her. She stared into his clear gaze. She lifted her leg over his and plopped flat on her back. Her heavy breathing sounded loud in the quiet room.

****

Joe shoved his back to the bed and forced his hands to remain at his sides instead of touching Ericka. Her soft, herbal scented skin and musky woman aroma tempted him. He wasn't a monk, but they were in a stranger's house and in all likelihood had been drugged by a potpourri concoction.

"Is it okay if I stay in here tonight?" Her voice

sounded little-girl weak, not the strong and rugged Ericka he'd grown to love.

He swallowed and gripped the covers. "Yes."

A man could die from sexual stimulation without release. He rolled off the mattress, grabbed a shirt from his bag, and held the stark white cloth in front of her.

"What?"

"Put it on. My will power is limited."

It sounded like she cursed, but she took the shirt and with jerky movements wrapped her delectable body in his clothing. She flung flat against the pillow and crossed her arms under her breasts making them plump.

His decision to let her stay would, indubitably, be a mistake.

Chapter Sixteen

Three o'clock.

Joe shifted his glance from the wind-up clock to the crescent-moon window at the peak of the guest bedroom ceiling. The darkness outside reassured him he had time to sleep. He couldn't. The tattler mechanism of the clock should have been a soothing sound, like counting sheep, but the furious wind muted the tick-tick-tick.

He'd always have the visions. Loneliness engulfed him. He wanted to be with his family, to feel the familial connection. It'd been almost a year. He wanted to play catch with his nephew and cradle his niece.

He sighed and relaxed against Ericka's soft sensual warmth. Her transition from being tightly wound to a relaxed sleeping state shocked him since he'd seen her in the library all hours of the night and into the morning. He hadn't been this personal with her since he'd managed to cop a feel when they sat snugly together on the sofa. She'd retaliated by tucking her fingers under the pillow and brushing against him; simple play, which tweaked the heat between them. Intermittent light moans flowed from between her plump pink lips. Yeah, she didn't play fair.

Tired of being alone, he wanted to settle down and to commit to one love. Ericka suited him. Her beauty, determination, honesty, and stubbornness tripped him.

His heart recognized love. Wolf hinted Joe could live with the prophecy gift. Easy for an outsider to pass judgment, but to live knowing at any minute a vivid color-filled vision depicting the death of someone you loved…was impossible to endure.

He vibrated with exhilaration as she snuggled, pushing her rear into his thigh. Three A.M., according to Brett's theory, paranormal activity occurred between three and five, a short span of time. Ironic Joe's visions always arrived in that slice.

He refused to sleep. A death prophecy would interrupt his quest. No sounds came from the rooms nearby, so either the healer slept or he was a specter—a ghost who tossed drugs into a pot, making them think they had arrived at Shangri-La and gave them unbelievable hope.

Joe would find out in a couple of hours. Why had Ericka felt compelled to cast a spell? What kept her from developing a long-term relationship with a regular guy?

He'd try to get rid of the foresight, even if it meant risk having a stronger vision. He prayed to God the prophecy, if one occurred, would be about an acquaintance, someone other than one of his newfound friends. The tick of the clock became distinct. He glanced at the hands, 3:58 A.M. One more hour and he'd rise and take a shower.

Ericka rolled to her other side. His thin shirt outlined the angle of her back, the indentations of her slim waist and the rise of her rear. Her dark wide-eyed beauty overwhelmed him at times. Someday she'd disclose her past, the one, which molded her into a future-fearing-spirit-seeker.

Where was the ley line located in Tennessee? He'd send Griff a text to arrange to use his truck a few more days.

Joe had visited churches, occultists, and researched paranormal until he could carry a decent conversation with Stephen King or M. Night Shyamalan. What if he couldn't change the present to Joe's pre-accident past? So many times, he'd prayed he'd been driving the car instead of Adam. Perhaps Joe wouldn't have lost control of the vehicle, and his partner would be alive. And…Joe wouldn't be searching for a means to rid himself of this ability.

Peace flooded him. Unreserved and swift, he relaxed and decompressed. A twelve-foot ladder rested against a snow-capped roof. A man hammered a board. Finished, the repairman crawled to the first step. He missed a foothold and the ladder fell to the side. The man dropped like a ball of lead. Heart striking panic raced through Joe, until he experienced the hard jarring contact with the frozen ground. He jerked upright and ran his fingers through his hair. Clammy slickness chilled the middle of his back. If the pile of snow hadn't been scooped away, the man would have had a softer landing and survived the fall.

Joe's heart vibrated his ribs. His breathing escalated.

Unlike the other visions, in this precognition he experienced the fear the person would feel…of dying. He exhaled and glanced at Ericka. She remained in a deep sleep.

He wiped sweat from his forehead, shoved the covers to the side, and slid from the bed. After stretching, he grabbed his satchel and trekked to the bathroom. Scrubbed and dressed, he gathered his day-old clothing and shoved them into the bag, then removed a comb from the pocket. He glanced into the mirror. Horror struck.

The person's face, in the dream, had been turned away. Fuck, he didn't know whom to save.

"Hey, are you done in there?" Ericka's scratchy voice came from the other side of the door.

He swiped the comb through his wet hair, and it flattened like a wet noodle. He flung the door open. "Good morning."

She bowed her head, but not before he caught a glimpse of the red infusing her cheeks. He caught her around the waist, drew her forward, and gave her a light kiss. "Nothing to be embarrassed about, not everyone's a morning person."

Her forehead hit his chest. Perhaps he didn't see the identity of the victim in the vision because he would be the one to die. Would she be his salvation? Could Ericka save him?

"What's wrong?" She took a step back.

When had she become sensitive to his body language? He mentally shrugged. As an attorney, she'd been taught to read a person's character through their actions, and his muscles had tensed.

"Nothing." Short and sweet, not what he intended to say, but it worked to divert her attention.

"Then move, so I can use the bathroom." Her soft words contradicted her lower back muscles tightening beneath his fingertips.

He contemplated what to do at this point, kiss her to make the situation better or get out of her way.

"Move!" She impelled his chest with her fist, and

then slid past him into the bathroom.

He pivoted as the door clicked shut. Damn, this woman confused him. He shook his head and followed the scent of coffee.

White Wolf sat at a scarred oak table sipping a steaming brew. Wearing a cream cable-knit sweater, jeans, and tall boots, he resembled a J. Crew mock-up and very unlike Joe's stereotyped image of what he'd expected.

The white-haired male-model stopped eating oatmeal and glanced at him. A grin spread, lifting his cheekbones and narrowing his eyes. "The coffee drew you?"

"Coffee and the mystery of the ley lines." Joe dropped his satchel and removed an earthenware cup from a rack near the sink. He filled the mug with dark rich java.

"Help yourself to the oatmeal. You'll need the energy and heat." The clever man threw out a verbal lure.

Joe would take a bite, but first he'd create a line of questioning. He glanced at the pot on the stove. Oatmeal was his least favorite breakfast food. Ham and eggs he could get into, but expanding little slivers of wood-textured cereal, no thank you.

"There's brown sugar in the crock."

Would he get used to the man's delving into his mind? Probably not. He removed earthenware bowls and spoons from a rack and prepared portions for him and Ericka. He sprinkled sugar in the oatmeal. He left her bowl near the heat source.

"I assume you want to wait for Ericka to explain about the trip." Joe used the point of his spoon to make tracks in his cereal. The thick consistency bordered on hard; although, the aroma of the sugar mixing in with the oats provided hazy warmth. He lifted a spoonful to his mouth and swallowed trying to prepare the way for the fiber.

"The ley line is located at Old Stone Fort, Tennessee." White Wolf rose, washed his bowl, and placed it in the rack. "It's a six-hour drive from here."

"I'm interested in the lines. Water is a magnetic source for spirits. At one time, I thought my visions were a result of something paranormal and tried to leave it in any spot of water. The approach didn't work." Dousing water had been one of his many attempts to rid himself of the visions.

A muffled chuckle came from the Wolf. "No, my friend, you do not have a spirit inhabiting your being." He sat down, leaned his elbows atop the table, and tapped. "Think of your gift as an actual package. Wrapped and sitting in your brain closet, after the accident, your brain shifted. When you woke from the coma the package opened and released the vision gift."

"Are you telling me I can't get rid of this?" The spoon clinked against the side of the earthenware bowl as he shoved his congealed cereal to the side. He lowered his voice. "The darkness is taking over my life."

If last night's vision meant he plummeted to the ground, maybe he wouldn't have to worry about the dreams.

Wolf jumped to his feet. He didn't appear to be a man who idled for very long. He poured coffee into the cup, leaned against the counter, and stared with his piercing sharp eyes. Joe wanted to squirm like a child being scrutinized. Instead, he returned the stare and raised his coffee cup.

The corners of Wolf's mouth lifted, then he sobered. "There are no guarantees in life, Joe." He nodded toward a wall lined with dried herbs and wrinkled pungent unknowns. "If you decide to spirit quest, when you return we'll try my version of the purification ceremony. Sometimes it's best to—"

"Good morning everyone." Ericka went to the drip brewer and poured a generous amount of coffee. She glanced at the sugar, lifted the spoon, and dumped a day's worth of brown crystals into her cup.

"Oatmeal on the stove for you." Joe nodded toward the now cool grain.

"Oh, thanks." Her attention focused on White Wolf. "Am I interrupting anything?"

"We were talking about gifts and, once unwrapped, how their value increases."

Why did Joe get the impression Wolf wasn't referring to prophecy? Wolf pulled out the chair for her to sit. He had the grace, verbal skills, and intelligence of an Ivy League college graduate. The corners of the medicine man's lips curved into a smirk.

"Okay, want to tell us more about the line thing and the spirit?" She sat on one of the wooden chairs and placed her cup and bowl on the table. The sun slipped its rays through the kitchen window and across her profile, adding to her luminescent beauty and glinting off her necklace. Joe wanted to spend every sunny day and starry night with her. Was happiness possible for him?

Wolf sat at the table and cupped the mug. "Alfred Watkins discovered the ley lines in 1921. Ley lines are a series of straight lines linking all the earth's networks, ancient tracks, and churches. Stonehenge was one of the first discovered sources, a line of power going all the way through the center of the earth. There were a couple of British theorists who connected the ley lines with subversive streams and magnetic currents, aptly naming them holy lines. A researcher by the name of John Mitchell claims the lines are placed in accordance with the laws of Feng Shui. The physics of the earth force influences the harmony of society. Men built their temples at the most powerful locations where the lines join together. You're familiar with the Roseline and the Knights Templar?"

"Just from the movie…something about a code. Are you telling us there is some fact to the story?" Ericka asked.

Wolf shrugged. "Skeptics say chance alignments."

"Assuming there's some validity to this ley line and powerful force idea, the closest crossing of the lines is six hours away in Tennessee?" Joe confirmed. He didn't care to fly to England's Stonehenge.

"Yes, America has a select few. We are fortunate to have one so close. Old Stone Fort is a historical Indian religious site. It doesn't resemble a fort. The area is a mound of sorts, about a mile or so in circumference, separating the pure from the impure. The consecrated site was constructed over several centuries ago." Wolf scraped fingers through his long white hair. The perfectly straight locks were messed in the process. "Pure, meaning the fort had been used for ceremonial purposes. The soil remains untainted and undisturbed for centuries."

"And the waterway is?" Ericka asked.

181

"Duck River and waterfalls." He smoothed his hair, his brown fingers tugging the strands into perfect order.

Joe had intimate knowledge with water. As a magnet to souls, he didn't question water as a conduit to crossing over into another realm. He had no fear of stream or lakes or rivers and often took a dip. On the contrary, he'd visited churches and doused himself the holy element. The liquid hadn't done anything except remove sweat and dust.

"How do we get there?"

"Take 41 to 24 south; go through Murfeesboro and Beechgrove until you reach Stone Fort Drive, Manchester, Tennessee." Wolf released the latest string of hair, rose, and rifled through a drawer in the kitchen cabinets.

Joe finger tapped a simple tune against the tabletop and glanced at Wolf. "Do we have to be physically on the bridge, in the water, or in the center of the ceremonial grounds?"

"Inside the grounds, in the circle. As you stated earlier, spirits are attracted to magnetic currents. They will be there." Wolf had gotten what he wanted, as he carried an accordion folded piece of paper and pen back to the table. "I can't guarantee your answers will be crystal clear, but you have today and tomorrow to find out."

"Who is Joe looking for and will the spirit just zap the prophecy ability out of him?" she asked.

"You both will find your answers at the religious ground."

"Both?" she asked.

Joe halted his tapping.

The flipping sound from the document pages

stopped. Wolf glanced at her and then Joe. "Yes, Joe must have you by his side in order to achieve his quest."

He held his breath. Wolf didn't tell Ericka what she would discover at the ley line. *You are the heart, his salvation.* Last night, Wolf declared there was a risk for Joe going to the site, to the ley line. He wouldn't put her in danger. He'd go alone.

"Six hours one way and less than two days. After that, the opportunity for Joe to find resolution will be closed?" she asked.

"Yes. He can't achieve his goal unless you are by his side." Wolf had unfolded a map. He held his pen in the air. Would he draw a set of ley lines across the map, directions guiding them to a quest in Tennessee? "Are you going?"

Chapter Seventeen

Ericka drew a deep cleansing breath and gathered the dirty earthenware dishes from William Wolf's kitchen table. It would be rude not to answer his question, but she had to consider the options and possible consequences. She turned around, wincing as the morning sun stunned her. A moment later, she scrubbed the soiled oatmeal bowls.

The herbal scented air in the large country kitchen added to her sense of unreal and helped to stifle her thoughts.

Neither man said anything. She didn't have an easy decision to make. Limited time. Nebulous band. Visions multiplying. She wasn't sure what the hallucinations consisted of or how the ley line would affect him and his revelations, but Wolf said he would have something tenfold.

Joe's trip to see the medicine man had turned into a quest. If she believed Wolf, then Joe couldn't purge his problem without her. Why her?

Her attributes, logical reasoning and the ability to defend a client in the courtroom, wouldn't make his world spin. Wait, he needed to meet his spirit guide. She could see spirits; at least she'd seen one. Could she see more?

She pivoted and crossed her arms, hugging the thin soft cashmere sweater snug to her middle. A few tendrils of hair had dried and tickled the side of her face. She chased them with a long exhale.

Joe remained hunched over the table, trailing his finger over the map. William nursed his coffee.

"Let me see if I've got this straight. You tried to see if a spirit took up residence in the necklace I always wear, because lost souls sometimes attach to an item or animal. I got lucky and no evil essence took hold. Yet, because I can see spirits I need to go with Joe to a ley line and within forty-eight hours." She nodded. "I'll help Joe find his spirit guide."

"Or not," Joe mumbled. The ladder-back chair squeaked as he rested against the rails and extended his legs.

William pierced her with a glower. "Correct. And..."

"If the spirit quest doesn't work or our timing is screwed, Joe will need to have his soul purified." She tucked her cold hands into her jean pockets. "I've a case I should be preparing to win. Travel to Tennessee and back will take time." She paused. "There's no guarantee I'll be able to see his spirit guide, which might help him get rid of his gift to see deaths right?"

Joe sat upright in the chair and placed his palms against the tabletop. "Not really a gift, Ericka, I see people die. Children die. No lucky lotto numbers, no impending births or happy marriages, only death."

"I'm sorry. How dreadful for you to see the death of a child or friend. That is a miserable way to live. Joe, I want to help you, but I'm afraid—"

"Joe will find the answer to his questions at the ley line, but the solstice will be over in two days." Wolf stared at her, as if searching for insight. She didn't have any, because more questions than answers plagued her mind.

"Is there a simpler solution? You said if Joe goes to the ley line, in Tennessee, his curse will intensify, and he could have sharper images. Hideous visions."

"Yes, a true possibility. However, in order to obtain his resolution he must try to connect to his spirit guide," the sage announced.

"Oh, that's right. My brain's still foggy because of the tea or incense. I'm usually very good at putting facts together." Not glancing at Joe, she resumed her seat at the table and lifted her mug. Snippets of the previous conversation, regarding women, rang through her mind. Heart. Weaving. Salvation. By helping him, would her life be forever altered? Would her nebulous role provide Joe relief from his difficult situation?

Grief washed across Joe's face, causing her a moment of introspection. Could she help him? To catch this spirit at a ley line would be unlikely, and Joe would be at risk.

William Wolf placed both of his hands around one of hers. "You need to go with him, because you're his heart. You have the power to create and transform. A ritual, such as the spirit quest, means changing something from one state to another. Your thoughts and practices are vital to his conversion, to realization and understanding. Although it's not clear to you now, your faith, your power, and your life is entwined with Joe's."

"Stop. It's decided." Joe stood and not in an angry jerky motion, rather slow, as if his willpower had depleted. "I'll go alone to the ley line. I assume I have to stay outdoors near this magnetic energy source. In a tent or what?"

Wolf rested against the back of his chair and tapped the table surface.

I see people die, children die. She shook off her selfishness. She touched his arm. "No, we will go together. You came to see Wolf and get help, make a transformation." She touched his face, so he'd look at her. "I want to help you solve your prophecy problem, and Wolf will explain the process or what to expect."

"All right." Wolf said, as if clapping his hands.

Ericka glanced at him.

William's smile widened. Yeah, he got what he wanted. She and Joe would be together in the frickin' cold on a mountainside. The upside, they'd have to cuddle to keep warm.

"Great, let's go." Wolf stood with his back to them and put his cup in the sink.

Joe stared, the one, which made her feel as if she was the only woman in the world. Her heart pounded harder, he made her want something…unattainable.

Joe captured her mouth before she could move. Public displays were never her thing, but the guy could kiss. He moved his lips in such a way she experienced a sense of being revered. She gave him a gentle shove, digging her fingers into his chest. His eyes glazed over. He stood and addressed William. "Give me the map. What should I take? It'll be about forty degrees warmer there?"

"Yes, there's the summery weather." Wolf's lopsided grin appeared. "I've everything you need."

"Now, why doesn't that surprise me?" Joe crossed his arms, and leaned against the countertop. He extended a black-booted foot.

William's face lit with joy as he grabbed the map

and handed it to Joe. Thick black lines designed a route straight to the unknown. The two men looked at each other. She felt like she'd missed something in the exchange. *Joe could be put in danger* became her chant and the drum accompaniment grew louder and louder.

The likelihood she could keep Joe as a mate was next to nothing. He'd ride his bike into the proverbial sunset. He had a curse, saw visions beyond the veil. Deep in her heart, she believed he loved her. She had to help him, and she'd hope for a future with him.

Her heart thumped like the ceremonial drums playing along with her chant. She'd go to the ley line. William Wolf had routed a clear path to her future, and by his smile, he rejoiced in their decision to venture forth. She should have a backup plan in case Joe got a vision.

Bundles of fragrant herbs, sweet basil, golden-yellow yarrow, and prickly purple-brown centers of leafless Echinacea stuck out among short stocks of white Chamomile with golden starburst centers hung from the rough-hewed racks mounted to the kitchen wall. She pointed to the dried foliage. "Any specific herbs we need to help us?"

William walked to a cupboard and withdrew a small clear glass bottle, filled with brownish-white power. A cork top sealed the container. "This is valerian. It's used to help with sleeplessness, cramps, and muscle spasms."

He rolled the tiny tube between his fingertips, and then extended the ampoule. She took the bottle from him. "And?"

"Best if used in tea or decaffeinated drink of choice." His smile made her wary. He knew the reason she'd need the herb.

She slid the container into her jeans pocket. "Won't I need to be awake to watch Joe's back?"

"It's not for you." His blue-eyed stare shifted between them.

Joe lifted an eyebrow, uncrossed his arms as if to reach for the vial currently bulging in her denim pocket.

"Come. I'll give you the gear you'll need." William strode down the hallway.

Joe hesitated and extended his hand. "Do you want me to take the bottle?"

Wolf continued along the short corridor.

Ericka stared into Joe's dark soulful eyes. "No, I'll keep it. He has a reason for giving the herb to me. We'll let it play out. Although, it'd be nice if he'd just tell us what was going to happen."

Joe chuckled. His low, sexy quiet laughter, the one her sensitive fingertips felt as the chortle traveled from deep in his stomach, vibrated his chest, and filtered out through those perfect lips. They'd gone beyond physical attraction. She inhaled, sieving the air through her teeth. His internal beauty far outweighed his gorgeous body.

As if he knew what she was thinking, Joe grinned. He clasped the handles of his satchel and trailed their guide.

Ericka took a final sip of coffee and placed the dish in the sink. She bit her lip, wanting to feel good about going to the ley line, but the image of his eyes darkening flashed through her mind. Something pricked the back of her mind. If the stars were aligned, they'd get rid of his devil and leave before…

She followed the men.

"Sleeping bags, lanterns, one crank flash light in case the others fail, matches, and water." William paused. "Ericka, a tiny notebook for you to record any activity in case you want to review it later. Maybe sell the story to a paranormal site."

She glanced in the mirror hanging in the foyer. Did she look like the type of person who'd do such a thing?

"She does have some of those sites in her favorites," Joe spouted.

Apparently, she did look like that sort of person. The paper would be helpful to create lists. Wolf finished his inventory of necessities. She'd ask about connectivity at the fort.

"Restaurants nearby?" Joe asked.

He held a bulging bag. "Dried food. You don't want to attract any creatures, at least live ones." William's gaze sparkled with impish laughter.

"How about the entrance into Old Stone Fort? Any problems getting admitted at this time of the year?" Joe focused on the map depicting their route.

"You'll have to park and walk. The route is marked and the ceremonial site has an L-shaped entrance. I imagine there won't be a group of visitors. I'm not sure if you can stay overnight." Wolf rubbed his ear.

"We need to be on the ley line, right?" Leather rustled as Joe slid his arms into his coat.

"What about the bridge? Isn't it the connection point, bridging life and death, earth and the, ah, white-lighted tunnel?" Ericka asked.

"Bridge is an expression, a euphemism," Wolf said and handed a pack to Joe. "You're right though. This is the holy ground, where the ley line crosses the magnetic current. It's not a physical bridge, but a"—Satchels

clasped in his fist, he smiled and extended the bags—
"jumping off point."

A smart-mouthed medicine man didn't please her.
Ericka took the bundle. "What about cell service at the
fort?"

Wolf lifted one black eyebrow, as if thinking about
what she wanted. Then, his humor-filled eyes glowed.

Joe slipped the strap of his saddlebag over his
shoulder and hoisted his pack. "You don't need a phone
to connect with the dead."

"Right." She hugged William. "Thank you." The
satchel between them made the hug an awkward
squeeze, but she felt compelled to acknowledge his
helpfulness.

"You're welcome." He held open the door. "Until
we meet again."

"Thanks. If this spirit doesn't remove the visions,
we'll need to find another way. I'll be back, and we'll
do the cleansing thing." Joe crossed over the threshold.

Ericka picked up her pace and followed.

"You're welcome in my home anytime," Wolf
said.

Joe threw the bags behind the seat, and then held
her arm as she climbed onto the cold leather cushion.
She usually tingled at his touch, but today her heart beat
damn fast. He shut her door and, through the window,
he gave a small smile, then loped around the front of
the truck.

The frost-laden morning air whizzed through the
cab as he arranged the bags behind the seat, then he
climbed behind the wheel. She blew out a steamy
breath hoping the window would remain closed and
knowing it couldn't. Oddly enough, she felt trapped and

welcomed the rush of fresh air.

"I think we'll be fine. We'll check the ley line to see if you get a jolt of electricity or something to alert you to powerful visions. Maybe because of the bridge and spirits you won't have precognition." Ericka exhaled. There, she'd shared a possible plan of action. She folded her arms close to her chest and tucked her chin in the collar of her jacket. Think positive, maybe Joe's visions would stop. An ache snapped through her stomach. She hoped the trip wouldn't be a pipe dream. Her heart double pumped. What if Joe found relief from his trauma and left Cyan for good?

Chapter Eighteen

The park ranger wore a dark green jacket with a badge emblem, golden background, and emerald trees in the foreground. Old Stone Fort had been embroidered in a shield over his heart. A smaller version of the shield had been sewn on the sleeve of his left arm. One of Joe's cousins had entered the park ranger battalion in Mississippi, so he understood the general responsibilities of the office, to provide resource management and scientific investigation. Not to mention park patron contact. Above all, the ranger provided protection and enforced legal rights of the people, animals, and nature. If anything happened to him, he was reassured Ericka would have a guardian.

The station looked well kept. Recently varnished walls, blue-black shingles, and the scent of tar. Windows glinted, in the afternoon sun.

The stern-faced, crew cut, officer might not like them settling down in the archaeological site overnight. All of the postings indicated the park closed at sunset. The ranger scratched his outer left thigh. The yellow-striped trousers didn't bunch. He walked closer to the truck and struck a military stance. Although not visible, a horse snorted somewhere close by. He must have chosen a mount instead of a bike, allowing him access to almost anywhere.

Joe lowered the truck window and dangled his

hand against the frame. Body language communication was key to gaining trust with a law enforcement officer. "Hello."

"Sir. Miss. Are you visiting the park today?" He stood within inches of the truck and looped his thumbs through his belt tabs. The leather squeaked with every movement.

Joe kept his gaze on the ranger instead of searching the perimeter as his cop's instinct warranted. "Yes, sir. We plan to hit the ceremonial ground. Maybe hike. Take in the waterfalls, and stay overnight."

"We're mid-renovations, getting ready for the season. The campground near the mound is closed due to the bridge being repaired." The ranger's dark-eyed glance scanned the truck interior. He didn't overlook the back of the vehicle either. "The park closes at sundown."

Joe respected his dedication to duty. "So, we'll still be able to go to the Indian religious site? Could we get permission to stay overnight?"

"Yes, but we don't allow overnight camping at the site. It'd be best if you left before dark." His thumbs slid from the belt loops.

"We understand. We're doing research. I believe Dr. Brett Firebach from Pennsylvania will call, or has called, your command center to try and get us overnight access." Joe had to call his brother-in-law the minute they were out of earshot range.

His eyebrows formed a V. "Researching?"

"Paranormal activity," Joe responded, hoping the man wouldn't laugh and escort them from the park.

The guard grinned instead of letting loose an outright guffaw. He shoved his hands into his pockets.

"Haven't heard from this doctor. I'll expect you to leave at sundown. If I hear otherwise, I'll ride over and give you the okay."

"Excellent. My name's Joe Reeves and this is Ericka Gilmore." He settled deeper into the seat and gripped the gearshift.

"Hi," Ericka shouted.

"Have a nice visit." The ranger turned to walk away, holding the radio transmitter closer to his mouth.

Several feet later, they came to a detour. "The bridge is out."

"I see that," Joe said. The suspension bridge connecting to the campground, as the park ranger had stated, was undergoing maintenance. "From what Wolf said, we need to stay at the ley line in Old Stone Fort. Look at the map we got at the entrance."

The brochure crackled in the silence as Ericka opened the stiff parchment. "An alternate route might be if you turn left up ahead. The lane winds, but eventually you should see a parking lot near the L-shaped corridor leading into the grounds." She folded the brochure and continued reading. "Two rivers drop off a highland rim plateau, plunging into a middle basin. The forks of Duck River cut down the peninsula. The promontory walls had been made by stacked stones covered with earth. Anthropologists and archaeologists, at first believed Welsh or Spanish troops created the mounds, but charcoal was found. Charcoal dates the grounds to Middle Woodland Period and the Hopewell people. Two thousand years ago."

She continued to read, while he navigated the small road.

"Does it describe the ley lines and magnetic

currents?" Joe asked as he pulled the truck into a parking space created by time and humans.

"Let's see, 80 A.D. Fifty acres. Ancient societies. North sunrise. Sacred ceremonies. Not a word about a ley line." She unsnapped her seatbelt and wiggled until she faced him.

"In an hour the sun will start setting. If the ground is dry, we'll toss our sleeping bags and settle for the night. No campfire." Oak, elm, and white birch trees lined the entrance and narrow walkway. Dry leaves splattered the ground, like confetti at a Thanksgiving parade. Strange, the dirt pathway remained clear. Right and left pedestal mounds marked the access of the fort.

Your ability will be tenfold. Joe had a moment of reservation. Wolf's forecast and Brett's skepticism kept running through his mind, not allowing him to rest. In addition, Ericka's soft figure had been snug, painfully snug, against him.

Her silent siren song continued in the daylight as she lifted her arms over her head. The sweet melody of excitement rippled from her tempting lips. "We're here and nothing dreadful has happened. What are we going to do if we don't connect with your spirit guide by sundown?"

Unable to stifle his desires, he turned away. Her actions seemed innocent of deliberate provocation, yet he wanted more. "I'll take care of it."

"Cool. Let's roll." She lowered her arms and dismounted from the truck.

"Keep the coat, although it's warmer with the sun, tonight it'll be freezing." Joe opened his door and slid from the seat. He removed his jacket and stuffed the material in the bundle Wolf had prepared.

"Don't you think it's odd, Wolf never told us what to do when we arrived?" Ericka wove her parka through her satchel handle, then shielded her eyes with a hand and glanced at the corridor.

"No, I think it's the way he operates, learning through discovery. Before we start walking, I need to make a call." Joe leaned inside the truck and removed his phone from the charger. One press of a button and he connected with Brett.

"Hi, Joe. Where are you?" His brother-in-law's deep voice rang through the line.

Ericka sidled a short distance and extracted a brochure from her handbag. She flipped through the pages.

"Tennessee. Hey, I need a favor."

"Shoot. Did you meet the shaman? Tell me what happened?" Brett's breath wheezed through the phone line.

"I can't go into it now, but the shaman is a medicine man—"

"Damn, there isn't enough information about the Coterie Nation." Brett's wheezing stopped.

"He didn't take offense. Wolf wants me to go on a spirit quest and maybe a purification ceremony. But first, I need a favor. We're at Old Stone Fort, near Manchester, Tennessee." Joe clasped the buckle of his bike saddlebag.

"Hold a sec," Brett murmured, keys tapped in the background. "I'm outside the Life Sciences building. I'll try to connect to the net. Archaeological Park. Indian ceremonial ground." White noise came over the line. "There is some belief the fort, which isn't a fort like in the west, was a celestial observatory. Parallel entrance walls seem to point toward the position of the sun at summer solstice."

"Yes, that's what we've discovered." Joe glanced at Ericka busy stuffing brochures in her purse. She removed her cell, stared at the face, and frowned.

Brett, a serial investigator, continued tapping keys. "Here's another, linking it to UFO's and lines running under the earth connecting locations together like Stonehenge, Anatom Island, Oracle at Siwa in the western Egyptian desert. Prehistoric trading routes. Here's another, Greek god Hermes, god of communication and boundaries, winged messenger. Druids—"

"Sorry to interrupt, but we've a time limit. The park closes at sunset. Will you call the ranger of the Old Stone Fort and get permission for us, as researchers, to stay near the ceremonial grounds? Overnight." Joe glanced at Ericka. She lifted her eyebrows and opened her mouth. A second later, she snapped it shut. "Do whatever it takes to get us an overnight pass."

"Yes, I'll take care of it. What is Ericka's last name again?" The phone clanked and street noise filtered through the connection.

"Gilmore. E.r.i.c.k.a G.i.l.m.o.r.e." Joe caught her gaze to confirm the spelling. Her smile widened and a spark lit her eyes.

"I'll have it taken care of within the hour. Wolf isn't with you?" Hopefulness rippled through Brett's voice.

Joe almost wished Brett could have been a part of this adventure, but not if Joe's death prophecies would multiply or deviate in some way as a result of visiting the ley line.

"No, we're here to connect with a spirit," Joe responded. Brett would be safe, and he could protect his family.

Ericka started down the path, toting her bag, with phone in hand.

"Joe, call me if anything happens. From what I'm seeing, your location could be rife with paranormal activity. We can't tell how you'll be affected." Brett paused. "I can take a plane and arrive in two hours."

Your ability will be tenfold. The partial dream from last night remained. Joe's stomach muscles clutched as beads of sweat ran down his back. Did this mean he'd see more than one death in a vision? Did he have the stamina to deal with more than one forecast, or even the time to prevent more than one accident? "Thanks for the consideration, but we'll return to Cyan tomorrow. I need you to keep Tess and the kids in sight, at least for the next two days." He exhaled. "Please stay off your roof."

"Ha, when have I ever done home repairs? No problem, bro, they'll be safe. I hope after this is over we can—" In addition to the warmth of love, Brett's tone held a hint of fear.

"Yeah, me too. Give 'em hugs and tell them...I love them." Joe clicked off the call and shoved the phone into his jeans' pocket. Damn, the next forty-some hours would seem like a lifetime. Hoisting a duffle, he put the straps on his shoulder, gripped another bag in his hand, and strode toward Ericka. Recycled oatmeal clogged his throat. Mouth gritty with apprehension, he feared for his friends and relatives. Actually, the notion of their lives ending scared him shitless.

Ericka clasped his hand, and they passed through

the mound entry markers. At the shaded entrance of the low-walled mound, he stopped to admire the peacefulness. She stood in the middle of the path and flipped open her cell. "My phone doesn't work. Does yours?"

Joe dug his mobile out of his jeans and pressed the slide bar. "Nothing. It's either out of range or blocked signal." He crossed into the celestial grounds. "Nothing on this side either. Maybe because of the forest or the magnetic fields running underground or because of—"

"Spirits." She flashed him a hopeful smile, and his fears receded.

"Sure. We'll find the specter and give him the prophecy package." His attempt to make light of the situation fell flat. A paradox awaited him. Had his spirit guide already changed from a blue light into the pure white one and crossed the bridge? Joe shook his head. Just standing in the center, he experienced a charge of energy. He took a deep breath. The forecasts would be stronger, more intense, maybe life threatening. However, the end result would be worth every minute of pain. He exhaled and committed, mentally and physically, to eliminating the visions.

Glancing around the enclosure, he looked for escape routes if needed. Had the park removed the leaves to keep the field section clean? As depicted in the brochure the mounds were a mile in circumference. Dark emerald grass and jade earth scented moss covered most of the rocks, making them appear rounded. A portion of the wall had smooth gray and brown pebbles poking through.

Scents of pine trees, brushes, wild honeysuckle and black-eyed Susan's created an aromatic ambiance, as they walked around the cul-de-sac, trying to get a sense of where to unload their burden and settle in for a long night's stay. Would he have horrific visions for the rest of his life? Of course, he didn't feel different. His mind didn't buzz with varied images. Perhaps because Ericka stood by his side he'd bypass a supernatural event. No, he'd had a dream last night. The visions couldn't be curtailed. He'd have to accept the inevitable.

Along the side, midway point, he could see anyone coming or going through the parallel accesses. Wooded areas closed the North and West entrances. Farther to the east, spumes of water gushed over rocks, burbling as loud as his Harley. The sound provided him a comforting balm for his soul.

"The Blue Hole Falls are thirty feet high and Step Falls are twenty feet high," Erica said, as if in tune with his thoughts. "Step Falls is self-explanatory, but I don't understand Blue Hole."

Fresh spring-generated water scented the area and grew stronger as they strolled the perimeter of the Wall Trail. "I assume the one in front of us is Step Falls?"

"If we're going by the description." She planted her feet against the edge of the steep precipice.

Tugging her hand, he pulled her back. The other waterway had notable differences in a tighter structure and lower height. "We should return in the summer and take a dip. I wouldn't mind seeing how the summer solstice affects the arena. Maybe we can see what's below the murky green water?"

She grimaced, and her eyelashes fanned her cheeks. Damn, he shouldn't plan for the future. He might very well have to hit the road again. A loner searching for...what? What he had right in front of him? Regardless, whatever happened today, tomorrow, or next month, one thing remained the same—he needed the prophecies to stop. "Do you pick up vibes of any sort, or get a glimpse of a spirit?"

Ericka dropped her bag to the ground. "Not really. There is a sense of sadness mingled with joy, maybe that's the atmosphere in general."

"I'm not certain what to expect. Here, this area is fairly clean." He handed her a satchel and carried the remaining bags to a slice of the mound, which didn't have overlapping dirt and vegetation. A canvas strap snagged against the edge of a stone. He jerked and the burden swung outward. Joe drew the bag closer.

The alarm call of a blackbird and the oppressing feel of the area sent quivers along his spine. He removed his Glock from his saddlebag and checked the cartridge. Fifteen rounds would be enough. If attacked, he'd shoot to kill, not caring if the invader was spectral or human. He slipped on the shoulder harness and secured the gun.

"Look at this big pile of grass." She pointed toward the ground at the other side of the fence. "The earth is flat, except for the slight rise at the edge. This mound hasn't been smoothed down."

"Maybe it's one of the burial sites." He sent a quick prayer for their souls and lifted his saddlebag.

She shot him a piercing stare. "How do you know? There aren't any crosses, headstones, or even sticks to mark them as being graves."

"Research. The Prairie and Woodland Indian Nations used mounds to bury their dead. At the museum, we discovered the Woodland Indians were credited with Old Stone Fort. Therefore, it's probably a grave." Joe swayed and righted himself. He hadn't been this lightheaded since he first stepped out of bed after his coma. "Why don't you take another walk and try to connect." He waved his hand toward the stars. His temperature went from normal to hot in seconds. His vision blurred.

She lowered her arms and gripped the sides of her trousers.

Joe hadn't meant his statement to come out as snarly has it had, but he needed to get rid of her. *Stalk off in a huff. Don't witness my weakness.* Slipping in the uneven dirt surface, he sat hard on the semi-warm stone ledge.

She frowned and half-pivoted. Her foot hadn't touched the ground. "Are you okay? You look pale."

"Yes." He straightened and fiddled with his saddlebag latch. "Go. I'll get camp set."

She turned and climbed over the gravesite.

The heavy beat of Tom-Tom's pounded in his head. He shifted away from the hard rock edge poking into his thigh and sat on a nature-indented seat on top of the four-foot stonewall. He dropped his head between his knees, inhaled and exhaled, hoping the dizziness would pass. Stomach acid rose to his throat, so he swallowed. The pounding behind his eyes increased. He licked his dry lips. "Tenfold."

He closed his eyes. "Leave me alone. Just for this one day, let me be at peace." He peered at Ericka. She stood at the precipice of Step Falls. His dry throat tightened. The queasiness would pass. *Water.*

The bag snagged on the jutting stone contained two bottles of water. Two straps appeared instead of one, and in his line of vision, the ties shifted. He gripped air.

Chapter Nineteen

Plop, slush, the swoop of water fell over the mossy rocks. Tears formed, and not the get-in-touch-with nature sort. Ericka resituated on a boulder. At the falls, she swiped her eyes with the backs of her hands. When would Joe's spirit guide appear? Why didn't William, the great healer, provide a means for Joe to talk to his guide? Guardian angels talked to their charges in every paranormal movie she'd ever seen. She wasn't certain she could, but if deciphering ghost chatter would help him, so be it.

She'd believed they'd connected. Two people heading toward similar goals gaining insight or losing phenomena. She immersed a hand into the edge of the waterfall. "Oh." She jerked her freezing fingers out and wiped her hand against her jacket.

The peacefulness of the ceremonial site soaked in and relaxed her. Birds' chirping merged with the splashes of water. She took a deep breath, absorbed the fresh rain scent, decayed leaves and the slightest hint of tobacco. Ready to move forward, she exhaled and stood. Odorous cigar smoke surrounded her, overriding freshness. From her research, she knew spirits sometimes announced themselves by firing tobacco plumes.

As a rule she wouldn't have rejoiced in the odor, yet a halleluiah stuck in her craw. She might get a connection, and they could get out of there. She spun in a circle, searching for a visual. "Hello."

Joe.

Slumped over the duffle bags, his neck twisted at an awkward angle. She evaluated the area, looking for a predator. Not seeing one, she ran. "Please let him be all right," the mantra gushed from her lips. She knelt beside him. "Joe!"

She pressed her fingertips to his neck. *Slow and steady pulse, thank God.* His sun-kissed skin had a gruesome pale hue. His saddlebag had fallen to the ground, and the other bag supported him. She slid the band of the saddlebag off the rock and shifted the canvas to prop his back. She clutched his leather coat and drew him forward. His head sagged to the side.

She bent, pushed her knee against his side, and held him steady with one hand, while tugging the second duffle to align with the first. She released her hold and eased him to the padded surface. *What happened?*

She ran her fingers through his thick dark hair touching the side of his head, but didn't locate any lumps or blood.

She pressed her cheek to his forehead. "No fever," she whispered. "Joe, wake up."

What could have caused his loss of consciousness? The visions. Wolf told him…what? *Think, Ericka.* What had he said? The herb. He gave her a remedy saying Joe would need it. She stood and groped in her trouser pocket. Gone. She'd put the vial in her satchel. What did the healer say? The drug should be used as a salve.

She turned in place, hoping to find the ranger in the

clearing. A cottontail and squirrel scurried into the underbrush, but not a human in sight.

"He's asleep, so the herb won't help him with sleeplessness. He doesn't seem to have any muscle spasms," she shouted, hoping the divine would interject.

Massive trees loomed stark against the deep violet skyline. The willowy branches reached out, twisting and turning, trying to capture her and Joe into their barren clutches.

Ericka exhaled, threw her backpack purse to the ground, and knelt beside Joe. She leaned her head against his side. How crazy she'd sound trying to explain this. Whom could she trust? She punched her index finger to the cellphone pad and waited.

No signal. Damn.

She stood and touched his forehead. Normal. Blue skin tint and all his breathing had regulated. She shut her phone, placed it in her jacket pocket, and rubbed each of his frigid fingers attempting to generate circulation.

Her jacket stuck from the top of a bag. She removed the coat and covered Joe.

Silence. Not even the birds twittered. No wind whistled through the tree branches. An omen?

She plucked her cellphone from her pocket and zigzagged the perimeter of the fort. Not one bar. They'd gotten signals at the truck. Should she leave him alone for a few minutes?

Joe hadn't budged. She'd done the basics, put him in a recovery position, and made sure his airways were clear. She needed reassurance. What if he started convulsing? Sick people weren't her thing. Tack a bandage over a wound, okay. Listen to woes of heartache, good. Give her an unconscious, helpless, human and she lost rational thinking.

She ran into the L-shaped lane, keeping Joe in sight. Before she could press the number one, her phone rang. A blank display. She hit accept.

"Hey, are you on your way home?" Jacey's voice blared through the line.

"Jacey, listen, I need—"

"You'll never believe what Griff did." Her voice faded and returned. "...not plowing our driveway, because he didn't want me to drive in this weather. The snow's three feet deep. Seriously." Jacey paused. "Are you there?"

"Jacey."

"Ericka, talk to me." A heartbeat later. "Well, hell."

Dead air.

Ericka shook her phone. No signal, no battery power, no aid at the other end of the line. Dead.

"Well, hell is right." She stuffed the device in her pocket and ran to Joe's side. Maybe the ranger would ride by with the news they could stay, and he'd get help.

She drew out a couple of tissues from her purse. The tip of a bottle peeped through the opening of a duffle. She dragged it out. Water. She soaked the tissues and stuck them to Joe's forehead. He didn't have a fever, but she had to do something.

Five minutes passed. How long should she wait before going to the ranger's station for help? She wove a lock of Joe's hair between her fingers. Could she rig a device to get him to the truck? Wind spun around and a spray of water sprinkled her face. She dropped the strand of Joe's hair and lifted another.

Jacey liked him, no doubt because he always agreed with her nonsense. He'd planed the door and after one glance at the wood Griff hired him.

A true-blooded-gentleman, Joe Reeves had a big heart as exemplified by helping the librarian and building a pot for Wolf.

The tissues dried and flew off, leaving fuzz balls behind. She caressed the sides of his face as if the action would bring him back to the present. Short barbed hairs, of his afternoon shadow, rasped under her fingertips. His perfect lips didn't move. She wished he'd awake and spread his movie-star smile.

They shouldn't have come. She bit her lip. She'd give him a few more minutes, and then drag him to the truck. He should be safe in Cyan instead of unconscious at the edge of a ceremonial burial ground. A mind tickle came forward: Joe's visions at the ley line would be stronger.

Was he unconscious because of the damn mystic line and a vision?

Sweat flooded her lower back. *Do something.* A tap to his face, not a smack just a hard five-fingered shove, didn't elicit a response. Her inability to bring him out of his stupor scared her, and the overwhelming silence pounded in her ears.

The wind increased, creating a macabre squeaking of tree limbs. Despite the eeriness of the situation, the splashing waterfalls reassured her.

Pure. Wolf said water was a purification agent. If she could tug Joe over to the falls, maybe the water would revive him. She evaluated the area. Could she tumble him over the short wall and drag him?

Idiot!

She spun the lid from the bottle and drizzled the water. Uncrossing her legs, she shook off the lethargic sluggishness and with shaky steps rushed toward the source. Her heart doubled its rate as she arrived at the edge of the mossy point.

Her knees buckled. She took a risk and leaned over the ledge. For the first time, since she was a parochial school girl, she prayed for help. "Whatever deity inhabits this place. Whoever is listening, spirits included, please help me revive my friend. He is a good man, who has saved lives. Help him."

She wiped away tears and shoved the bottle into the frigid splashing gush of water. A shadowy pool swirled, disturbing the glassy surface and stirring the mineral aquatic odor. She reached, trying to capture algae free liquid. Intoxicated by the rapid ebb and flow over the dark rocks and rippled the glimmering starlight. She pressed flat against the ground and pulled the bottle from the water. Spirit renewed, she switched the container to her other hand and wiped her cold-wet palm against her cheek. "I love him. Have I put Joe in danger by coming with him?"

She shook her head, trying to focus instead of babbling into the brook. He would recover.

Facing the star-studded pool, she used her free hand, gripped the moss and rose. What would it hurt to wish on a reflected star at a ley line in order to put her fears to rest?

She glanced into the water and screamed.

Chapter Twenty

Joe touched her shoulder. "Shh, it's just me."

Her shudders changed to quivers. Her clothes were damp and getting wetter as the waterfall spray splashed her. He knelt beside her and gripped her shivering forearm. "We need to go."

Ericka had mumbled something about love. He wanted to pursue her comment, but they needed to leave. At least this time the vision revealed a face. Griff perched at the ledge of a rooftop. The slope's angle resembled his home. The scene blurred and a struggle between three men occurred. One man died. Griff was the identifiable one of the three.

"What about—"

"If possible, we'll return." His queasy stomach irked him. The hammering in his head multiplied. He extended his hand, hoping she wouldn't ask for more information. She clasped his cold fingers and steadied her stance. An open bottle of water precariously tilted as she did.

"You okay? I didn't know what to do. Were you in a trance?"

"Yeah. Sorry you had to see that. Let's get on the road." The pressure to act, to go to Cyan was priority. "Griff's in danger."

She jerked, but without saying a word she wrapped her arm around his waist. In the past, post vision, he'd viewed his image in a mirror. He knew he looked like hell, pale face, pupils dilated, and blue lips. Although his gait held steady, he accepted her assistance as it provided comfort and closeness. Even during a crisis, she made him whole again.

"I need to find the bottle cap. Where is a flashlight?" she asked while running fingers through the grass.

"Leave it."

"Can't."

Joe searched through an outer pocket of the saddlebag and handed over the torch. The instant the flash shone, she dipped to retrieve the cap.

"Pure water from a ley line site. It might be helpful, like holy water. We need to take anything in order to prevent a death right?" She tucked the bottle into her purse and dragged the strap over her shoulder. "Ready? You look sick."

"I'm okay." He gathered the remaining bags, pausing a moment to catch his breath. The prophecy had shaken him, more powerful than any prior vision and more confusing because he couldn't identify the guy falling to his death? Would Griff or another faceless man die? Bottom line, a man would plummet from a rooftop. He had less than twenty-four hours to find Griff and seven of those would be consumed in travel time. He prayed snow covered the ground in Cyan.

They threw the bags behind the seat of the truck and climbed inside.

"You're still very pale. Should I drive?" her voice quivered.

"No. I'm fine. Please call Jacey. Make sure they

don't clean off their sidewalks or driveway. Ask Griff not to..." He swallowed the vomit erupting in his throat. "Not to climb on a ladder."

"He's not cleaning the driveway. Not sure about the sidewalk." Her hand shook as she removed her phone from her purse and punched a number.

As the truck engine turned over, Joe knuckled the window and took a deep breath. She hadn't questioned or doubted his prophecy. He appreciated her due diligence. She remained steadfast during a time he needed a clear mind. The second time she punched a key on her cell, a dee'dal sound rang through the cab.

"It doesn't work. I haven't recharged for two days." She dropped the phone into her bag and held her head between her hands.

He dug into his jacket pocket and withdrew his cell. "If it's not powered, I put a charger in the consul."

Tweets and punches rang through the dark interior. The red and white dashboard lights blinked at him, insisting he go faster. His head roared in pain, blocking out the engine and her voice.

"Joe," she shouted.

He shook his head, trying to rid himself of the dizziness. "Did you get them?"

"They're not answering. I left this telephone number on both of their cells." She twisted in the seat. "I didn't think leaving a doom and gloom message would be good."

He frowned. Damn. "What about the ladder?"

"I said to stay off of a ladder. They'll call. Its dinner time and one of their *things* is to turn off the phones during dinner, so they can have uninterrupted conversation." Her pale fingers glimmered under the dashboard light as she strangled his phone. "They'll call back. No worries."

Out of the park, he turned onto Highway 41 North. A seatbelt indicator flashed red making spots appear in front of his eyes. Ready to give her a firm reminder, he glanced at her face. Her throat moved up and down. No sounds came from her beautiful mouth. He hoped the water at her temple came from leaning over the ledge of the falls. She understood he might not be able to save her friend. Damn, she feared grim-reaper abilities or his inability to save everyone.

"Don't worry, Ericka. I've saved…some."

She knuckled tears from the tops of her cheeks. "Griff…"

"Yes, he's repairing a roof and misses the step. If we can't prevent the fall from the ladder, then we need to make sure snow is below to cushion him." His dry throat convulsed. He coughed up saliva and swallowed. "I'll do everything to save him. They're my friends too." Distract her or a blasted flood of tears would flow. "How long have they been married?"

"Almost six months."

He had to prevent the fall, even if he became the sacrifice.

"Could I have a sip of water?" He pointed toward the bottle sticking out of her purse.

She twisted the cap and extended the bottle. "We have plenty of time, don't we?"

He took a sip of the water, enough to lubricate his throat and then put the bottle in the holder. It tasted clean, but not extraordinary. Liquid gurgled in his stomach, but the ache in his chest didn't subside. Easing into a stop at a red light, he dragged the nylon strap across her front and fastened the seatbelt in place. Their gazes hooked and held. Her amber eyes glimmered with hope. Her claret lips drew his attention. He kissed her, pressing soft, a reassurance of promise and underlying love.

A horn blared. He wanted to continue the connection with her sinuous lips. He drew away and re-situated, and then pressed his foot to the pedal. "There were three men in the vision. Does Griff have a brother who helps him with his home repairs?" *Let there be a brother?*

"His brother is an impersonator. A singer. Performer. He doesn't do anything outside of his zero-work comfort zone. Why do you ask?" Her eyes blazed with anticipation and hope.

"I didn't see the face of the man who fell to his death. But I did see Griff fall. My vision was scattered. Next, there were two men. I struggled with one of them."

"Was this when Griff was on the rooftop?"

"Hard to say. This vision was different from any I've had before. Wolf and my brother-in-law, Brett, warned me the ley line or combo ley line and ceremonial site might have an effect. I can't help but wonder if I had more than one vision. Seems like all the scenes overlap."

"You've always seen the person who was to die?" She rubbed her forehead.

"Yes. Always. Very lucid visual." He glanced at her. "There was never any doubt of who I needed to save."

She exhaled. "You've been dealing with so much."

He flipped a dial and soft rock surrounded them.

"It's easier with you here. Other than the no phones at dinner, what other things make Griff and Jacey special?"

"They're trying to find nicknames for each other. Some of them are humorous and some of them make me want to puke." She faced him, leaned her head against the headrest. "For as long as Jacey and I've been friends she's not the endearment type, at all."

He envied their relationship, of having a best friend and wife. "What names did she try out?"

"The usual. Honey. Sweetie-pie." She chuckled. "Griffy-poo."

For the duration of her chatter, she changed from the topic of newlywed endearments to Jacey and her own business ventures. Through her words, he heard angst about starting a new business in a small town. She'd moved from the state capitol where she had a long line of clients, to Cyan and one client.

Her meandering through the past and voicing her fears kept his mind off the amount of heavy traffic backing up near the off ramps. The stopping and starting at stop lights grinded his nerves. Each intersection equaled further delays, and with every interruption, his mind shaved away the hope to reach Griff before or if he fell from a roof. They drove out of Tennessee and entered southern Indiana. Cyan drew near and so did the dreaded snow-covered roads.

"There's a road block ahead," she whispered, then pressed a hand to her mouth, and the other gripped the truck door.

"We have plenty of time." He told her, but there weren't any guarantees. The fall could have happened. Hours had passed since the first, unclear, premonition occurred at Wolf's house. Damn the curse. Damn the traffic as they crept forward in miniscule increments. An hour later, he pulled beside a highway patrolman. A plastic cover protected his billed hat and a slicker kept the rain off the dark blue uniform.

The scent of cold wet air flowed into the space as Joe lowered his window flush to the frame. "Officer?"

"Due to a mud slide and an accident, the highway's been shut down for the next five miles. You'll need to take a bypass." He lifted his light saber, nudging them forward.

"How much time will it add?" He cringed as the cop lowered his hat to shade his eyes from the pelting sleet.

He shook his head and waved the wand. "Move on."

"Another delay." Ericka punched numbers into his cellphone. "Voicemail."

Needing, wanting to touch her, he caressed her arm in rhythm with an up tempo song currently playing. "Don't worry, we'll get there. He'll survive."

"It's my fault. I delayed the trip. If I wouldn't have been so selfish, you'd be in Tennessee trying to connect with your spirit guide and maybe the forecast wouldn't have happened." She gripped his hand. "Hurt. I don't want Griff to be…"

"Not your fault. The visions can't be controlled. The forecast would've come anyway." The howling wind shifted the snow across the bypass, making the road treacherous. Balls of ice slipped through the crack of his window. Joe kept reassuring himself he'd save his friend.

He glanced at Ericka. What could he say? You'll

need to be able to hold Jacey if he failed to prevent Griff's death? Remain strong if Joe was the one to die. That dark faceless shadow falling to the ground bothered him more than he cared to admit.

"Why don't you take a nap?"

"I hate Indiana when late winter storms arrive at the beginning of spring." Her voice caught. "It's frustrating."

Soon thereafter, her neck relaxed and like a rag doll, she fell against the seat. In the darkness, he couldn't determine if she slept, but he hoped so.

Joe continued driving home to his true north. His compass pointed toward the magnetic Ericka Gilmore of Cyan, Indiana.

****

Joe parked the truck in Griff's driveway. The sun peeked over the horizon, giving the ice-capped snow a pristine diamond appearance. Innocent snow. No, it was cold slush ready to sever the life or maybe had already ended the life of his friend.

He glanced at the A-line rooftop of Griff's house as he got out of the truck. Joe removed his coat and tossed it on to the seat. The monster tree outside the bay window clicked its icy branches together. Griff's dog, Mac, would have raised all kinds of hell, but no disturbance came from the front of the building. Joe repositioned the leather holster over his shoulder. He gained some comfort in the strap. He checked the safety. Off. He replaced the Glock in its sheath and turned to Ericka.

She'd fallen toward him, as if seeking him during her sleep. His heart ached with desire, longing for her love. He shook off the sappy romantic notion. Anyway, he couldn't live a normal life, and she remained in her own personal haze.

He placed his palm at the side of her face, touching her one last time. "Ericka, we're here."

She jerked awake. Falling forward, she strained against the seatbelt. Alert, she scanned the perimeter of the house. "The sidewalk's been cleared."

"You go inside, and I'll check in the back." A nagging doubt pricked his mind. The sun wasn't in place. In the vision, he fell and the sun shadowed him. Had they arrived too late? His lungs tightened and squeezed against his rib cage. Had the paramedics taken his friend to the morgue?

"Yes. Sure." Click, snick, the seatbelt returned to its holder. She glanced at him, as if asking for reassurance.

He caught a bunch of her hair, adoring the soft luxury. "Let's go."

Her eyes held a mysterious expression, a mix of confusion and satisfaction. Her cute raspberry-tinted lip pulled between her teeth. She slid her legs over the seat and jumped to the ground. Ericka took off running with the grace and agility of a gazelle, her open coat flapping behind her. He slammed the door and chased after her, coming to a stop at the back of the house.

"Shit." Joe mumbled.

Griff hung from a broken gutter.

Ericka tugged a ladder from its cold grave in the snow.

"Griff, we're right below." His heart pumped blood so fast he knew there wasn't a chance it'd freeze. "Let me." Joe took the twelve-foot ladder from Ericka and propped the rail, in line with his friend.

"Hey, buddy, good timing," Griff called. He didn't look down. "Ladder fell, gutters coming down."

A squeak cracked through the air, adding validity. The metal bent in the center, the outsides edge tore apart sending him closer to the ground.

"Ladder," Griff shouted. In short, order his hands propelled to the left, away from the splitting gutter and higher on the roof.

Joe shot the ladder, closer to Griff and steadied it. "Step to your right."

Griff wrapped a gloved hand around the side of the ladder frame and slipped a foot onto a rung. With great care, he descended. Joe breathed easy when Griff's camel-colored boots hit the ground.

Joe took a step away from the ladder and glanced at the sky. The sun would cast a shadow at the opposite side, the north side.

Griff snared him in a two-fold hug. "Thanks. Thought I'd be plastered to the ground."

A man hug? Sure, after a couple of eggnogs, at Christmas, his brother-in-law gave him the one-armed version. Okay, friends experiencing a renewal of life should share a hug. "What were you doing on the roof during a snow emergency?"

Three feet of fluffy white had been piled to the side. He would've hit the frozen ground or worse, the sidewalk.

"Cause he's an idiot. That's what you are, Griff. Is Jacey aware you're out here climbing around the roof like a careless teenager?" Ericka's face, angry red not a chilled blush, scrunched.

"Leak in the roof, water damaged one of her treasures." Griff's forehead furrowed as if to say *women, who knew what to do with them.* "Hey, how'd it go with the healer? I need a drink."

"We're not done. Thought we'd make a trip to Ericka's, she wanted a change of clothes, and then we'll finish. Griff..." He'd just created the scenario, but he wasn't opposed to stopping at her house for a shower. He'd been sweating through his clothes for the past several hours. He had to deal with vision part two, if he didn't die first. Joe blocked Griff's path as they walked to the back door. "Until spring arrives, could you please stay off the roof? Send one of your guys."

The odd expression, a mix of surprise and question on Griff's face, wasn't unfamiliar. Precisely the reason Joe didn't want other people to be aware of his ability. Once they found out about his aptitude, one of two things happened: they ended the relationship because of fear they'd be the next to die, or believing him to be irrational. The newspaper article Ericka had read described him as malicious. How else would he have known Billy planned to ride by the boulevard at the exact time of day, unless Joe wanted to execute an evil plan?

If ignorance was bliss, more often than not people preferred ignorance.

Joe waited, breathing out cold mist and clouding the air between them. He'd hate to lose Griff's and Jacey's friendship. Tremors shuddered through him, hard and fast—waves like an electric prod had been attached to his heart. He prayed one more time *please grant me a cure.*

"I didn't hear the last part." Griff lifted the earflaps of his hat.

"Come on, let's get some coffee." Joe flagged him

forward. "And stay off roofs until spring."

Griff's comical grin spread, as he shoved Joe's shoulder. "Thanks, buddy."

"All men are idiots." Ericka's shoulders dropped several inches. She stomped ahead of them and stormed into the house, allowing Mac to exit.

"Let's keep this between us. No reason to get Jacey all clenched." Griff rubbed Mac's ear. Reassured, the dog took off to investigate.

"Right, I imagine she'd yell like a banshee," Joe added.

Griff lifted the ladder. Snow crunched beneath their feet as they made their way around the house. He propped the ladder outside the door and they walked into the kitchen. Fresh-brewed coffee aroma warmed Joe, for a brief moment masking what he had to do next. He grabbed a paper towel from the holder and blew his nose. Looking for a trash container, he met Ericka's wide-eyed gaze as she entered the room. She stumbled forward as Jacey shoved her out of the way and plowed into Griff's back. Brown liquid fell over the cup's lip and spread over the counter.

"Hey, what—"Griff said.

"You told Jacey," Joe accused. Winter wind scent filtered from her skin straight into his senses overloading him with want and humanity.

"Had too, she's my best friend. If our guys were at the edge of death, I needed her to be there with me, as support." Ericka's slender arm gripped his waist, taking away the chill of cold sweat.

Just looking at her escalated the cattle prod jitters another notch.

"Our guys?" he whispered into her ear.

"Griff is her other half, which means he's one-fourth of my family. You're...my friend. Aren't you?" She kissed his neck, confusing him, making him want everything life could offer. Enjoy this bit of loving, his mind insisted, it might end soon.

"Yeah, we're friends. I need to go." He broke the embrace. The thrill of saving Griff subsided. An unfulfilled forecast beat at his door. Someone was slated to die.

"Why? You saved him." Fear re-entered her stare.

"There wasn't a third person. No struggle. No sun shining on the shingles. Gotta go." He gripped the butt of his gun and turned toward the couple. "Who has a roofline similar to yours, but with a north sunrise?"

"North sunrise was in the Old Stone Fort brochure. Are you getting your dream confused with the legend?" Ericka asked.

"Old Stone Fort?" Griff asked. He tugged Jacey snug to his side.

"Tennessee and a long story, I'll tell you later. Who has a roofline like yours?" Joe grabbed the cup of coffee and downed a good deal of the steaming fluid. The roof of his mouth burned like hell, but he appreciated the warmth.

"Ames Mansion." Griff replied. "I'm coming with you."

"No," Jacey shouted.

Terror lined her face. From this day forward, she'd probably avoid Joe, fearing Griff's death or because of his view of the future in general. Death and the possibility of dying had different effects on individuals. And most people wanted to fault someone for the loss of a loved one, especially if the person lost his life before he'd aged to life expectancy. Joe had visions of the future, and it was always bleak.

"Thanks for the offer, but this is something I have to do alone." He twisted the doorknob, leading to fresh air and maybe to his demise.

Ericka's soft hand touched his. "No you don't."

Part of him tried to deny the draw, but the other went with instinct and kissed her, merging their lips with heat and intensity. Maybe for the last time. She didn't pull away, and although reluctant to end the bond, he had a life to save.

"I'll return and get you. Then, we'll go to the ley line so you can see your future." The pressure of his heart splitting would kill him before the fall did. He loved her, and for this moment in time, he convinced himself she loved him.

"But I'm the heart, power and your salvation." With those words, she severed his bit of willpower. He couldn't fight. Love for her would be everlasting.

"Okay, but you stay in the truck." He entwined their fingers and turned to Griff. "Will it be all right if we keep your truck for a couple of more days?"

"Sure, take as much time as you need."

A burst of wind blew open the fireplace screen and tiny flares sprang from the hearth, reminding Joe the past didn't lie in cold ashes, rather blazes could be created by the smallest of embers. He still had his ability to see death. "We need to hurry."

"Good heavens where did that come from? It's calm outside," Jacey asked.

Griff ran to put out the sparks scorching his wood floor.

"I need to go, thanks." Joe tugged the kitchen door

open and Mac galloped inside.

"I'll get my coat and meet you at the truck," Ericka said.

"Hurry." He rushed outside and glanced at the sun's location. He might have time to save someone, perhaps one of the men he couldn't see in his vision or save himself. Would Ericka be his salvation, as she seemed to think?

Right now, dealing with her contradicting actions and words flayed his heart; layer-by-layer she tore from him more than he'd ever imagined.

****

Ericka gripped the edge of the cloak closet door and took a deep breath. She attempted to relax the pulls in her stomach. Stop. She wanted to stop. But she could not stop wanting Joe. His touch created a thrum of happiness. He always considered her wants first.

She pounded her head against the door panel.

"You okay?" Jacey rubbed circles on her back.

Ericka came to grips with her chosen path. She jerked her coat from the doorknob, pasted a half-hearted smile, and pivoted. "Yes. I'm overwhelmed with everything."

Jacey held the jacket so Ericka could find the sleeve. "You like Joe?"

"We need to leave. Someone else might die." She strode toward the kitchen.

"Ericka," Jacey shouted. "You can have a future with Joe."

Her heart pounded. She halted, but didn't turn around. She'd been waiting for months for Jacey to voice aloud what her facial expression had always declared.

"Maybe. It seems as though the night I conjured a lover, Joe had been created. Would our love also be built on a foundation of mist?"

"Nonsense. Return to earth and burn those damn magic books."

Ericka snuggled into her coat. "Sounds like something my best friend, who always supports me regardless of the outcome, would say." She broke through the backdoor, running toward her future and from her past.

Chapter Twenty-One

Joe pulled into the Ames Mansion's circle drive, and his sixth sense went berserk. The 3D full color prophecy replayed and weighted his chest. He lowered the window, until the glass became flush with the frame. The cool air hit him and the brick resting on his chest eased. He breathed, long deep pulls. The truck spit loose gravel when he drove around the curve. Two automobiles were in the driveway. His heart raced. His mouth dried and he worked his throat muscles, as he drove closer to the black van and the ghost buster license plate, a joke from his nephew.

Please God don't let it be Tess. Brett had been insistent about joining them. "My brother-in-law's van. Brett..." He swallowed. "I assume the—"

"Wa-ard." She struck the name hard making it two syllables.

"Your psycho client." Joe pressed the pedal, rocketing the truck across the grass and in front of the car.

"Yes." She bit her bottom lip.

Joe slammed on the brakes, an inch from the bumper now sandwiched between the van and the vibrating truck. He unsnapped his seatbelt and scanned the front of the house. "Don't get out."

"Are you crazy? I can help." The click of her belt being released sounded loud in the unnatural eerie silence. Fear skittered along his nerve endings, ramping his testosterone to equal a Bull Shark.

He gripped the handle and the door flew open. He attempted to control his emotions and choose his words with care. "Look Ericka, a man is going to die today. I don't want you to be a witness or involved. Please, stay in the truck."

She held the door handle.

Would she honor his request? He couldn't waste more time debating with her and stepped to the ground. The drive had been cleared, but snow surrounded the exterior of the house.

The fluff would be a cushion if he couldn't stop the fall. His recent vision kept replaying through his mind like a bad dream. Someone would plummet.

He ran to the rear of the house and scanned the roofline. The sun crested at the bottom of the flashing, shadowing the widow's walk.

The fall would occur from the rail outside Ericka's bedroom. The ornate balustrade slats ran horizontal instead of vertical, imitating a ladder. Perhaps this added to the confusion of his vision. A man had slipped or fallen off the rail of a rooftop platform. Two visions, entwined? Joe wouldn't let anything happen to Brett, and he didn't want to fall face down in the stone cold snow either. If he couldn't prevent the prophecy from playing out, he wanted Ward to die.

Joe ran to the kitchen door and twisted the knob. Locked. The jiggle caused snow to fall from the ledge. He lifted his hand and drank the ice. The coolness soothed his scorched throat. No sign of activity in his bedroom, they had to be in the master suite. He sprinted to the front entrance and stole a glance at the truck.

Ericka wasn't there. Fuck!

He followed her tracks through the snow and into the house. Size seven water pools led to the left, into her office and out again. Brief imprints marked a path toward the kitchen, and without looking, he knew they'd lead up the staircase.

Low murmured voices came from upstairs. The sun would hit the widow's walk in mere minutes. Joe gripped the banister and pulled his weight missing every other step. He avoided the squeaky stairs. At the top of the landing, he glanced down the hall. No sign of Ericka, but the sun peeked through the window. A few seconds. Blood pumping, he removed his gun from the holster, and crept forward.

"It's illogical she'd store her legal records in her bedroom," Brett said, "and very unlikely they'd be hidden in her underwear."

Good. Brett instead of Tess.

"Shut-up." Ward's muffled demand didn't give Joe notice where he stood.

He peered around the doorframe. Brett's arms were tied with clothesline. Another rope held his legs to the rungs of a chair.

Brett twisted his hands, tugging the binds. "You can get help for your sniffing problem. Hell, you'll get drug counseling when you're in jail."

"Bitch. That's what she plans to do, send me to jail. You want to smell the panties, don't you? Here!" The floorboards vibrated with each of his steps.

The creak-scratch of the chair's legs moving rang through the room. Sounds of a struggle ensued, followed by a garbled voice and insane chuckle. Joe shifted to the other side of the doorway and glanced inside. A chair had fallen backward and a pair of silver panties had been stuffed in Brett's mouth. They connected gazes. Brett nodded to the left.

Joe slipped into the room and assumed the position. Like riding a bike, knees slightly bent, the stance felt natural and so did the gun secure in both hands. He unlatched the safety. "You're done, Ward."

Ward held a little .22 in one hand and a pair of pink panties in the other. "You ass," Ward said. "Look behind you."

Unwilling to give him the advantage, Joe didn't take his attention from Ward. He smelled magnolia and hoped Ericka had grabbed a gun instead of the damn sword.

"In a matter of seconds I can take out pretty-boy squirming around the floor or my beautiful lawyer-bitch. Your choice. Bullet holes or surrender?" Ward's straight white teeth gleamed, as he pointed his weapon toward Ericka.

"Neither." Joe wouldn't shoot or surrender. Two years ago, he would have taken a chance and blasted a slug into the man's black heart, but not now. Out of practice, he would hit Ward but in all probability not kill the man. In this type of situation, a cop shot to kill. Joe wouldn't take the chance of a wild bullet from Ward hitting Brett or Ericka.

He let his shoulders fall and the tenseness in his hands eased. The chair clacked against the floor. Brett struggled. He coughed, and gagging followed.

"Now, that's more like it." Ward took a step forward. "Drop the gun."

Not going to happen. He had a gun, no knife strapped to his ankle, no backup, no friend protecting his ass.

"Slut, come here." Ward wagged his gun.

Joe obstructed her path. "No. Let her go."

Ericka blew out a mumbled curse. "I'm the reason—"

"Put the gun down," Ward's insane bark bounced off the walls.

"Ward, you want to be a big man—take a gamble with me." Joe knelt, removed the cloth from Brett's mouth, and placed the gun on the floor. Close enough he could snatch it up. "Let them go. Hell, I'll even give you the advantage."

"Don't do this, he's unhinged." Brett worked the ropes, trying to get free. The chair banged against the floor. Joe's gun slid under a table.

He flung a kick, catching Ward at the calf. His heavy biker boots worked, sending Ward to his knees. Ward's trigger finger set off a bullet into the high ceiling. The crack of the shot and the splitting of wood rumbled like thunder.

"Ericka, untie Brett and leave," Joe shouted. He managed to keep the panic out of his tone, but his heart raced.

Despite his stocky build, Ward sprung up like a gymnast, fast and steady. Arm extended, he fumbled with the grip until his index finger pressed the trigger.

Joe embraced his anger, collected it into a powerful force, and then jabbed with his left, aiming for the wrist and round kicked at Ward's gut. The man's hand shook. A bullet exploded, shattering the glass door. Joe got the opportunity to block with a left cross, then smashed Ward's carotid artery. The sickening thud proved he'd been on target.

Ward fell backward, plunging through a French door. Shards of glass sprinkled throughout the room. He would be going over the banister. Joe glanced at Ericka. A raw emotion flooded her gaze. He followed Ward to the widow's walk.

****

Ericka's heart raced as she slipped the parry knife from her coat pocket and sliced through nylon cords holding Brett's wrists. She gave him the blade to free his ankles. A shot blasted, cracking wood and glass. Ward's bullet had shattered her French door. Brett struggled to get free from the ropes. She positioned her father's service revolver between her sweaty palms, trying to control the shakes. Never having shot a person, she wasn't even sure if she could. She'd grabbed the pistol from her desk drawer downstairs, checked the safety, but did the antique work?

From behind her, Brett said something, but she ignored him and walked to the door and flung it open. With Ward in sight, she took aim. She'd try for his upper left shoulder. If he'd hold still she could get a shot off. Ward ducked, dodging a punch from Joe. She realigned. Ward slammed the butt of his gun into Joe's ribcage. He struck Ward in the throat. Eyes wide, in shock or pain, Ward stumbled backward.

Shards of crystal crunched under her feet as she moved closer. Ward held the revolver, clutched in his hand, pointed at Joe. She had a clean shot. She had to pull the trigger.

"Give the gun to me," Brett demanded.

"No, I'm the one to save him," she shouted. A gust of air whipped through the room, creating a wind tunnel and spinning flecks of glass with the icy snow. Out of the corner of her eye, Joe fought to get the gun released from Ward's tight grip.

"Ericka. Let me." Brett held her trembling hand and pointed the gun toward the floor.

She had to get control. Tremors coursed through her arm. Brett removed the silver barrel from her cramped sweaty hand. He gripped the small black handle.

"Fuck." His hand shook, but within moments, he'd gained control.

She understood the phrase, life passing in a blink of the eye. In a second's time, her insane client hurled Joe over the banister of the widow's walk. He caught the ledge and held tight. Unable to grip the wet surface, he swung his leg trying to get a secure foothold.

Ward pounded the butt of his gun loosening Joe's fingers. Her heart slammed against her ribcage. She ran forward.

Too late.

Joe plummeted to the ground. *He'll die*. Her chest constricted. She tried to breathe. Snow flew around her, flooding her with an epiphany.

She loved Joe, and regardless of her predecessor's historical failures, she'd try to have a relationship with him.

A projectile wheezed past her ear. Powder and metal bits from the .38 liberally sprayed the side of her face. The tiny pinpricks dug into her skin. The hollow-pointed lead bullet entered the sinew of Ward's upper right arm.

She swiped a hand over her cheek, ignoring the metallic scent of blood. The impact of the slug loosened Ward's hold on his pistol. Splattered with Joe's blood, the weapon dropped to the balcony floor. Screaming in agony, Ward clutched his shoulder and dropped to the snow-laden deck of the widow's walk.

Ericka flew forward, stepping across Ward's legs to peer over the railing. Joe's dark form, flat against a pile of snow, didn't move. She gripped the icy ledge, willing herself to follow. Heart racing, her blood pressure rose to a dangerously high rate as she placed a foot on a banister rail. She had to get closer to see if he lived.

"Ericka, get away from there." Brett's calm low-toned voice didn't relieve her anxiety.

Ward, whimpering, scuttled to the edge of the walk, closer to the open door.

"Move the slightest bit and you're a dead man," Brett hissed.

Chapter Twenty-Two

Ice dug into Ericka's knees as she pressed her hands to Joe's chest. His eyes remained closed. "Live, damn you."

Resurrect: to breathe new life into. The resurrect chime pierced her thoughts. She forced air into his motionless form.

Water. Wolf proclaimed she needed to use water to purify Joe. The liquid from the waterfall at the ley line. For the first time in her life, she loved a living man, and she'd make him survive. She overlapped her hands on his ribcage. Arms straight she pressed the twentieth compression.

Noise drew her attention to the balcony. The sun beamed its rays to the snow, reflecting in prisms and blinding her. She blinked and glanced at the truck a few feet away. The bottle was in the cup holder. She couldn't leave Joe.

"Thirty." Chest compression finished, she pinched his nose, pressed her lips to his chilled mouth, and breathed new life into him for one second. She sucked in cold air and shoved another second of air into his lungs. His chest rose.

Tears slid down her cheeks. She aligned her hands to compress.

"Ericka, let go." Brett's words didn't match his begging intonation.

"No," she screamed and shoved Joe's chest. Rivulets of her salty tears dripped and spotted his dark shirt. She caressed his bruised jaw. "There's a bottle of water in the truck, go get it."

Her fingers shook as she closed Joe's nose and blew all of her love and hope into him. *I'm your heart. I have the power to create and transform. Damn you, live.*

Sobs clogged her throat. She pumped his chest. Wolf's edict continued to reverberate through her mind. *A ritual, such as the vision quest, means changing something from one state to another. You are vital to his transformation. Although it's not clear to you now, your faith, your power, and your life are entwined with his.*

Hand fisted she thumped Joe's chest a final time and then fell on top of him. "Please God, take me, not him."

Her howls filled the silence, making her tears trek faster.

If she'd comprehended how much she cared for Joe before today, she'd tell him of her love. They'd live in blissful happiness…for as long as possible.

An arm covered with light brown duck cloth covered her shoulders and pulled her upright. Brett held out the water. "Take a drink." His other hand pressed against her shoulder. Was he afraid she'd pound on Joe again?

Beaded tear splotches fell to her jacket. Shards of agony pierced her knees, yet she couldn't move.

"No. Pure water for Joe." Her throat ached. She lifted a hand and wiped the wet ooze from her neck. Blood, she assumed from the glass cuts, mingled with tears and melted snow.

"What happened to your face?" Joe's deep voice croaked.

The bottle of water bounced against the ground. Brett tilted against her. She elbowed him and leaned into Joe.

"You're alive," she whispered.

He arched his back against the ground and moaned. "Yeah, just lost my wind. You're a very aggressive kisser. Damn, I've a hell of a backache. The snow wasn't as good of a cushion as I'd thought it'd be."

"Hey, man, I thought you were a goner." Brett helped him sit upright.

Joe wheezed. "Well, I'd prefer we tell people the wind was knocked out of me."

Brett swiped snow from Joe's back. "Tess would never have forgiven me."

"Or me if you'd fallen."

Ericka met Joe's gaze. Brett would not have been revived. An adrenaline rush shot through her, a surge of heat and understanding. Joe lived because of their connection. He hadn't had a heartbeat. Wolf's prediction had proven to be true—together she and Joe had life and power because of their love.

"Help me up. I'm freezing."

Brett pulled Joe to a stand.

Ericka took a deep breath, exhaled, and then wound her arm around Joe's. The cold leather of the holster bit into her hand. Should she tell him now? It'd be easy enough to say, "Joe, I love you."

"What happened to your face?" Joe asked, his voice cop-like cool.

"Flash gap," she muttered. She wiped her tears on

the sleeve of her jacket.

"What?" Brett held the door open. He must have unlocked it when he'd joined her.

"You used the old .38 in the desk drawer." Joe grimaced as he limped into the kitchen.

"You looked through my desk?"

"A cop tends to investigate," Joe mumbled.

"Ericka let him be. I'd have done the same thing. What's a flash gap?" Brett pulled out a chair at the table. The wood scraping against the tile floor sounded loud in the sudden silence.

****

Joe fell onto the seat. "The Smith and Wesson .38 revolvers were used by cops over twenty years ago." He raised his voice. "They're antiques now." He coughed "Between the front of the cylinder and the forcing cone there's a gap, bits of metal and smoke spray laterally when the gun is fired."

"Look, I could hurl all over you right this minute. Do you really want to reprimand me?" She took a towel from the top of the dryer and wrapped it around his shoulders, keeping her arm snug against him. "It was my father's gun, and it's very serviceable."

"You didn't shoot it because you were sprayed." He glanced at his brother-in-law and lifted an eyebrow. "Seriously, a man of peace?"

Brett shrugged. "You were in danger. I guess instinct takes control when someone you love is in a life and death situation. This changes the premise of my paper regarding—"

"Where's Ward?" He wanted the man dead, but hoped he wasn't because Brett wouldn't be comfortable having committed such an act.

Brett nodded to the side. "In the foyer, tied to a chair. The bullet traveled through his upper arm, so I wrapped it in a towel and duct taped it."

Joe moaned and glanced at the doorway. A bottle of water hit the tabletop. He squinted. Ericka extracted the glass vial from her jeans' pocket.

"Valerian. It's used to help with sleeplessness, cramps, and muscle spasms." She tapped the small container against the rim of the plastic bottle of water. A layer of grayish dust floated on top of the liquid. She recapped the vial, screwed the lid, and shook the contents mixing the herb.

"Is that for Ward?" Joe asked.

"For you. Remember, Wolf said you'd need it?" She unscrewed the water cap and gave him the container.

"It'll make me tired, and we're leaving in a minute to return to Old Stone Fort." He rose from the chair. Muscles tightened and cramped, making his entire body ache.

"No. We must stay and talk to Caleb about the..." She flicked her fingers toward the hallway. "Ward incident."

"Brett will give them the report." He placed his bloodied hands on the table, using the leverage to motor forward. "I'm going to take a quick shower. Maybe the heat will help."

Even to his own ears, he sounded pathetic, but his muscles throbbed and his joints felt frozen.

She gave a quick headshake. "Drink the water and talk to the cops."

"Maybe she's right. You should stay and talk to the law," Brett said. His arm shook. Some of Ward's blood had splattered over his skin. He shoved his hands behind him, typical professor mode.

"Can't, the magic of the ley line ends in less than ten hours. Ericka needs to see her future and I…want to end the misery of foresight." He took the bottle of water and drank a small sip. Pain or not, there wasn't any way he'd admit defeat.

"I'll drive then. Go shower." Brett lifted the phone from the receiver hooked to the pale cream painted kitchen wall.

"Someone needs to be here to explain how the guy got shot." Joe entered the bathroom.

"You haven't asked me if I want to go. I don't want to put you at risk again," Ericka shouted.

A flutter entered his heart. Could wishes come true? She said the words, the ones he'd hoped to hear. He would insist she go to the ley line. Her fears had to be put to rest.

"We'll go. Brett will stay and explain." He shut the bathroom door and turned the shower dial to hot.

Chapter Twenty-Three

The Archaeological Park consisted of the same road, trees, and guard shack, but now Ericka's stomach muscles clutched in knowledge of what would or could happen. She couldn't prevent the anxiety gripping her. Could she handle Joe's next vision?

Joe stopped near the ranger. The same man they'd met the day before—tall, six-five at least, bony frame with a big-knuckled handshake—greeted them. She hadn't taken in his height before.

The ranger swaggered to the driver's side with stereotypical arrogance. Ericka chuckled deep in her throat and met Joe's glance. His eyes held a glow, a look that filled her with tenderness. He grinned, then lowered the window.

"Officer Rendfeld, we've returned. Fresh batteries and all." Joe held a bag of essentials they'd pilfered from her pantry. Batteries included.

"The camp's still closed." He ambled and evaluated the interior and exterior of the truck.

Joe curled his hand on the frame and stuck his head out the window. Ericka wished they could've disguised the enlarging bumps and dark blue bruises marring his face.

Joe tapped the metal truck door. "We should have all the research and evidence gathered tonight. Are you going to allow us to pitch a tent on the grounds?"

"The university guy said you'd be making a hefty donation to the park." Rendfeld's hand wedged between his armpit and side. "When should we expect the contribution?"

"I'll have Dr. Firebach transfer the money pronto. Two grand sound about right?" Joe offered the endowment as if it were a piece of penny candy.

"Sounds about right. No fires. Make sure you cleanup after yourselves. If you need anything contact the station." He extended a card. "I'll see you tomorrow morning." Officer Rendfeld slapped the door, the ding of metal from his ring clanked against the tin.

"Will do." Joe raised the window to his standard three inches from the frame top. She didn't mind. At least Tennessee had elevated temperatures. He drove to the ceremonial grounds, winding along the paths, chasing birds from the trees along the way. He stopped in the same spot they'd occupied the day before.

She got out and rushed to retrieve her bag. Joe had already opened the rear door.

"This is insane." She caught Wolf's prepared bundle as it fell. "Drink the rest of the herb water."

"I'll think about it." He moved a little slower, but pink cheeks and bronze skin reassured her he would mend.

At the house, she'd stuffed the bottle of Valerian into her purse. Her hair had dried into uncontrolled waves. Taking a shower had been worth the extra ten minutes of travel delay, because she wanted to get the blood splatter off.

Wolf intimated she and Joe belonged together. She'd have to tell Joe of her past, with the hope they could work though her history and have a future together. In the meantime, if he expected to get rid of his visions, she'd help him.

Old Stone Fort looked exactly as it had the day before. She didn't smell cigar odor or feel mystical vibrations. Maybe they wouldn't connect with Joe's spirit guide. If not, would he be more accepting of the visions and the drama that came with them?

At the Indiana state line, she'd turned to look at him, ready to say *I love you.* She'd never spoken the words to a man before and the notion of rejection made her pause. What if he looked stunned? Or worse, said nothing at all? At a sudden stop, he grimaced, so instead of a tremendous heartfelt declaration, she offered to drive.

She'd battled bullies in and out of the courtroom, but at the prospect of saying *I love you* she lost all confidence. Time slipped past and words were left unspoken. She glanced to the religious site. Where was the ley line, under the ground or in the wall where Joe had passed out?

Joe parked and started to get out of the cab.

Despite the queasiness in her stomach, and the constant fast thump of her heart, she held his arm. "Joe, I want to tell you something, before we cross into voodoo pass. I—"

At the chime of his cellphone, Joe held up his index finger. "Just a sec."

As he answered the call he opened the truck door and dropped to the ground. He got his saddlebag from behind the seat.

She jumped from the truck and walked closer to the entrance of the park. A bright red Cardinal joined a Robin on a sturdy barren tree limb. "Traitor, you belong in Indiana. Don't you honor your state bird status?"

"Yeah." He talked into the phone, but stared at her. Concern rippled across his eyes. "Any trouble?"

He lifted his saddlebag. "Sure, use a map app. Will you transfer two grand to Old Stone Fort before you leave? Yep, see you in seven or eight hours." A lightweight chuckle filtered through the air. "You told me three was the bewitching hour." He held a hand against his ribs. His sexy laugh erupted again. "Later."

He disconnected the call and slipped the phone into his pocket. His gait seemed slow and awkward but his mission was evident, to get to the ley line.

"Hey, aren't you going to tell me what happened? Brett called, right?" She grabbed his arm. The muscles bunched beneath her fingers. The man had to drink the herb water. "Joe, regardless of how much you want to deny our bond, we're a team. Trust me."

"Sure." He started forward again. "Sorry, it's been a stressful day."

She jogged in front of him. In line with the opening of the ley line and near the location his vision had occurred, she stopped and faced him. "We are partners, right?"

"Yeah, we're partners." He dropped his bags and sat on the mound at the entrance. "The police arrived and carted Ward to the hospital. Brett gave his statement. The house was sealed, and the guns taken into evidence. Your friend said it would be all right for us to give our statements tomorrow."

"And Brett's coming here, to Old Stone Fort?" Her declaration of love would be very difficult if she had to pull every word from him.

Joe's fingers dug into his lower back, and then

rolled a couple of shoulder circles. He rose, gathered the bags, and met her gaze. "Yes, he'll arrive at midnight.

Ericka took his hand. Although his jaw was firm, his gaze had softened. She parted her lips and exhaled.

Her bags fell to the hard ground with a thud. Now. Seize the moment. "I don't want you to be in jeopardy. I want to tell you..." She twisted a lock of hair and shoved it behind her ear. Her stomach muscles flip-flopped.

"What?" He clasped her upper arms.

"I love you, Joe Reeves. I've fallen in love with you, and I don't need to cast a spell to know we're good together." Rapid firing words lessened the power to the announcement. He'd had a flash in his gaze.

His gentle touch comforted her. Their gazes connected and the glimmer of emotion held strong. She hoped the spark was a result of love.

"It's about damn time." His fingers tightened. "I love you, too."

She released her breath, but her heart continued to pound against her ribcage. He kissed her, strong, assured, working from the top of her lips to the bottom. This kiss was like nothing she'd experienced before, not even compared to the night he'd arrived at her house. His perfect lips merged with hers, the pressure points in line. She fit snug against him. His hard bulge nudged her thighs. The flip-flopping in her stomach doubled, and a whimper escaped from her lips. He released her arms and cupped her rear. She clutched him. The heated slick of moisture flooding her prepared the way for their joining.

She'd make love to him anywhere, even at a

supernatural site. His tongue outlined her mouth, then caressed. She leaned into the lip lock, enjoying the thrust and pulls replicating what would occur once their clothes were removed.

She ground her hips closer to his, desiring the feel of him inside her, wanting the connection.

He moaned, reseated on the mound, and tugged her closer.

Already missing him, she recaptured his hot lips.

He framed her face with his thumbs stroking the sides.

"Let's go to the truck." She touched his hand.

His arms fell like heavy weights to his side. "Not here. However raw and exciting, it's not very romantic."

The vial of Valerian must have opened, and the drug seeped into her system, because she had to be hallucinating. No, the sweet ache between her thighs was real. She dug her fingernails into her scalp. "What?"

"Let's find the spirit." He patted her butt like a basketball player going onto the court. "Sex later though."

"Let's go to a hotel, now."

He shook his head.

"How can you be sure the second sight will leave? What if you pass out again?" She took a step away. What if you don't wake?" Frustration pounded through her brain. She struggled to understand what he was trying to say.

"If it happens, it happens. The one thing I've learned, since I began seeing death, is people need closure. I love you, and I'm excited about the possibility of a future together." He stood, entwined her fingers with his, and dragged her close. "Since I've known you, you've been trying to avoid a relationship. You need to put the past to rest, to say goodbye to whatever you fear and embrace a future. Our future."

He loved her. Joy raced through her, until she glanced at the ley line. The place where he'd had the vision before. "On two conditions."

His eyes glittered as he drew their hands to his chest. "What conditions, my dear?"

"Take the rest of the Valerian to ease your aches and regardless if the spirit shows or not, we leave at the crack of dawn." She hovered near his mouth. "Those are my conditions."

He moved his hands to her sides. His thumbs caressed the lower curve of her breasts. "What if—"

"Doesn't matter. The longer we stay the more of a chance you'll have a vision, and I need a day of rest before we go save another life." She finger-combed a dark lock from his forehead. Surges of desire swept through her.

"We're a superpower team, fighting death?" He grinned.

Her heart tripped. She loved him, despite his quirky sense of humor. She fell against his chest. "You better believe it. We're like the wind, twisting and turning as one major force."

He grunted.

She kissed him. "Hopefully for all time."

****

"Faith, power, and life." A shock wave of energy rushed through Joe. He'd bask in the glory of her love.

"Do you think we can use the ceremonial ground

for our own sacrament?" She took little bites of his lower lip.

"The ranger could make a surprise visit, and I'm not an exhibitionist." He slipped his hands beneath her sweater, snapped the bra clasp, and released her breasts from their skimpy confines. He caressed the soft under-skin, then skimmed over her protruding nipples.

"He said later or in the morning. We've been here a few minutes and rain is predicted," she urged. She made quick work of unzipping his jeans and folding the sides to his hips.

"Not..." He caressed her beautiful rounded rear. Aches and pains took a backseat to the thrill of being with her.

"Not in the open and on sacred ground. The ghosts of Indians past would track us for life if we desecrated their ceremonial site." She stroked him. The hardness surged to life.

His heart pattered a quick beat like drum taps. The anticipation of a sacrament grew. He'd never felt as alive as when his lips touched hers. Visions of death abated, life existed. "There's a grouping of white pines behind you with a clearing in the middle."

"Good." Her sly smile animated her gorgeous face.

He drew a deep breath as her fingernails twisted his hair. "I've slept outside a few times. As long as you don't break off a twig or get close to the base of the tree you'll be sap free."

She lifted her head. Her pale cheeks bloomed with a beautiful soft rose blush.

He met and held her gaze. When she licked her lips, he considered disturbing the natives of the past to take her right there on the short green grass of the ley line.

"Do you want to wait?" she whispered.

He tugged her close. Lust ripped through his veins erupted like a shooting star. The pounding savagery of her lips and touches made all rational thoughts flee. He wanted her. "Come."

He led her outside the ceremonial circle, near the cover of balsam fir trees with overhanging branches at least three feet above the ground. He dropped the cloth bundles on top of the carpet of pine needles and the scent infiltrated the area. Ericka flung her backpack purse to the ground, then unzipped her jacket and jerked it off. He retrieved a sleeping bag for their bedding. She nudged him. The liquid heat in his groin turned up a notch.

She'd removed her sweater and kicked off her shoes. Her luscious round breasts, cupped by soft magnolia scented see-through lavender material lured his gaze. Part of him, the stupid romantic side, wanted to slow down. His hetero instinct won.

He'd fantasized about her for weeks. He tossed off his coat, adding it to hers. Before he could strip off his shirt, she dragged the cotton shirt over his head. Her nails bit into his collarbone, but he welcomed the pain. She'd given him life and now her love.

Her chest heaved. She licked her lips, and then kissed him.

He unfastened her jeans and eased them to her ankles. She stumbled backwards, pulling him into her fiery warmth. She caressed him. He lowered to the sleeping bag and tugged her toward him.

She landed on top. He grunted as his already tender body screamed in agony. She kissed his skin just above the nipples. Single-minded and versatile, she laved her way to his manhood.

When a cool wet path led to the tip of his erection she stopped. He hoped, beyond hope, she hadn't finished. She grasped his jeans and boxers and dragged them away from his pulsating nerve endings.

He cupped her breasts through the filmy blue bra, rubbing the rosy nubs. She moaned and pressed against him. She snaked her way until their bodies were aligned.

She tilted backwards and pressed her fingers into his arms. He caressed the backside of her knee, moving to her inner thigh. His hot tongue flashed across one nipple and then the other. Her chest lifted and lowered with each rapid breath. They belonged together, like the sun and the moon. Ying and yang.

He moaned and shifted putting more pressure on his right side.

"I don't want to hurt you. Switch places."

"Your wish is my command." He ignored the pain and rolled to the side.

She stood and like a practiced striptease shed her undergarments. He took her hand as she lowered to the ground. His hips touched hers, and he kissed the side of her neck. Her musky scent drew him as he settled on top.

She lifted her hips and ground her pelvis against his. "Please don't make me wait any longer."

"Okay, my love," he murmured into her ear. He tasted her, stroking his way to her mound.

She tugged his head. He rose and nudged his tip into her slick entrance, begging to drive forward. He wanted to be superior to any supernatural lover she would've created.

He breathed, and her star earrings moved. He shifted the shiny bits aside and nuzzled her neck, then captured her lips. She arched her neck, allowing him full access.

She grabbed his hips, dragging him until they connected. "Foreplay another time. Please take me."

"As you wish, my love." Limbs, from the under-hang of the pine tree, scraped along his spine as he lifted.

He thrust inside her welcoming warmth and exhaled. She gripped him, sucking him deeper inside her ready entrance.

She kissed him, tugging his lips with her teeth. He ground against her, matching her gyrations. He plunged higher into her soft heat. She moaned in response and inspired him to drive into her full throttle, pull away and press forward again. He pulled out and held his cock at her precipice, caressing her sweet spot, wanting to make this moment last.

"I've waited…wanted…needed," she stuttered.

He silenced her words with a soul-touching kiss and entered her full hilt. She stretched, accommodating his thickness and dug her fingers into his rear.

He broke the kiss and nuzzled the side of her face. Pulled out. Thrust.

He withdrew and plunged again. She wrapped her legs around his waist, keeping him attached. Twigs bit into his ankles, but he ignored the pain, nothing mattered except making love to his woman, his salvation.

She placed her hands at the sides of his face, dragging his lips to meet hers. He kissed her, putting stored passion into the connection. Her tongue darted into his mouth, exploring all the inner aspects. Parry and withdraw, his tongue matched the tempo of their bodies.

He kissed the side of her face, blazing new paths along her neck. Her rapid breathing sounded loud in his ear, but pleasure followed as her fingernails pressed into his rear. She nipped at his neck. Heated excitement met each thrust. Ripples of her pleasure massaged him, and her orgasmic shriek saturated the area.

A blaze of passion burst through him as she climaxed, then he allowed himself to join her. He touched his forehead to hers. Connected, he rolled over, dragging her to his side. She exhaled and kissed his shoulder soothing the nips she taken earlier.

After a moment, she unstuck their sweaty skin and rested her head on his shoulder. "I never thought this would happen, us coming together. I do love you, Joe."

"And I love you." Pleasure rushed through him. He loved her, but to remain by her side, he'd have to deal with the devil. He kissed her plump lips and shifted on the twisted cloth beneath them. "I'm thirsty. Do you have water in your bundle? I drank mine yesterday."

He scraped his fingers over his chest. They would be lucky if they didn't get poison ivy or oak, rolling over the weeds like two teenagers. How unromantic could he have been?

"Umm, the herb water. Want it?" she asked without moving an inch.

He rolled over and opened the end of her bag. The water bottle popped out and the colorful packaging of a protein bar. Although Wolf claimed the herb would help with sleeplessness, he doubted any herb, or drug, would allow him to rest. Relaxed, his body hummed with sexual satisfaction.

He gave her the energy bar. She ripped into the package, split off half, and extended the partial crunchy chocolate-coated snack. Shadows and darkness had overtaken the area and by the look of the clouds, indeed rain was probable.

"Want some?" He held out the bottle. Tiny speckles of the herb splattered the bottom.

"No, thank you. I've an energy drink in my purse." Paper crinkled as she unwrapped the remainder of the protein bar and handed it to him.

"Thanks." He took the treat and ate it in two bites. He lifted the water, drank the clear upper half, and then sat upright. Every single muscle in his body ached and a few bones beneath, but he needed to be alert. He wouldn't be drugged and tipped the herb-tainted water into the earth.

"I'll share my drink." Rustle. Scrap. She dug through her bag, extracting a pear-shaped container filled with clear fluid. She removed the cap and handed him the bottle. "Here."

"No thanks. I'm good."

"We should do this more often." She took a deep drink, then handed him the container. "Go ahead."

He took a swallow and returned the bottle to her. Joe rearranged the duffle, so the bulk could support his arm. "Anytime and obviously anywhere."

She laughed, the sexy loud one.

He sniffed her neck. "I think I fell in love with you the first night we met."

"Umm. Ditto."

He stroked her arm, and she shivered. "Cold?"

"A little. Maybe we should get dressed and climb inside the sleeping bags to cuddle?" She jumped to her feet with the agility of a life-long dancer.

Pinpricks of intense pain jolted through his sore muscles. In their feverish need to make love, clothes had been tossed everywhere. He snagged her jeans and as she reached for them their fingers touched, reigniting the flame of passion existing just beneath the surface.

Dressed, he gathered their gear and the water bottle. Black sweater and jeans, she'd blend into the night. Twigs stuck out from her tumbled hair. He plucked a small pine needle from a strand.

She hoisted her bags. Her nails scraped against the duck cloth of Wolf's bundle. "Where are we going?"

"Same place as before, near the ley line." He jerked his saddlebag to his shoulder, ignoring his bruised knuckles, and entwined his fingers with hers.

She held tight and whispered, "The source of energy is high there. Let's settle a few feet away and observe."

"Why are you whispering?" He fought off the stiffness and kept pace with her leggy walk.

"Feels like we should. Don't you sense the excitement?"

"I thought it was because of great sex."

She flashed a smile and dropped her duffle at a high point in the wall. "That too."

The four-foot wall of the mound would provide a nice headboard for their makeshift bed. His bundle fell open, separating the flashlights, candles, matches, and another energy bar into colorful bits across the grass. He spread the duck cloth across the ground, unzipped the sleeping bags and zipped them together.

She tossed unnecessary items into her purse, leaving the flashlights within reach. He held the top layer, as if an invitation. "I'm going to the falls and get fresh water. Need your bottle filled?" He nodded to the near empty container.

"No, I'm good. I should go visit the bushes." She glanced throughout the area.

"Okay. I'll go this way," he pointed to the north, "and you'll go."

"East."

A thick pillow of clouds hid the moon, so the light grew dim. He handed her a flashlight and took one himself. Drips and tinkles from the waterfall gave him a location of the stream, but he didn't want to trip over the edge and free fall into the basin.

A mist rose from the edge of the cascade. Soon the haze would encroach over the ceremonial ground. He flipped on the flashlight at the same time a beam came from her light. The ley line and earth-less portion of stonewall needed to be crossed. Using one hand, he catapulted over the ledge. Odd, his muscle aches seemed less invasive. He could breathe without a catch in his lungs. Wolf knew his stuff. The Valerian he'd consumed had indeed eased his pain.

Near the falls, Joe took a sharp right and edged past the spiked thorn bushes. He propped the flashlight under his arm, relieved himself. A sense of foreboding came over him.

He zipped his jeans. "Okay, prophet. I'm ready when you are." The falls splashed, chiming through the air.

He went to the stream and plunged the container into the stream. The water acted as hydrotherapy on his bruised knuckles. He recapped the bottle and slid the flashlight beam toward Ericka's last location. The ray had stayed with him most of the way, but where was the spotlight now?

The beacon pointed in the direction of the ley line. She stood, dead center, with her arm in the air, fingers outlining crepuscular shadows. Her words of love tripped his heart. He jogged, scaled the wall, and slid to a stop beside her. "Ericka?"

She turned toward him. "Joe. Do you see him?"

He saw something. Joe closed his eyes and opened them. Adam, his partner, wavered in a cloudy form.

"Joe."

"Adam?" Could this be real? Had he drank more of the drugged water than he'd thought?

"Yes, my friend. I'm here." He grinned. The same sappy smile he'd grown to love during their partnership with the force.

Dressed in a long white robe, Adam's shape solidified. "What's with the toga?"

Adam laughed, a deep barrel laugh. "Jealous much?"

"Hi, I'm Ericka."

Joe rubbed his eyes, trying to clear his vision. Was he in the midst of a dream? A foresight? No, because Ericka was having a conversation with Adam.

"No. You're not dreaming. I'm here."

Like the few leaves clinging to the tree branch a few yards away, Joe clung to the idea he wasn't hallucinating. He pressed his eyes shut for a moment, and when he opened them, Adam stood in front of him, white robe and all.

Ericka took Joe's hand into hers. "Please listen."

He nodded, trying to force his mind to accept the impossible. "Okay."

Adam tilted his head. "Your gift is part of your destiny. You'll have many years of dealing with life and death. Some of the people you'll be able to save and others, fate will be as it should be."

His gut clutched. Death prophecies would always invade his life. "Why?"

"Why do you have the gift? Or why are some saved and others not?" He crossed his hands in front of him. No bloody runs and no crack to his skull. No injuries. No remnants from the wreck.

"Both." Joe couldn't look away. He ignored the glow beneath Adam's skin, radiating outward and illuminating the space, because it'd force him to admit the truth.

"Don't sound so sad, you're doing a great service," Adam replied.

Ericka resituated, snuggling against Joe's side.

Joe calmed and put his hand on her waist. "I assume you're aware of the events. Who lived and the ones I couldn't save?"

"Yes, and I thank you." Adam shot a grin to Ericka. "Thank you for your efforts to save him."

"My pleasure. He's given me more than I've helped him," she said.

Joe squeezed her arm. "Why me and not you?"

"You are just and honest. You'll be able to intercede when necessary. Brawn and brains."

"That's what you said right before we took a perp down. I was the brawn, and you were the brains."

Adam chortled, a deep belly laugh. "Yes, but we both knew I was both."

Ericka flattened her hand on her chest.

"You were given this opportunity. Some men, women, and children will be saved, and others will not."

Joe clenched his jaws, not wanting to hear more.

"You're wondering why you're to try and save a life if that person will die anyway." A tear glistened on his cheek. Did Adam cry because of the changes in their lives?

"Yes. Tell me a logical reason for a child to die underneath the wheels of a drunk driver's car?" He attempted to relax, willed his mind to accept the illogical, to no avail. All of the muscles tightened. Wolf's herb must have worn off, because his legs cramped and his back contracted into tight burning bunches.

"One child died to influence thousands of other people. Memberships to support groups increased. Law enforcers became more proficient at getting drunk drivers off the streets and if caught more penalties were applied. The parent, a woman I believe, unconcerned for her son's welfare now volunteers at a homeless shelter, assisting mothers with their children." Adam's calm soothing voice rang through the celestial site.

Joe's mind continued to rebel. "The child gained what?"

"The boy's lack of parental love and guidance would have allowed him to go down the wrong ethical path: theft, abuse of women, and he would have died in prison. His soul has a second chance to find a loving family. He will become a valued asset to society." Adam stepped closer, the brilliant light within inches of Joe's face.

Joe swallowed. "What are you trying to say?"

"I'm sorry I caused you grief when I died. You'll help so many people. My death was of no consequence."

His chest constricted. His friend stood in front of him, looking like an angel of sorts. His tranquil voice, sounding omniscient. Did he say he had to die so Joe would see death?

"Adam, are you saying Joe's destiny is tied to the gift?" Ericka asked.

"Yes. Don't carry the guilt around anymore. Your life path had been decided years ago. I left so you could save lives."

Joe gulped air. "You were my friend." He exhaled. "You drove the car. You left me. I was in a coma." He released Ericka's arm and took a step closer to Adam. "When did you decide all of this? Why didn't you tell me your grand plans before the accident? Perhaps I should've had some say in my life."

"Our lives are on paths decided before we're born. Joe, the life you're leading is your destiny."

Earlier he'd dunked his head under the purifying waterfall, hoping to eliminate the oncoming vision and to wipe out the gift. Nothing on earth, or beyond, could alter his state of being. He did a 360 looking for other possible spirits, ancestors and friends. "Are there others?"

"Yes, there is a procession along the ley line. Despite what we've heard, a person doesn't immediately pass through a gate, St. Peter's or anyone's."

He tucked the flashlight under his arm. "No. Are there others like me?"

"Yes." Adam nodded to a dark spot in the wall. "I need to hurry because dawn is approaching and many souls need to cross the bridge."

Joe pointed the flashlight in the same direction. Could his mother and father be in the procession line?

"Joe, do you see the spot where you had your vision? The bit of wall without grass growing on it?" Adam pointed.

"Yes." Nothing had changed. The stonewall remained intact. Their sleeping bags softened the harshness of the celestial site. No other visible spirits, just Adam.

"The smooth places on the ledge are the first step of a stone staircase leading to a suspension bridge. It's not grand like the London Bridge, but a plain wooden planked one with stone pillars marking each end. At the other side of the link, the life force will be met by their loved ones." A mere second later Adam leaned forward, as if bowing.

"The staircase is made of stone?"

"Yes, plain old-fashioned rock, burnished to the point it resembles marble." Adam tipped his head. "I'm sorry you couldn't see your parents, but they passed a long time ago. And now it's time for me to go."

Regret made Joe's heartbeat faster. He'd have given anything to see his parents again. "I guess this is goodbye."

"You're my best friend, man. I felt honored to be the link to your superpowers." Adam drew him into a hug. "I'll see you in the afterlife."

"You know it." His voice came out raspy. Something became clogged his throat.

Joe couldn't see *the bridge* where Adam entered,

but his peaceful luminescence highlighted his route. When Adam disappeared, Joe turned to Ericka. "I'll always have visions."

She bit her lip. A habit he found endearing. "Yes, but now you'll have me...to help."

"Yes, I'll have someone to share my challenges." He wrapped an arm around her waist.

"Full disclosure from this point on." She shoved a lock of hair behind an earlobe. "I need to tell you about an inheritance, er, a condition the females in my family all have had."

"Okay." He made his tone of voice reassuring. Regardless of what she had to say, he would always love her.

"Let's sit down." She pointed to their sleeping bags.

He took her hand and led her to the wall. She dropped to the mat, cross-legged and rested her elbows against her knees, then scrubbed her face. He leaned against the cold stone.

"In the past, I simply broke off the relationship before he got commitment close. I'm not sure how to tell you."

****

Joe's cool fingers touched her wrist. "Just tell me."

Ericka swallowed. "The only long-term romance I've had was with a ghost, because women in my family, from the early 1800's, don't remain with their husbands. Great-grandmother, third generation, Mildred MacLeod had an arranged marriage. She tolerated the loveless union, until she left him and disappeared into the west. Her daughter and granddaughters married, but all abandoned their families. My mother left when I was ten. My ancestors couldn't maintain long-term relationships. Knowing this, I thought a non-human would be the perfect choice for me."

He knelt beside her. "Don't you think the women all had it in their minds to leave? I believe it's called predetermined destiny."

She grabbed his hand. "Yes, that is what I'm trying to say. If we marry, I will leave you."

He kissed her cheek. "I'm sorry, not the phrase I wanted. I meant self-fulfilling prophecy?"

She turned into him. "What?"

"Because you think it will be true it becomes real. Belief and behavior. If I dream I can shoot my gun and get a bull's eye, and I succeed due to imagining the event was real, when the gun fires and hits the target, the action becomes real. Maybe in your case the women in your family falsely believed the marriage would not last. The fear caused the marriage to fail. But you can break the pattern. Marry me, and we'll have a long and happy life together. I promise you, I'll love you until my last breath." He exhaled. "The future is ahead of us, and the past will remain in the past." His tone reverent and sincere.

She shimmied, disconnecting from his loose hold, stood and reached into the darkness. Like that night she attempted to conjure a lover, she dropped her hand to her side and twirled crossing over the supposed waiting line to heaven. "This is the last spell I'll ever cast. I'm breaking ties with my past. My relatives' activities are not mine. I'll be happy. I'll love and remain with Joe until I die."

He stood. "We don't need spells. We've got love."

She stopped her dance and ambled to his side.

"Will we be safe staying here tonight or should we pack and go to a hotel?"

"Let's stay. If a vision comes, we'll act on it."

"Together." Ericka withdrew the flashlight from its tight hold between two stones and then scooted until she bumped him.

He kissed her. "I think we're safer right here, right now, than we would be at the Roseline in Paris."

"I've made the right choice." She tucked her face into the nook of his neck.

"Lady, there isn't any doubt you've made the right choice. Together, we'll make our own magic."

"Magic is relative. It's best if we join our lines as much as possible." She pecked his mouth.

"Yes." His lips were a breath away from hers. "Since we're on holy ground and on top of ley lines, let's sanctify our vows."

"What?"

"Become my wife?"

"Oh." Wolf had been correct. She'd discovered her future, and it was linked with Joe's. Why not jump? She clasped his hand. "I take you, Joe Reeves, to be my mate during our earth-years and who knows, maybe thereafter."

"And I take you, Ericka Gilmore, forevermore."

Chapter Twenty-Four

Joe jerked upright and glanced at Ericka. Wrapped tight in the sleeping bag, she remained in a deep sleep. The ceremonial area had mist rising from the ground. Was the Old Stone Fort now spirit free? Maybe.

A vision started, but he woke. Had he really stopped a divination? Did he have a new playing field? Could he alter the forecast, enabling him to deal with the prophecies in a different way?

Fully awake, he stuffed a tiny flashlight into his pocket and staggered to Step Falls. He knelt at the edge and flung his hands into the cascading waterfall, then splashed the cold water to his face. The strain of the visceral response his visions always created eased.

"Joe?" Brett's voice came from behind him.

He sighed. Compelled to see the ley line, nothing would have stopped his brother-in-law from coming.

"Yeah. A sec." He braced his palms at the bluff's edge, then jolted to a stand. Water flowed along the sides of his face and soaked his jacket. He shook his head. Sprinkles shot from all sides. In the shadows of the tilted flashlight, he glimpsed Brett's indistinct shape.

Brett came to his side and gazed into the water. "Vision?"

"The beginning. I've never been able to stop a revelation before tonight. This place, devil's hollow protected by God's angels, allows mixed visions, but I was able to prevent a prophecy from playing out." Joe pressed his hands against his cheeks and hair, trying to feel pain or anything.

Brett squatted and braced an elbow against his knee. He pulled his chin. "Never happened before?"

"No." Could he figure out how to make a bad dream into a positive change?

"Probably the currents or the inflow of spiritual energy."

Joe nodded. "You're going to try and record the spirits?"

"Yes," Brett responded. "If there is a procession of spirits, I might get some data on my monitors to support my paper." He glanced toward Ericka snuggled in her sleeping bag. "Did Wolf tell you where the entities hovered?"

"There's an invisible celestial bridge over there." Joe didn't want to tell him about Adam Long appearing in front of them. Brett would treat it as a research endeavor, and Joe wanted their conversation to remain sacred. "A straight line from the edge of the wall."

Brett held the flashlight steady and examined the area. The mist had become a fog and covered the terra firma, rising three feet from the cold surface. Faint outlines of naked trees created a ghoulish backdrop. Not one spiritual light though. The revelation had indeed faded.

"Logically the spirits would be in a straight line through the center of the ceremonial plot. It's a beautiful religious ground." Excitement zinged through each word Brett spoke.

Joe surveyed the perimeter of Old Stone Fort.

Nothing. "Can't see them, but I hope you get some data." He flung waterfall from his jacket. With each swipe the beam of light moved.

"Do you mind if I set my equipment here? I don't want to interfere. This is your challenge. You need to get rid of your ability," Brett said. His focus was on the ceremonial site. Did he try to capture charged vibes?

"No. I won't have a change in my visions. Still got them. Although, I did find love."

Brett laughed, a deep chest gurgle. "About time. Damn, I owe Tess twenty-five bucks. A celestial bridge? Point out the location of this bridge."

He missed his family more and more. "What time is it?"

"Three o'clock." Brett burrowed in his coat pocket. Paper crinkled and coins clicked.

"What happened to midnight? Did you get delayed?" Concern for Tess and the kids tore through Joe's mind. His stomach gurgled and the muscles tightened. He should have let the vision come instead of cleaving it off.

"Minor things, stopped to get a new SD card. I want to try and record paranormal sound activity. I hoped to get limited noises, spirit chatter in the form of energy. From what you've told me, I might get straight communication." Quick as a streak of lightning, he placed a set of headphones around his neck and flipped the player in his hand. "Where's this bridge you mentioned?"

Joe jerked Brett's jacket sleeve. "Tess and the kids?"

"They're good. Safe. Considering your gift, do you see a bright rainbow glow of souls snaking through the center of the circle?" Brett shoved the headphones to the top of his head, and lifted several bags near his feet.

Joe needed reassurance. His disappointment in Brett's lack of concern created a fresh anger in him. "No." His tone came out sharp and hard. "I can predict when a person will stand in the after-life line."

Brett stopped and dropped the bags. A narrow frown creased his face. "I talked to Tess three hours ago. They're fine."

Damn, he'd offended his brother-in-law. "I'm sorry, but I'm in a place where I try to prevent loved ones from becoming ghosts. Whereas, you want to discover what happens after their human bodies become glowing bits of dust."

Brett's beefy hand pounded on his back. "Not a problem. You saved my ass yesterday, and I thank you. Are we okay here? Do you mind if I try to get spirit noise?"

"Yes. Go ahead. The staircase leading to the transitional bridge and after-life is at the east end." He nodded to the area. A dried strand of hair tumbled to his forehead and he shoved it aside.

"You're okay?" Brett asked.

"Sure, enjoy your time with the phenomena. I hope you get some bites," Joe said.

Brett gave a short nod and walked through the thick mist. His form was scarcely visible to the human eye.

Ericka had her rear propped against the mound wall. The thick sleeping bag acted as a barrier between the cold earth and her sweet figure, the top layer of the cloth was braced under her chin.

"Hey." Joe held the flashlight's beam to the right

of her face. The glow from the light gave him a clear shot of the concern marked in her eyes.

She pushed the sleeping bag alongside the wall and scooted over.

He eased between the materials. His saddlebag was to his left, so he propped the torch against the leather. The light provided a hazy glow in the encroaching fog.

She wove her fingers through a few wet strands of his hair. A significant sigh passed across her lips as she leaned her head against his shoulder. "Are you all right?"

She must have been aware of his oncoming vision and witnessed his run to the falls. He'd frightened her and no doubt would again.

"Sure. I'm fine. I went to get some water. Brett's here." A full bottle of water rolled off the bag and into the light beam. He put an arm around her shoulders. "You watching the stars?"

"Like falling bright orbs circling earth. It's an amazing sight to behold." She shifted, crossed one leg over the other, and grabbed his hand. "Joe, we need to come to terms with our arrangement." Her breath hitched as she said the words.

"The vows aren't legal, just between us." His stomach knotted, but he didn't regret his rash decision to bond them. She'd need time to adjust to their pledge. Maybe he shouldn't have pressed the commitment issue.

"No. Not that. It's…"

He met her gaze and exhaled. His heart quit its erratic pumping. Maybe all of the songs were right, love would save the day.

"We both agree we should be a couple, right? Love

and trust each other?" She rubbed her thumb along his palm.

"Yes. I love you with every breath you give me."

"I love you, too." She kissed him. "So we need to deal with the visions, and how we should communicate."

She didn't negate their oaths. Her unfettered love would indeed help sustain his life. She was the most beautiful, charming, direct woman he'd ever met. "Words are overrated, I like action."

The gentle stroke of his palm ended, and she pressed her hand flat against his chest. "We'll go home."

Home. The mantra played over and over, igniting his heart. He'd have a semblance of a normal existence, something he hadn't believed could happen. "Home sounds great."

"Ground rules. Always trust me to hold your confidence. Speak openly and honestly with me. Tell me when a vision occurs."

"Done," he declared, regretting the avoidance of the topic. "Trust each other."

"Joe, all the people you save or don't save influence others in some way. The people, even bystanders, are or will be changed because of your gift of prophecy. You need to quit running from what is your destiny and embrace the visions." She lowered her voice. "Together we can save lives and change the world as we know it."

"So much to take in at one time. It's difficult to accept." He kissed the top of her head. "I guess love and destiny are tied."

"Yes." She glanced toward Brett. "What's he doing

on the ley line?"

"He's a professor and paranormal researcher. He's getting sound bites for evidence." Joe exhaled and pressed his head against the wall. With all of their movements, the sleeping bag had fallen so his aching noggin rested against the dirt and stonewall.

His body hurt like hell, but he would not utter a word about the pain. They were side by side, and he rejoiced in the connection. He swallowed the lump in his throat, and hoped she couldn't feel the pound of his heart. "What if I have a vision about you?"

"You'll save me," she shot back.

"You sound confident." His heart rate slowed, somewhat.

"I am, because love means always holding onto hope."

"You won't invite a supernatural into our lives, right?" The idea of her conjuring messed with his mind. He quaked with the image of the unsaved invading their space.

"No. I'm burning the books," Ericka pointed. "Do you see the line of spirits waiting to cross into ever after?"

"No, but maybe we'll cross the bridge together," he said.

A sly little upturn of her beautiful, plump lips spread across her face, then she kissed him. Intense passionate kissing wooed him into forgetting about the spirits surrounding them. She caressed the side of his face. "I want you. I need you. I love you."

"Ditto." Hugging her close, he glanced behind her. The darkness would soon disappear because the sky had changed from purple and red and would be pink and golden. Soon the sun would peek above the horizon in its resplendent hues and cast its glow over her.

"Do you think he's crossed?" she whispered.

She wasn't talking about Brett. Joe glanced into the distance, wishing he'd had the gift before the accident, so he could have saved Adam. Who knew the day would come when he wanted the gift of prophecy. Overwhelmed with fear of not saving those he loved, he'd lost valuable time with Tess, the kids, and even Brett.

"I hope so, he deserves bliss."

She rested her head against his shoulder. "You're a fine man, Joe Reeves, and I'll be proud to call you husband."

"Then you're okay with a church wedding. Maybe with a little ring bearer and flower girl?" He wanted his family near.

"Are you thinking of a winter or spring wedding? A spring wedding would mean we could have it outside the manor."

"Whatever you want is fine with me."

She yawned. "Wonderful. I'll talk to Jacey and make plans when we get home." She slipped farther into the sleeping bag. "I'm going to take a little nap."

"I'll be right here."

An hour later, Joe stood stretched his sore muscles and searched for Brett. He found him near the ley line stuffing the recorder and wires into his coat pocket. Brett's buff, duck cloth, coat blended with the morning light.

"Did you get anything?" Joe needed confirmation Adam had crossed.

"Nothing obvious. I'll know more when I listen to

the recordings on my equipment."

Joe had a better understanding of the relevance of death and afterlife. "I get how important it is for people to say good-bye before someone they love passes into another dimension. Do you think the spirits made it to the other side?"

"Yes." Brett nudged him. "Ready to come home?"

"Yeah." Joe grabbed one of the satchels, with an antenna peeking out of the corner. "Ericka and I are getting married. Interested in being the best man?"

"I'd be honored."

Joe glanced at Ericka, curled inside the sleeping bags, the moon to his sun. Perhaps they could save a life or two, and even change the world bit by bit.

A word about the author…

JJ inherited her name and creativity from her grandmother. A love of reading and adventure took her to many wondrous places. Studying literature provided a solid foundation in which to express her ideas and storytelling became a part of her world. She wants to share with you all of the magic, so please enjoy pieces of her life through her tales.

www.jj-keller.com
www.romancewithjjkeller.wordpress.com
~*~
Other JJ Keller titles
available from The Wild Rose Press, Inc.:
TRADE AGREEMENT
THE TAROT CARD
THE VALKYRIE AND THE MARINE
PIPPA'S RESCUE
MEMORY OF LOVE